BLUE SKIES OVER WILDFLOWER LOCK

HANNAH LYNN

Boldwood

First published in Great Britain in 2024 by Boldwood Books Ltd.

Copyright © Hannah Lynn, 2024

Cover Design by Alexandra Allden

Cover Photography: Shutterstock

The moral right of Hannah Lynn to be identified as the author of this work has been asserted in accordance with the Copyright, Designs and Patents Act 1988.

All rights reserved. No part of this book may be reproduced in any form or by any electronic or mechanical means, including information storage and retrieval systems, without written permission from the author, except for the use of brief quotations in a book review.

This book is a work of fiction and, except in the case of historical fact, any resemblance to actual persons, living or dead, is purely coincidental.

Every effort has been made to obtain the necessary permissions with reference to copyright material, both illustrative and quoted. We apologise for any omissions in this respect and will be pleased to make the appropriate acknowledgements in any future edition.

A CIP catalogue record for this book is available from the British Library.

Paperback ISBN 978-1-80549-661-8

Large Print ISBN 978-1-80549-663-2

Harback ISBN 978-1-80549-660-1

Ebook ISBN 978-1-80549-664-9

Kindle ISBN 978-1-80549-665-6

Audio CD ISBN 978-1-80549-655-7

MP3 CD ISBN 978-1-80549-656-4

Digital audio download ISBN 978-1-80549-657-1

Boldwood Books Ltd
23 Bowerdean Street
London SW6 3TN
www.boldwoodbooks.com

To Em, Michaela, and all the readers that find strength in stories and respite in reading.

1

Daisy May closed up the shutters after another successful day at the Coffee Shop on the Canal. It was hard to believe this summer was almost over. June and July had whizzed by in a blur – a very hectic blur. Getting the coffee shop up and running hadn't been as smooth sailing as she'd hoped, with issues from licensing to broken windows, and a slight turmoil in her love life to add to the mix. But she had got through it. And the last six weeks had been plain sailing, relatively speaking.

From learning to bake to waking up at five-thirty seven days a week, it was a steep learning curve, but no matter how tired she got, or how much she wished she had just a little more free time to see Theo, Daisy knew she could never go back to her previous office job. Just like she could never go back to living in a normal flat.

The situation with Theo was less than ideal. Having had her heart broken when she was younger, Daisy had actively avoided getting into another relationship and assumed she'd be single forever. But Theo had changed that. Unfortunately, Daisy's fears about having her heart broken, combined with the very charismatic Christian – who swept onto the scene, and nearly swept her off her feet too – meant she and Theo took longer than necessary to get together. Thankfully, Daisy finally saw sense and they had officially been a couple for just over two months. Theo was everything she could have hoped for in a partner – encouraging and supportive, as well as being a dab hand in the kitchen. He made her laugh more than anybody else, and being with him truly made Daisy feel as though she was capable of anything. In fact, as far as Theo went, there was only one issue – he wasn't there.

Daisy hated that she only had herself to blame. While she'd been trying to cope with the unexpected love triangle she'd found herself in, Theo had taken a job on the other side of the country – a three-and-a-half-hour drive away. With the coffee shop open every day of the week and Theo wanting to make as good an impression in his new position as he could, the time they had to spend together was limited. Which was why Daisy was shutting up shop fifteen minutes earlier than normal; so she had time to get showered and clean through the boat before he arrived.

As she finished the final wipe-down of the counters, her phone buzzed on the table. Theo's name flashed up on the screen, causing her stomach to flutter with excitement.

Dropping the cloth where it was, she hurried to pick up the phone.

'Hey, you,' Theo said as soon as she answered. His voice was enough to make her heart race. It was crazy how much she loved hearing from him. And in only a few hours, they would be together. 'How are you? How's your day been? You're not still open, are you?'

'No, I've just closed up,' she said. Her cheeks were aching as she grinned.

'Good. Does that mean you have time to talk, then?'

'You know I always have time for you.'

Theo chuckled. 'That's a nice line, but you know it's not true, right? You're almost always busy.'

Daisy grunted. It was true. The only time their schedules seemed to align was late in the evening and often, she was so tired, she could only manage fifteen minutes of conversation before she fell asleep. Lesser men than Theo might have been insulted that their girlfriend started snoring half the time they spoke, but Theo knew how hard she worked.

'So, are you on the road yet?' Daisy asked as she flopped down onto the sofa. 'It feels like forever since I've seen you.'

'I know. I'm really sorry about last weekend.'

'You don't need to apologise. It wasn't like you put those otters in the canal.'

Theo let out a wistful sigh. 'They were amazing, Daisy. Honestly. I wish you could've seen them. But we had to stay up there, make sure none of the boaters or borders disturbed them.'

Theo's job involved general maintenance and monitoring of the canals, which meant that, just like Daisy, no two days were the same. It also meant he could be called upon at the most inconvenient hours, including when the pair were meant to be meeting.

'Honestly, you don't need to explain,' she said. 'I get it. It's completely fine.'

As much as Daisy meant it, it didn't stop the knot twisting in the pit of her stomach. It had been so many years since she'd been in a relationship like this and yet, since Theo had moved over six weeks ago, they had seen each other a measly four times. Three of those times were on weekends when he'd come down to the coffee shop, and it had been so busy, he'd had to spend the daytime working with her. It had been nice, of course, just being close to him, but by the evening, they were so exhausted, they could barely even manage a decent conversation. The other time was just for the evening when he'd managed to score the following morning off work.

'So, are you on your way?' she asked again, realising he hadn't yet answered her question.

'Actually…' Theo paused. The knots in Daisy's stomach tightened. It'd all seemed so straightforward before he'd left. They'd had a plan. Any time the weather forecast was terrible for more than two days in a row, she was going to head up to Slimbridge. Any weekends when Theo wasn't called in for emergency jobs on the canal, he was coming down here. But the weather had been perfect, with barely a cloud in the sky, and Theo's new job had far more responsibility than expected and emergencies always seemed to happen. Now, she sensed it was going to be even longer until she saw him.

'Actually, Daisy, I hate to do this to you so much, but—'

Whatever Theo was about to say was drowned out by a heavy hammering on her front door.

'Sorry, Theo, did you say you're not coming?'

The hammering knocked again.

'For crying out loud,' Daisy muttered to herself. She couldn't imagine who it could be. Perhaps some irate customer who expected her to be open until six, even though the sign clearly said she closed at five. They'd knocked on the hatch doors before, but on her front door was a whole different level of rudeness. Besides, whoever it was, there was no way it was more important than hearing when, or if, she was next going to see Theo.

'Actually, do you know what, Theo? I'll ring you back. Don't go anywhere. I'll be two minutes.'

She strode across the *September Rose*, where her paintings hung from the wall, and the afternoon light filtered in through the windows. Once again, the knocking came.

'Will you just hang on?' she said as she swung open the door. 'Do you—'

Daisy stopped, staring at the sight in front of her. His long hair was tied up in its normal bun, while the hint of a smirk twisted on his lips.

'Sorry, I know you were on the phone and everything, but I thought I might come down a bit earlier, if that's all right with you?'

2

As Daisy lay in her bed the next morning, she prayed for rain. It wasn't something she prayed for often. After all, her business depended on the bright sunshine to bring out the dog walkers and paddle boarders who were always happy to spend their money at the Coffee Shop on the Canal. But that morning, with Theo lying in bed beside her, she wasn't in the mood for serving coffee. She wanted a day for just the two of them. Maybe they could take a walk together, or better still, take the boat out.

After an incident involving a drunken stag do, the boat had been out of action for the best part of a month. Thankfully, she'd found someone who could fix it without taking it out of the water, meaning the cost had been kept to a minimum and she'd only had to shut up shop for half a day, but despite now having a fully working propeller, she hadn't been out on a trip for weeks.

'You know, you haven't told me how long you're planning on staying,' she said as she nestled into Theo's shoulder.

'I know, because I have to leave later today.'

'Today?' Daisy sat upright. 'You're not staying for the whole weekend? You drove all this way for one night?'

Theo shifted slightly in the bed and raised an eyebrow.

'Would you prefer it if I hadn't? Maybe I should've stayed in the Cotswolds.'

'You know that's not what I meant.' Daisy hit him playfully on the shoulder as she spoke. 'It's just, I'd love to have some real time together. It feels like the minute you arrive, you're getting ready to leave again.'

'I know, I get that. But it's not forever, is it? When the weather turns, you can shut the coffee shop and spend some more time up in Slimbridge.'

Daisy let out a long sigh as Theo's words rattled around in her head. To visit him for any length of time meant closing down her business, and that was a hard pill to swallow.

Despite the *September Rose* being a fully mobile canal boat, the likelihood of Daisy opening up anywhere other than Wildflower Lock or Heybridge was slim. All because of where she was. Wildflower Lock was positioned on a canal on its own strip of perfect countryside. She could head all the way to Chelmsford, or down to the estuary which lead to the sea. But that was where the problem arose. Canal boats weren't designed to go on the open water. Even Theo had been nervous about doing it. And that was putting it mildly.

The closer and closer to the move he'd got, the more nervous Theo had become. Not because he was leaving, but because of *what* he had to do when he left. Getting from Wildflower Lock onto the main canal network that spanned across the country meant going, however briefly, out of the estuary and onto the open water, after which it required a trip on the tidal River Thames, before finally joining the network of canals on the west of London, which he could use to get to the Cotswolds and his new home.

'It's a boat,' Daisy remembered saying as they sat down for dinner one evening, when Theo had told her his fears. While she was a long way from considering herself a canal boat expert, she no longer considered herself a complete novice, either. However, it was clear from this situation that there was still plenty she needed to learn. 'What's wrong with going out into the estuary? I thought people crossed the channel on narrowboats?'

'Crazy people cross the channel on narrowboats,' Theo had replied.

'Normal people stick to the canals and rivers. The hulls aren't designed to cut through the water. One big wave can capsize you, with no way of righting yourself again.'

It didn't sound great.

'Surely there's another way?' Daisy had replied, her previous doubts and worry about Theo leaving amplified by the fear that he might not make it to Slimbridge at all. 'Is there something else you can do? Another way of getting there?'

He had shaken his head and let out a long sigh.

'Short of getting a lorry, loading the *Escape* on, using a ton of my savings, no. It's fine. It's summer. The weather is great. This is the time to do it. As long as we have a smooth day to leave, with no wind, we'll be fine.'

'We?' There was something in his use of the plural that made Daisy stop. Did he think perhaps she was going too? Or was he referring to himself and the boat?

Theo saw her concern and smiled.

'Don't worry, I'm bringing a friend with me. Dominic has done the route before a few times. It's not that I'm not capable; it's just that I feel safer having somebody else do a trip like that with me.'

Daisy did too.

Theo reached across the table and grabbed her hand.

'Don't worry, it'll be fine, I promise.'

And of course, it had been, but that didn't change the fact that this separation was a big one. There was no chance of him just packing up the *Narrow Escape* and bringing it back to Wildflower Lock. Not for a long time.

'Hey, don't do that.' Theo's voice brought Daisy back to the moment and the fact she was now sitting in bed next to him, the crossing weeks in the past.

'Do what?' Daisy said, flopping back down onto the pillow with a sigh.

'Get stuck in your head. It's fine. We're fine. Like I said, as soon as the weather turns, you'll only need to be down here on the weekends. And then we can make up for all the time we've lost not being together.'

'And how do you propose we make up for this lost time?' Daisy asked, rolling over onto her side and propping herself up on her elbow.

'You know, I've got a couple of ideas.'

Theo leaned in to kiss her. It was a morning-breath kiss, something she'd have previously avoided at all costs, but given how rarely they got to see each other, she took whatever she could get. Unfortunately, no sooner had their lips touched than the sound of voices reached them.

'Well, that's a shame,' she heard a masculine voice say on the towpath outside. 'I thought it'd be open by now. Never mind, we'll fetch a drink on the way back.'

Daisy rolled onto her back and groaned.

'I could put up a sign,' she whispered to Theo. 'A sign saying I'm sick, that the coffee shop is closed for the day.'

She wanted nothing more than to sink back into the bed and forget that her job was waiting for her, but Theo ripped the duvet off.

'Come on, where's that hard-working woman I fell in love with?'

Daisy froze. The L-word hadn't been mentioned before, apart from in conversations with Bex and Claire, where her friends had mercilessly asked her to admit how she felt. But she wouldn't do that. Besides, she told them, she was sure Theo felt the same way as her, so what did it matter if he used the actual word or not? But now she'd heard it, she wasn't sure how to react. After all, saying 'woman I fell in love with' wasn't the same as saying 'I love you'.

Was she meant to respond? And if so, what was she meant to say?

With a flood of heat rushing to her cheeks, Daisy jumped out of bed and marched towards the bathroom.

'Come on,' she said. 'If you're here, I'm putting you to work. You've got a lot of cappuccinos to make.'

3

When working in the coffee shop by the canal, days went at a pace that Daisy had never known. Her last job, before inheriting the *September Rose*, involved eight hours sat behind a desk, staring at a computer screen while her eyes constantly flicked up towards the clock, praying that time would speed up. Now, however, she wished it would slow down.

As much as she hoped there might be a quick shower of rain, or at least a cold spell to break up the day, there was no such respite. She and Theo didn't even get as much as a lunch break to stop and talk together. Instead, they grabbed a slice of cake each while they were on the go. It didn't help that Daisy's lie-in meant she hadn't done the early-morning bake like normal, and so was running back and forth to the kitchen, tipping scones onto baking trays while whipping up cream-cheese icing for the carrot cake.

By the time five o'clock rolled around and Daisy finally had a chance to restock the paper cups above the coffee machine, Theo was already checking his watch, a sure sign that he needed to leave.

'Are you sure you can't stay tonight? It is Sunday tomorrow,' Daisy stressed as if Theo might not be aware of what day of the week it was.

'This is not forever,' he told her as he wrapped his arms around her waist and pulled her in for a hug. 'Honestly, when winter comes, we'll be so sick of each other, we'll be laughing about this.'

'Do you think?'

'I know. We'll be praying for the summer days when we get to be apart.'

Not for one second did Daisy believe it was true and yet, for Theo's sake more than anything else, she forced herself to smile.

'Come on then,' she said. 'I'll walk you to the car park.'

As their fingers remained intertwined, the weight in Daisy's chest grew heavier and heavier. Her last relationship had ended because her ex didn't want to do long distance. And she had been so mad about it. But now, as she was saying goodbye to Theo after only twenty-four hours together, she couldn't help but wonder if he had been right.

'Please don't look like that,' Theo said when they reached the car park.

'Sorry.' Daisy forced herself to look slightly more upbeat. 'You're right. It's not like it's going to be long until we see each other. You're still planning on coming down next weekend too, aren't you? It's meant to be a scorcher.'

Rather than confirming his next visit, as Daisy had assumed Theo would do, her boyfriend's eyes shifted to the ground, causing a lump to fill her throat.

'Theo?'

There was no denying the look in his eye, which only intensified as his gaze met Daisy's.

'I didn't want to say this in the boat, but these next few weeks, they're going to be manic for me.'

'Manic? What does that mean?' Daisy asked, the pit in her stomach taking on a new churning feeling.

'They're doing some bridge work that I need to oversee. It's meant to last for five weeks. I'm not even sure where I'll be. I might moor the *Escape* in Bath for some of it, at least on the River Avon somewhere.'

'So, what does that mean for us?' Daisy hated how she sounded insecure, but it was hard when the only other relationship she'd had bolted at the thought of anything long-distance.

'It doesn't mean anything for us,' Theo said. 'I love you, Daisy May.'

There was no ambiguity now. No way to misconstrue those words. He had said them, clear as day, staring straight at her.

'I love you, and just like I said, when winter comes around, you and I will spend so much time together that we'll be sick of each other.'

Daisy could feel the tears prickling behind her eyes as her heart swelled. The way Theo said things just made everything sound so simple. Like she had nothing to worry about. This was it. They were a properly committed couple. A little bit of distance wouldn't be enough to split this relationship up.

'So?' Theo said.

'So what?' Daisy replied, before suddenly realising. 'Oh, I love you, too,' she said, grinning from ear to ear. She didn't even move to kiss him, the way she thought they would when they finally said those words. Instead, she just covered her mouth in half shock.

'Are you sure?' Theo said, mockingly wiping sweat from his brow. 'You know, I was getting worried there. You took your time to reply.'

'I did not.'

'You did too.'

She laughed and placed her hands on his cheeks.

'I love you, Theo. Is that enough? I love you with my whole heart.'

'I love you too. And I will love you tomorrow, and I will love you next week and I will love you when I finally see you again. Now, though, I better go.'

Daisy didn't object again. Instead, she watched as he climbed into his car, not sure whether she wanted to cry at the sight of him leaving or laugh at the fact he'd finally said those magic words. Either way, she stayed there, watching him as he reversed out of the car park. When he reached the road, he wound his window down and yelled across to her from the gate. 'I love you, Daisy May!'

'I love you too,' she called.

And with that, he was gone.

4

It didn't matter how upset Daisy was at Theo leaving; hearing the words 'I love you' yelled out over Wildflower Lock car park was enough to forget it all.

Daisy May was in love. She wasn't just dating; she didn't just have a boyfriend. She had a boyfriend who *loved* her. It was enough to put a skip in her step as she headed back onto the towpath. There, the closest boat moored to the car park was the *Jeanette*, which was owned by none other than her mother's new boyfriend, Nicholas. For a split second, she considered knocking on the door to see if her mother was visiting. After all, she desperately wanted to share her news, though she decided quickly against it. No matter what her mother said, Daisy hadn't yet seen a pleasant side to Nicholas. Besides, she could simply text her mum to let her know on the phone.

Her second thought was to message Bex or Claire, only she immediately discarded those options, too. Bex was spending the weekend on a work retreat that she'd been talking about for the last two months, and not positively. Two days full of team-building activities, like leading one another blindfolded through an obstacle course, or completing personality tests to find out what sort of leader you are. All activities that Bex pretended she had no interest in. But deep down, they all knew how much she'd enjoy it when she was there. After all, a bit of competitiveness always brought out the best in her. Unfortunately, it meant she wouldn't be free for a chat.

Claire, meanwhile, was currently on holiday in Croatia. The last thing Daisy wanted was to disturb her while she was getting some well-needed family time. For a split second, Daisy thought she was out of people she could divulge this amazing news to when, as she walked up the canal and reached the *September Rose*, she noted the boat on the other side of it.

The beautiful *Ariadne* was owned by Yvonne, the elderly lady who had been on the canal even when Daisy's parents were married and living there. She had been the one who'd told Daisy about her past on Wildflower Lock, and let her browse through the dozens of dusty photo albums she kept, allowing Daisy a glimpse of her father and mother in a life she had never known.

Daisy always promised herself she would drop in on Yvonne more often. After all, Yvonne invited her around for a cup of tea every time they saw each other, but Daisy struggled to find the time. After talking to people all day at the coffee shop, the last thing she wanted when she finished was yet more chatting. Only today was different. Today, she wanted to talk, and maybe, she thought, she could kill two birds with one stone, giving Yvonne a bit of company while somehow slipping in the news of her and Theo.

Having decided what she was going to do, Daisy popped into the *September Rose*. She grabbed the unsold slices of cake, popped them into one of her takeaway boxes and crossed over the bridge.

The *Ariadne* was identifiable by sight but also by aroma, as it was the only houseboat on the canal that smelled strongly of incense. The scent, which rose from constantly burning candles and incense sticks, formed an invisible fog around the moorings and, for an instant, Daisy regretted the decision to visit her friend. Thankfully, she spotted Yvonne sitting on the stern of the boat enjoying a cup of tea outside.

'Fancy a slice of cake to go with that?' Daisy asked as she approached.

Yvonne turned to face her and grinned. 'I never say no to cake.'

Daisy returned the smile. 'I thought you might say that, though I brought a slice for both of us too, if you want some company?'

A slight pause followed, after which Yvonne waved her hands impatiently.

'What are you waiting for, then? Pop aboard!'

A minute later, Daisy was sitting on the hull of the *Ariadne* with the box of cake open between them.

'So I saw your young man last night,' Yvonne said between mouthfuls. 'He popped in to say hello to me.'

'He did?' Daisy wondered when that could have been, as from the moment Theo had arrived at the *September Rose*, the pair hadn't separated. Then again, he probably arrived earlier, while she had a queue, and came here first. That would explain why she hadn't seen him coming up the towpath.

'Oh, he couldn't stay. He was rushing to get to you.' Yvonne confirmed what Daisy had thought. 'But he wanted to make sure he said hello. Tell me, how's that new job of his going? Sounds like it's keeping him busy.'

'Too busy,' Daisy said. She didn't mean to sound so down. After all, that was the exact opposite of why she had come here. But it was how she felt.

'That doesn't sound good,' Yvonne commented. 'Everything all right between you two?'

'Oh, yes, everything is wonderful. He told me he loved me.' Daisy grinned, happy to have shoe-horned the comment in almost naturally.

'Well, of course he loves you. Any fool can see that,' Yvonne remarked, almost rolling her eyes.

Daisy smiled to herself. Others had said that before. That it was obvious how crazy Theo was about her from the way he looked at her. Still, there was something about hearing those words from his mouth that made it all the more concrete.

'It's good. It's really good; I just wish I could see more of him. He's going to be away for a month now. Honestly, if I could take the *September Rose* on the sea, I swear I would head straight to him tomorrow.'

Yvonne frowned. 'What do you mean, "if"? Of course you can take it on the sea. Well, not the open sea. And it's been a long time since I've done it, but...'

Daisy paused, her fork poised just above the cake. 'What do you mean? You took the *Ariadne* on the sea?'

'The *Ariadne*, and the *Minotaur* before that. It's the only way to get out of the estuary.'

Daisy could hear what Yvonne was saying, but she was still shaking her head in disbelief.

'But I thought you couldn't? The hull, the flat bottom. I thought if a wave hits you...'

'Oh yes, if a big wave hits you, you're done for,' Yvonne said matter-of-factly. 'But we're not talking about crossing the Atlantic here. Get a calm day, get your tide timings right, and you can get round to Southend easily enough. And after that, well, the world is your oyster. Or at least, the rivers and canals are.'

Daisy sat back in her chair, ruminating over what she just heard. She'd always thought that the *September Rose* could only be moved off this stretch of canal on the back of a trailer. But Yvonne was saying she'd done the journey, and multiple times at that.

As she sat there, pondering the idea, Daisy couldn't help but think how nice it would be to turn up and surprise Theo. To moor up alongside the *Narrow Escape*. That way, they wouldn't just have to spend one or two days together. They could spend weeks, months even – assuming she could find a suitable spot for the coffee shop.

She looked at Yvonne, unable to suppress the giddiness that was flooding through her.

'Would you fancy doing that trip again?' she asked.

5

Daisy immediately regretted her words. After all, it was a ludicrous suggestion. Theo had been anxious enough about making the trip and had needed to take a more experienced friend with him to help pilot the boat. It was preposterous to think Yvonne would want to undertake such a journey at her age and especially with someone as ill-equipped as Daisy. Though, as Daisy looked up from her tea, she noticed the slight twist at the corners of Yvonne's mouth.

'We'll have to get going soon,' she said. 'While the weather is still nice. The moment it turns, everything becomes a lot more challenging. But I think I've got one last adventure in me. Who knows, this trip to Slimbridge might be exactly that.'

'Well, yes, I was only joking,' Daisy said, hoping to divert the conversation to another topic. 'Just voicing my thoughts aloud. Now tell me what you think of the cake. It was my mother's recipe, but I added some lavender to it. Do you think it worked?'

With the conversation successfully shifted, the pair carried on chatting about day-to-day things – how busy it was with the paddle boarders, how many of them had been kicked off the canal for not having a licence, and which of the canal volunteers were retiring after the summer. After about half an hour of nattering, Daisy felt herself yawn. And once she started, it was near impossible to stop. It might be the weekend, but she was working seven days a week and couldn't see that stopping anytime soon.

'Sorry, Yvonne, I should head back,' she said. 'I think I need an early night.'

'No need to apologise. Thank you for coming over. Perhaps I could swing by one evening if you like? Make you my famous yellow curry.'

'That sounds fabulous,' Daisy replied. 'Just let me know when.'

After a hug goodbye, Daisy stepped onto the towpath and started her walk towards the bridge. She had just reached it when Yvonne called out to her.

'And I'm in, you know. If you change your mind, I'm definitely in.'

* * *

The next morning, when Daisy opened up the coffee shop, she was surprised to see her first customer ready and waiting. Early patrons weren't unusual, but seeing this one at such an hour certainly was.

'Mum? What are you doing down here?'

'You know, I was just... here...' her mother said.

It didn't take long for Daisy to connect the dots. For her mum to have been at Nicholas's so early in the morning, it was more than likely she'd spent the night there and that wasn't a thought Daisy wanted to dwell on. Taking a deep breath in, she reminded herself that her mother was an adult, and said, 'Well, what can I get you to drink? Or would you like something to eat? I've just baked a Bakewell tart. It won't be anywhere near as good as yours, but it's not too bad.'

'No, no. Nicholas made me breakfast, thank you.' Her mother kept her expression neutral. 'An Americano would be lovely, though. And make it a double shot; I'm feeling particularly tired this morning.'

That was more innuendo than Daisy could handle, so she turned her back to her mother and got to work on the coffee machine.

'How's Theo doing?' her mother asked as Daisy placed a cup under the filter.

'He's good,' Daisy replied, still not ready to turn and face her. 'He came down for the night on Friday, but had to leave yesterday evening.'

'That's a shame. I'm sad to have missed him again.'

'Me too, actually.' Daisy pulled the cup from the coffee machine, though she held on to it rather than handing it over.

Like her mother, Daisy was exceptionally tired that morning as she'd struggled all night to fall asleep. Her mind had been too busy flitting from one idea to the next. Normally, painting was the key to resolving any of her issues. She could open up her palette of watercolour paints, swirl her brush around in the water, and within minutes, she'd be thinking about nothing but the washes of colour on the page. But after she'd got back from Yvonne's, her mind had refused to settle. Instead, it kept returning to the same thought: Could she do it? Could she take the *September Rose* not just away from Wildflower Lock, but all the way to see Theo?

She cleared her throat and began to speak.

'This is probably going to sound a bit strange, but when you were here with, with...' She paused. She never referred to her father as 'Dad.' That was too personal. Those words implied a relationship between the two of them, and there never had been one. But, as ridiculous as it was, since moving into the *September Rose*, Daisy couldn't help but feel a bond forming between the pair. Still, she knew where the land lay with her mother and her ex-husband. 'When you and my father lived here, did you ever take the *September Rose* out of the canal?'

'What do you mean?' Her mother looked confused by the question. 'Of course we did. We travelled everywhere. I thought you knew that. During our honeymoon, we spent months on the boat.'

'So you actually went out of the estuary? Onto the open waters?'

At this, her mother's expression changed, her lips pressed together tightly.

'You mean out into the sea?' She reached out her hand, and it was only then that Daisy realised she had not yet given her mother her cup of coffee. 'Once. Yes, for our honeymoon. The most terrifying thing we've ever done, I can tell you that.'

Daisy clicked another round of coffee grounds into the filter, deciding she needed to pour herself a drink, too.

'And the boat made it?' Daisy asked, trying to sound as casual as possible. 'Obviously, she made it. You're fine, the *September Rose* is fine.'

'Oh, yes. It was an adventure, that's for sure. We picked a beautiful day for it. Honestly, the sea was so calm, it was like glass. I swear, not a single wave. Or a cloud in the sky. But I tell you what, I was sick with nerves. Well, that's what I thought at the time. Turns out I was pregnant with you. Didn't change the memory though, and the way back was just as terrifying. But your father, he knew what he was doing with boats. Just like Theo.'

Daisy nodded, accepting the truth of her mother's words. There was no way she could head out of the estuary in the *September Rose* on her own. But then again, she didn't have to be alone. She already had an all too willing and experienced volunteer to come with her.

'Well, thank you for this, darling. Nicholas does a lot of things well, but honestly, his coffee tastes like dishwater. We'll catch up soon, right?'

'Of course,' Daisy said, her mind still thinking of a boat trip she couldn't possibly take. Could she?

6

The morning influx of customers didn't stop, although not all of them wanted coffee or cake. By midday, it felt like every other person asked if Daisy had ice cream on board or if she knew where they could get some. Unfortunately, she had to let them down on both fronts.

More than once, she'd looked at whether it would be feasible to sell ice creams, even if it was just the frozen-lolly type, but she and Theo had both concluded that it wasn't. It didn't matter how she looked at the space – there was no room for an ice cream freezer unless she wanted to sacrifice some of her living room or a bedroom. The space in the *September Rose* was one of the things Daisy adored the most, as was the ability to have friends stay over. She wasn't ready to give either of those up yet. So the customers would have to go without until she could think of a creative solution.

At four-fifteen, when the majority of visitors were packing away for the day, Daisy finally closed the shutters. Without even bothering to tidy up the machine, or restock, she dropped onto the sofa and allowed herself a proper deep breath for the first time all day. Tidying up would have to wait.

With all the windows open and the breeze sweeping through, the *September Rose* was pleasantly cool, yet even as she kicked off her shoes,

Daisy couldn't get comfortable. Even after she got back up, cleaned up the coffee machine and washed the milk jugs, she couldn't rest. Her gaze continually drifted outside, onto the water. It had been such a calm day that the only ripples on the surface came from the paddle boarders and the waterfowl. It couldn't possibly be like that on the estuary, could it? Or the open sea? But then what had her mother said? When she had made the trip, the sea had been so calm, it was like glass. Surely taking the boat on the water when it was like that would be no different than driving it on a canal and she was perfectly capable of that.

With her pulse increasing ever so slightly, Daisy stood up, slipped her shoes on, and marched over the bridge.

'Are you serious?' She didn't even bother with a greeting but started talking to Yvonne the moment she saw her sitting out on her hull. 'Would you do this trip with me?'

'The trip? You mean to see Theo?'

'There won't be lots of room,' Daisy said, her thoughts spilling from her mouth before she had time to think through them. 'You could take my berth, and I can take the smaller one. That's fine, but there's still not going to be lots of room.'

'Well, I don't need that much room—' Yvonne started but Daisy hadn't finished yet.

'And I'm not sure I'll be able to have all your incense and candles burning, not with all the cooking I have to do if I'm going to keep the coffee shop going while we're on the move. And I would need to open the coffee shop, at least for a few days, otherwise I won't be able to afford fuel.' The more Daisy spoke, the more issues rose to the front of her mind. 'And I'm not sure about getting back, either. I don't know how long I plan on staying there. But, I can stay on the *Escape* with Theo, or you could?' She was thinking through the process as she spoke. 'I'm sure he wouldn't mind at all. And then we can come back together after a couple of weeks? If that suits you, of course? You can come back sooner if you want.'

The reality was that Daisy needed to be back for winter. Mooring fees were due in September. If she wasn't back by the end of the month, with the money to pay them, she would lose her spot. Her father's spot. Still, that gave her several weeks to drive up to Slimbridge, spend some proper time with Theo, then drive back again before the weather turned and the crossing became impossible. Assuming, of course, that Yvonne really was up for one last adventure.

Having got everything off her chest, Daisy finally allowed herself to take a breath.

'Obviously, I haven't got all the details sorted,' she said, only then realising exactly how insane she must have sounded. So insane that she was about to offer Yvonne an apology and blame her outburst on overwork and lack of hydration. But instead, when she looked at Yvonne, she found a smile breaking on her face.

'Oh, I don't need to bother with all the details. They only bog me down,' Yvonne said. 'I'm in.'

7

Daisy and Yvonne spent the next two hours poring over maps of canals that spanned the width of Britain, along with photos of the places from Yvonne's previous travels. She had dozens of booklets containing tide times, lock information and telephone numbers for various marinas.

'The thing I love about the canals is how nothing changes,' she said. 'So many of these places still look the same as the first time I visited them. It's a miracle, really. Everywhere else, buildings are going up, history coming down, and yet the canals get to stay. Do you know there is a bridge over the canal in Maldon that still has holes in it drilled during the Second World War, just in case they needed to blow it up?'

'Is that right?' Daisy didn't know whether to feel awed or terrified that she was going to be driving the boat under bridges with holes in them.

'It's got a very interesting history, you know. Very interesting indeed.' Yvonne picked up another of the photo albums, only to rest her hand on the top without opening it. For the first time since Daisy had come to the *Ariadne*, the pair fell into silence.

'What is it?' Daisy asked. 'Is something wrong?'

'Wrong?' Yvonne said, before shaking her head. 'No. No, it just brings back memories, you know. And your dad would've liked this. I bet he'd have given anything to be the one talking to you about these routes. Telling you about all the places we're going to see.'

'I'm sure he would have,' Daisy agreed. A slight melancholy had fallen between them, yet before it could form any depth, Yvonne reached forward and took Daisy's hands.

'It's probably very selfish of me, but as he can't be here with you, I'm glad that I get to do this. It makes me feel a little closer to him, you know?'

Daisy knew exactly what Yvonne meant. And she was equally grateful. Perhaps this time spent together travelling to Slimbridge would be a time for Yvonne to teach Daisy more about her family, her past and, most of all, her father.

'I need to figure out where I'm going to get business for the coffee shop,' Daisy said, breaking the nostalgia with practicality. 'I still need a couple more weeks of trade to have enough to cover me for the winter, which means I need to stop at as many points as we can. Maybe we can do one day travelling, one day opening the shop?'

Yvonne pondered the question with a shrug of her shoulder.

'Well, it'll take some planning, but there are definitely a fair few places we can stop, though it might be easier when we're through London.'

'Through London?' Daisy said, her stomach squirming. There were several days travelling between here and the big city, and she was hoping she wouldn't have to keep the coffee shop closed for more than two days at a time.

'Don't worry, there are a couple of places this side too,' Yvonne assured her. 'We can stop on Burnham. It's on the River Crouch, the next estuary along from us. It's a pretty little place with a nice seawall. I'm sure we'll get a few customers there. After that, it'll be Southend. Again, you should manage a bit of business. It's not going to be quite so grand going through the Dartford Canal, though. You might have to swallow your pride and stay closed there, I'm afraid.'

Daisy nodded. The places Yvonne had mentioned sounded vaguely familiar, but not enough for her to know exactly where she was talking about. Still, it would be fine. Once they were on the canals, they would be limited in the ways they could go. And beneath those flurries of fear were definite bubbles of excitement, too.

'You're not allowed to mention anything to Theo, please?' Daisy said to Yvonne half an hour later as they were packing up the maps and photographs. The longer they'd talked, the more excited she had become, though Daisy was determined not to get ahead of herself. There was still a way to go before they could leave.

'Don't be silly,' Yvonne assured her. 'And don't worry about me bringing too much stuff either. One suitcase, that's all I need. Just my precious bits and bobs. You concentrate on the coffee shop. Get a good couple of days' sales in. I'll focus on the rest of it. I've got all the information we need here.' She patted the pile of booklets in front of her. The top was yellow with a torn cover and while Daisy couldn't read the full title, the words 'Tidal Thames' were boldly typed across the centre. 'I'll get us there. I just need a couple of days to check times, book some moorings and I'd say we'd be good to go in... three days?'

'Three days?' Daisy's nervousness hitched in her voice as she spoke aloud. Three days – that was absolutely ridiculous. Three days until she left not only Wildflower Lock but the entire canal system she knew. Was she really going to do it?

She answered the question in her mind without a second thought. If she was going to do it, then she needed to do it now. Any later then Theo would be coming down to see her anyway, and they would risk the bad weather.

'Three days it is,' she said, before squeezing Yvonne tightly. How she was going to keep this a secret from Theo was a mystery, but that was part of the fun, too, wasn't it?

8

With her mind set, Daisy just had a few housekeeping issues to deal with before she could focus on the journey ahead. And the first thing on the list was telling Bex and Claire.

After her retreat – which was entirely teetotal – Bex was happy to meet at a nearby pub on Monday evening. While Claire couldn't join them in person, she was there on Daisy's screen, looking more than a little sun-kissed, sitting on a lounger by the pool with a margarita in her hand.

'That's insane.' Bex made no attempt to mince her words about the upcoming adventure. 'Wicked, but completely insane.'

'Are you sure it's safe?' Claire asked, straight in there with the practicalities.

'I think "safe" is probably the wrong word. We just have to be cautious, that's all,' Daisy said. 'And the *September Rose* is capable of the journey. She did it with my mum and dad.'

'When she was brand new?' Claire said, though thankfully, before Daisy had time to respond, Bex was asking her next question.

'So you're going to be living with Yvonne in your boat? For how long? How long will it take you to get there?'

Daisy blew out a long puff of air as she picked up her drink and took a sip.

'Well, this is the thing. It's a bit hit and miss, really. To start with, we have to rely on the tides. We can only go out when it's high tide, so that'll put some restrictions on us. And I'll also need to make some money, so we can't travel all the time, but assuming we're travelling for most of the daylight hours, then I reckon we can make it in three weeks.'

'Three weeks? That's ridiculous. Just get a bus. Or a car.' Claire said.

Yet once again, before Daisy could reply, Bex was talking.

'Wait, hold on a minute. You're saying you're going to drive the *September Rose* and keep the coffee shop going? I thought the whole point of you buying the licence was because you were only going to run the coffee shop here, at Wildflower Lock?'

'I know.' Daisy let out a slightly exasperated sigh, aimed more at herself than anyone else. 'But I had to get the licence for Wildflower Lock, otherwise I wouldn't have been able to get the propeller fixed, which means I couldn't move. It was a catch-22. Besides, it's not like I'm not going away for that long, really. It's just going to be a few weeks. Six at most. So I'd still need the licence for the rest of that time.'

Bex and Claire exchanged a look, or rather, Bex raised her eyebrows while looking at Claire on the phone screen, and Claire crinkled her nose in response. It was even less subtle than when they did things like that in real life.

'I don't know why you guys are being so strange about it. I just thought you'd be happy. Theo and I are a proper couple. In love.'

Bex rested her chin on her hands as she dropped her head. 'Well, I suppose if that's what you want to do, that's what you're gonna do. But six weeks? How the hell are we going to cope without you for that long?'

'I'm sure you'll find a way.'

Surprisingly, the girls didn't say any more to dissuade her. Instead, they simply asked more questions about her plans and, if anything, they made her more certain she was doing the right thing.

'This isn't just about seeing Theo,' Daisy told them. 'Since I've had the *September Rose*, the furthest I've been is to Heybridge. That's not what my dad wanted a boat for. It's not why my grandad gave her to me. She was meant to travel. She was meant to go around the country. I need to do this, almost... almost...'

She didn't manage to finish her sentence, but she didn't need to as Bex reached across the table to take her hands.

'It's for your dad,' she said.

'An apology, you know. I thought he abandoned me. I thought he wanted nothing to do with me. Doing this. Spending this time on the water... It's going to be my apology to him.'

She looked at her friends, awaiting their reply.

'Well, there's no way we could not support that, is there?' Bex said with a smirk. 'But you need to stay in touch, okay? Every place, we want photographs and videos. And you need to make sure you've got life-jackets.'

Daisy rolled her eyes. 'You know I've already got a mother, right?'

'That's true,' Claire said. 'An overprotective one, if I'm not mistaken. What's she said about it?'

Daisy picked up her glass and took a long sip of wine. The girls might have been all on board for this adventure, but somehow, she didn't think that her mother was going to feel the same way.

9

Daisy sat opposite her mother, the ticking clock echoing through the room, a potent reminder of the rapidly approaching departure time. It was now only forty-eight hours until she had agreed to leave with Yvonne, and yet she had still not told her mother about the impending adventure. It was cowardice; she knew that. She was scared of her mum's response. Scared that it would put a wedge back between them when they were only now starting to heal their relationship. Not to mention the fact she was scared of the trip itself. And so Daisy had asked if she could come to the shop before she opened up on Tuesday morning.

'So, it must have been very important if you needed to see me this early?' her mother said, forcing Daisy to take in a deep breath.

'So, here's the thing...' she started.

Daisy told her what she'd told the girls, almost word for word. That she was eager to spend some real time with Theo before winter set in and would need to leave now to make sure she could get back before the weather turned. She also told her how it was going to be a last adventure for Yvonne, and how Daisy was lucky she was going to be with someone experienced on the trip. However, she omitted the part about the journey being an apology to her father. If they were honest with each other, it was her mother who owed both Daisy and Johnny the biggest apology.

When Daisy finished speaking, her mum folded her arms. Her lips were pinched together and an unusual number of lines creased her face. It wasn't the most enthusiastic expression.

Daisy held her breath as she awaited her mum's response.

'Right, I'm going to say this now, just so that it's out there,' she said. 'I don't think it's healthy you chasing after a man you haven't been with that long. This is your first proper relationship in a long time, if you don't count that other fella. I think you're going headfirst into this without thinking it through.'

Daisy felt a surge of annoyance sparked by pure irony. Her mum jumped headfirst into every single relationship she had, most of them adorned with red flags. Still, she allowed her to express her concerns.

And she wasn't done yet.

'Maybe this time apart is what you need,' her mother continued. 'You know, your relationship will only be stronger after it. Or you'll find out that it wasn't meant to be after all. And that's before we get started on Yvonne. She might have done all those crossings before, but it was a long time ago. Besides, do you really want to spend all that time cooped up on a boat with someone you don't even know that well? She can be quite... *alternative,* you know.'

'We will hardly be cooped up,' Daisy said, her voice tight with indignation. 'And I know all about Yvonne's hippy ways; I can smell the incense from here. But she and I get on well. And it'll only be until we get to Slimbridge. If we fall out that badly, she can get a train or a bus back to Wildflower Lock. Once we're on the main canals, I'll be fine on my own, anyway. Not that I think that's going to be a problem.'

Her mother hummed, clearly not agreeing. Once again, she pressed her lips together tightly before unfolding her arms, only to refold them again a moment later.

'This should not be a spur-of-the-moment decision,' she said. 'Taking the boat on a trip like this. Is it even in good enough condition to do the journey?'

'Of course it is,' Daisy snapped back, as if the comment about the *September Rose* had somehow been a personal insult. 'She's just had the propeller fixed. And the engineer said the engine looked in brilliant nick.

Of course it can make it. The *Escape* did.' She realised she sounded slightly petulant, but deep down, she'd been hoping her mum would be supportive of the idea. Encouraging even, though she'd known the chances of such a response were slim.

With a sigh, her mother placed her palms together, steepling her fingers.

'Look, love, I only ever want what's best for you. I hope you know that. And even if I've got my doubts – like you and Yvonne sharing that space and whether I think the boat can actually make it – I won't interfere in your life. I made that mistake once and I won't do it again. But just be careful with this man. You fell hard once before, remember, and I don't want this to end the same way.'

'This is nothing like that,' Daisy assured her. 'Theo is nothing at all like Paul.'

'Well, I'm sure we'll find out soon enough.'

Daisy let out an internal sigh of relief when a queue of customers started forming outside the hatch.

'Sorry, Mum, I should get to work. I think it's going to be a busy day.'

'Oh, yes, right,' her mother said, looking equally relieved that the awkward conversation had come to an end. 'Just stay in touch, will you?'

'Of course I will.'

Without speaking, her mother wrapped her arms around Daisy in a tight hug. When she broke away, she had tears welling in her eyes.

'You know, you can always ring me, whatever happens.'

'I know, Mum. Don't worry. It's going to be fine. Trust me.'

10

Over the next two days, Daisy informed every customer that she would be heading away for a short while, but it would not be permanent. Wildflower Lock was her home and she would be back before autumn to serve them cakes and coffees. Sometimes, she told them more details about her route – out of the estuary, into the tidal Thames and onto the network of canals that would lead across to the west of the country. If the people were regulars, or knew the lock and the boats well, she told them how she was off to see her boyfriend, who had previously lived there on the *Narrow Escape*. Other times, she just told them she was off on holiday. Still, every time she mentioned what she was about to do, it caused a flurry of butterflies to fill her stomach and it was hard to keep them under control, especially with Yvonne appearing at her hatch every half hour to tell her she'd booked another marina or to show her a photo she'd taken from the River Thames decades earlier.

The buzz of excitement was constant, yet there was one place Daisy couldn't show it – on the phone to Theo.

'You look very happy,' he said, as they spoke that Wednesday night. 'I assume it's been a good day.'

'It has. A really good day,' Daisy admitted.

'Well, I definitely want to hear all about this.'

She was sitting on her sofa holding her phone out in front of her, looking at Theo, but also the scenery behind him, where hills of every shade of green rolled off into the distance. Soon she would be there with him, and he had absolutely no idea, although a slight sliver of worry struck as she considered their evening calls. She wouldn't be able to talk to him like this, on the sofa with the curtains wide open so that he could see Wildflower Lock behind them. Or their morning calls, which normally took place when she was sitting out on the stern with a cup of coffee in her hand. But it was fine. She'd think of a way around that.

'Oh, nothing special happened,' she lied. Her expression remained flawlessly casual, despite how much she was bursting to tell him the truth. 'It was just a lovely day, that's all. Nice weather, great customers. What more could I need?'

She missed out on the part where Yvonne came to tell her she was all packed up and ready to get going the very next morning.

'Well, it sounds like you don't need me there at all,' Theo joked.

'Oh, I do. I absolutely do.' She was about to ask him what he was up to – and if there had been any more sightings of the otters – when there was a knock on the door.

'Daisy, dear, it's me.' Yvonne's singsong voice sang through into the boat. 'I was wondering if I could trouble you for some help with my suitcase.'

Daisy blanched, terrified Theo had overheard and jumped to the completely unobvious conclusion that Yvonne was moving onto the *September Rose* so that they could travel to the Cotswolds to see him.

'Is that someone at the door?' he asked.

Daisy breathed a quick sigh of relief. The fact Theo hadn't mentioned Yvonne by name meant he most likely hadn't heard who it was. Still, she needed to get off the phone now, before he did.

'Yes, sorry. Mum said she was going to pop over. But I'll speak to you again tonight, right? Before I go to sleep.'

'That would be nice. Love you.' A rush of warmth and adrenaline flooded through her at hearing those words again.

'Love you too.' Daisy hung up the phone before holding it momentarily against her chest. She did. She really loved him, and this was going to be fun. She smiled to herself. A massive game of trying to make sure Theo didn't find out what she was doing. In a way, it was going to be part of the adventure.

Putting the phone down beside her, she stood up, walked across the boat, and opened the door to Yvonne.

The old woman's eyes glinted with mischief, which was highlighted by the flawless green winged eyeliner she currently wore. Perhaps, Daisy thought, when they were moored up for a bit, she could ask Yvonne for some make-up tips; she certainly seemed to know what the latest trends were and pulled them off perfectly.

'So, how are you?' Yvonne grinned. 'Ready to go?'

'I have no idea,' Daisy admitted. 'I was hoping you'd be able to tell me that.'

The old lady chuckled. 'Well, I've got my suitcase all packed and was going to bring it over, but I'm not as strong as I used to be. I've got it out of the boat, but I could do with a hand getting it over the bridge. I don't suppose you could spare me five minutes, could you?'

Daisy frowned, concerned by the comment. She had hoped that bringing Yvonne with her would make things like locks easier to manage. Given that Yvonne often took the *Ariadne* up and down the canals locally, Daisy had assumed that she was strong enough to do some of the legwork, but perhaps that wasn't the case. Without Yvonne's help, Daisy knew she'd have to rely on the kindness of strangers and those who worked along the water.

Still, the thought was fleeting. Yvonne's knowledge of the Thames and the waterways was more important than her physical strength, and she would have to steer the boat through the locks while Daisy dealt with opening the gates.

'No problem,' Daisy said, trying to quash the new feeling of anxiety that was flickering within her. 'I'll come and help you get it.'

11

Following Yvonne, Daisy crossed over the bridge and walked towards the *Ariadne*, where she immediately saw the issue, and it didn't lie with Yvonne's strength at all but her choice of luggage.

Rather than bringing a suitcase or rucksack, as Daisy assumed was normal for someone about to embark on a trip, Yvonne had packed a trunk. An actual trunk, the type in which Daisy could easily imagine a child in the fifties carrying off all their belongings to boarding school.

'Yvonne, what is all this?' Daisy asked as she stared at the wooden antiquity that looked like it belonged more in a chapter of *Malory Towers* than in any modern environment. 'I thought you said you were bringing a suitcase?'

'Oh, it's near enough,' Yvonne said cheerfully. 'Besides, this here has stood the test of time. Mark my words, nothing keeps my belongings safe like my case. I've taken this across the world. And if this is the last journey I'm gonna be doing on the water, then I'm taking it with me.'

It was hardly something Daisy could object to, but looking at the item, she was having a hard time figuring out how she was going to lift it on her own. It was a miracle Yvonne had got it this far; she would never doubt the old lady's strength again.

'Okay, I think you're gonna need to help me with this,' Daisy said. 'Are you okay to grab one end? I think we can manage it that way. Ready when you are?'

Together, slow step after slow step, Yvonne and Daisy heaved the antiquated trunk back to the *September Rose*. With each step, it seemed to get heavier and heavier. Daisy knew she had gotten stronger since taking up this new life on the canal – the fact she was spending her days on her feet and had to walk or cycle over a mile to the nearest shop had seen to that – but as they reached the other side of the towpath, her arms were already feeling like jelly.

'What is in here?' Daisy asked, struggling to believe that simple clothes could weigh that much.

'Odds and ends,' Yvonne said. 'Things I didn't want to leave in the *Ariadne* while we're away. I've got some first-edition books in there, jewellery, and so on. Oh, and some brass that my grandmother left me when she passed away. You know, things I couldn't leave behind.' The last one explained the weight.

When Daisy and Yvonne reached the *September Rose*, they placed the trunk down on the towpath, catching their breath.

'I'll clear out some wardrobe space for you,' Daisy said as she rested her hands on her knees. 'It's on my list of jobs for tonight.'

'No, don't worry about that. I don't want to put you out,' Yvonne said. 'I'll take the smaller berth too. I'm fine with that.'

Daisy shook her head. 'Actually, it's easier for me if you take the main cabin. The second berth opens up onto the coffee shop. The last thing I want to do is wake you up every morning to open up.'

'Well, as long as you're sure…'

For a moment, the pair fell silent. Daisy was looking at the *September Rose*, an amazing vessel that had already done so much in its life. By contrast, Yvonne was staring at the *Ariadne*. It was then Daisy realised what a big ask she had made of her friend. After all, in all the time Daisy had been at Wildflower Lock, she had never once heard Yvonne mention going away. It was no surprise then that she wanted to hold on to those little bits of home. However heavy they made the trunk.

Daisy lifted her hand and patted her friend gently on the shoulder.

'Come on, then,' she said, bending down and taking hold of the trunk. 'Let's get this thing inside so we can both get a good night's sleep. It's going to be a big day tomorrow.'

12

Daisy yearned for a good night's sleep. She wanted nothing more than to wake up fresh and revitalised, ready to start the next morning. And she had curled up in bed early, hoping it would happen, but the butterflies had different ideas.

Over the past year, she'd gotten used to the feeling of nervous anticipation. It was the same when she moved into the boat full-time, leaving her life and flat in London. And again when she opened up the coffee shop for the first time. But this night felt different.

It didn't help that she desperately wanted to share every detail of her upcoming trip with Theo. When they spoke again that evening, while she somehow resisted telling him, she couldn't help but drop a few hints.

'Did you know Yvonne had taken the *Ariadne* out of the estuary too?' she asked, randomly shoe-horning the question into their conversation. 'All the way up the tidal Thames.'

'Of course,' Theo said. 'She was quite the skipper in her day. She's been all round the country. Not just out of the estuary, she's done the Wash too.'

'The Wash?'

'It's in the north and takes you right out at sea. Some tricky piloting that, what with the tides and everything. Lots of high sandbanks to avoid too. Takes some real skill.'

As strange as it was to be keeping her upcoming adventure a secret from Theo, Daisy couldn't help but feel assured by his praise of Yvonne's narrowboating skills.

'Do you know, she once thought about doing the Channel, but that's completely insane.' Theo said. 'Thankfully, she seems to be past all that now. She's far better off in the safety of Wildflower Lock and the canals there, if you ask me.'

'Yes, absolutely,' Daisy agreed, with only a niggle of guilt tickling her. Why would anyone want to leave the safety of Wildflower Lock? That's when she knew she had to end the phone call there, not sure how much more truth-stretching she could deal with. 'I'd better go to bed now,' she said. 'Speak tomorrow?'

'Of course,' Theo replied. 'Oh, and Daisy?'

'Yes?'

'I love you.'

'I love you too.' She grinned.

Unfortunately, the conversation had left her wide awake and full of adrenaline, and it took a binge-watch of five true-crime episodes before she finally fell asleep.

* * *

The late night falling asleep, and lack of alarm set for the morning, meant that it was gone nine when Daisy woke up. As was her normal habit, she rolled over to grab her phone and immediately spotted the missed call from Theo. Her heart sank, but it wasn't a surprise. Morning and night were the times they spoke to each other most. However, given how hard it had been to keep quiet the night before, she wasn't ready for another conversation so soon afterwards. And so instead, she sent him a text:

Opened the cafe early. Weather's great. Speak tonight.

She hoped changing *speak soon,* which she normally wrote, to *speak tonight,* would prevent him from trying to ring her during the day. And then, because it was something they now did, she added another line to the message:

Love you.

She had just pressed send when there was a knock on the door. A flurry of excitement twisted in Daisy's chest as she stared at the empty area in her closet where Yvonne was about to place her clothes. Were they insane? Daisy wondered, glancing out the window at the picture-perfect morning that was waking up on Wildflower lock. She had everything she needed right where she was. And did she really need an adventure? After all, she'd got this far in her life without having one. Would it really hurt just to spend the summer here, on the canal, the way she had originally planned?

As she sat there, a saying flickered through her mind. She couldn't remember where it had come from – whether she had read it in a book, or heard it on some television show – but the moment the words came to mind, they resonated deep within her.

'Better to regret the things you do, than the things you don't do,' she said aloud.

The excitement surged within her. She was right. If she didn't leave now, she'd regret it forever.

Another knock on the door reminded Daisy that someone was waiting so, jumping to her feet, she strode through the *September Rose.*

Yvonne was standing outside, a large rucksack on the ground by her feet, and the broadest smile Daisy had ever seen on her face.

'Come on then, Skipper,' she said. 'Let's do this.'

13

As excited as Daisy was to start the journey, it didn't take long to fall into a sense of normalcy. Well, as normal as driving a narrowboat with Yvonne could be.

'I was in my late thirties when I moved to Wildflower Lock,' Yvonne told her. 'But before that, I lived all over the place. I was what you might call a nomad. Left home at seventeen, determined to see the world.'

'You did?' Daisy asked. They were moving along nicely, hoping to reach Heybridge in time for high tide.

'Oh, yes. Well, a fair bit of it. There are so many places I'd still love to see. I never got to South America. Sometimes, I think maybe I could do the trip now. Not travelling like I used to, but maybe join one of those tours. You know, with busloads of people and a tour guide who drives you to all the popular places and charges you three times as much to go to a local restaurant?'

'So why don't you?' Daisy asked.

'Oh, I don't know. It seems like a lot of hard work. Not the travelling so much as the people. I don't know if I've got it in me any more, all that conversation with people you've probably nothing in common with.'

Daisy struggled to believe this was true. After all, Yvonne had had no trouble introducing herself into Daisy's life. But then maybe that was because she wasn't a stranger. Not completely.

As she pondered the point, Daisy remembered how Yvonne hadn't actually been the most welcoming when she'd moved in, slamming a noise complaint on the *September Rose* the first time Daisy and the girls spent the night there. Maybe she was right; strangers weren't her strong point.

'So, less about where you haven't travelled,' Daisy said. 'Tell me about where you have. Where did you love the most?' She was keen to learn more about her travelling companion, along with different places in the world.

'Well, motorcycling around Vietnam has to be one favourite,' Yvonne reminisced.

'You motorcycled around Vietnam?' Daisy exclaimed.

Yvonne looked at her with a twinkle in her eye. 'Like I said, I was young and wild and wanted to see it all. That was fun. I was terrified, mind you. Some of those roads, and those drivers... But you don't forget things like that in a hurry.'

'Who did you go with?' Daisy asked. Several times, when they had enjoyed coffee and cake back at Wildflower Lock, Yvonne had let slip about a husband, but then each time, she swiftly moved the conversation on before it could settle. Now that Daisy was going to be living with Yvonne for what was likely to be a lengthy period, she felt like she really ought to know more details about her shipmate.

Surprisingly, Yvonne looked at her with a sense of confusion.

Her face paled, her eyes drifting beyond the water, before she came back and looked at Daisy.

'Of course, you wouldn't know about Harry, would you? Funny thing is, I still think about him – all the time – but when I lost him, it became easier *not* to talk about him. It didn't matter that he was always in my thoughts. I didn't talk about him. I don't even think young Theo knows, nor some others on the canal. I guess I've just found easier it not to mention him at all.'

'Sorry, I didn't mean to pry.'

A surge of guilt flooded through Daisy as she regretted bringing up

Yvonne's past. After all, they were less than a morning into their journey together. The last thing she needed was for Yvonne to change her mind before they'd even reached the first estuary. And it wasn't like she didn't understand; Daisy wasn't keen on talking about her past relationship either, and that had been a normal breakup. By the way Yvonne was talking, this had been something different.

Still, Yvonne waved away Daisy's apology and pushed a smile onto her face.

'No, don't be silly. I should talk about him. He'd be embarrassed by how mournful I've become. Let me tell you, I met my Harry in an ashram in Kerala.'

'Kerala? As in India?'

That twinkle returned to Yvonne's eyes. 'I did tell you we travelled, didn't I? Well, I'd been travelling about for a bit by then. Been to lots of places, around Europe mostly. India was my first big trip. The one that had my parents really worried.' Yvonne grinned, and Daisy couldn't help but smile at the thought of this older woman's parents. It didn't matter what generation you were from; it seemed parents would always worry about their children. 'Well, he was there on my first day, and that was it. I was hooked.'

The way Yvonne said that made it sound as if there was nothing more to tell about the situation, and yet Daisy wanted to know more. She needed more than that tiny insight.

'So what happened? Did you marry him? Where was he from? Did you have children? I assume you travelled with him? Did he live with you on the canal, too?'

Daisy realised she'd probably overdone it with the number of rapid-fire questions. Yet Yvonne's face lit up with a glow Daisy had never seen before. As much as Yvonne had resisted discussing her past relationship, it was clear this Harry was still very much in her heart.

'Oh, we travelled. We did some wonderful travelling. Thailand, Cambodia, Laos. He was the one I motorcycled around Vietnam with. He was Dutch, actually. Beautiful and tall and blonde. Spoke four languages, would you believe, and his English was better than mine! We had such fun. Oh yes, we had a great deal of fun. And then we came back here.'

Her voice wavered, and a quietness settled around them. A quietness filled only with the constant whirring of the boat's engine.

'He didn't like life in England?' Daisy asked hesitantly.

There was something in the way Yvonne had spoken that led her to draw this conclusion.

Yvonne shook her head.

'No, he loved it. Settled in here like a duck to water. Mind you, he settled anywhere. He was a bit older than me. Well, twelve years, actually. You can imagine my parents weren't too keen on that for their nineteen-year-old daughter. But even they succumbed once they met him. He'd lived in America – New York, no less – and spent time in New Zealand too. And everywhere he went, everyone fell in love with him.'

'It sounds like he was a wonderful man,' Daisy said, the use of the past tense making her feel awkward.

'He was. Oh, he was.'

Yvonne's eyes drifted away again, but Daisy didn't ask any more questions. Instead, she just waited. If Yvonne didn't want to share more about her past life, that was fine. They had an entire journey together.

'Right, enough chatter. We're coming up to a bridge.' Yvonne spoke with a renewed focus, implying that the time for reminiscing was gone. They needed to get to work.

14

Daisy was nervous. She'd done this journey before with Theo, all the way to Heybridge and the estuary, back when he was helping her out on the *September Rose*. It was a memory she reflected upon with mixed emotions. Theo had still been dating his ex, but the more time Theo and Daisy spent together, the harder it became for Daisy to ignore her feelings for him. It was here, in the marina, after she'd been cleaning out the water tank, that they nearly had their first kiss. Thankfully, she'd come to her senses before that happened. Less thankfully, it took her a lot longer to realise she really did want to be with him.

But all the things that had gone wrong were behind them now and she wasn't going to waste time thinking about their past when they had their entire future in front of them. When she passed through this lock, she would be on the River Blackwater, which would mark her first step of the voyage to sea.

Daisy shouldn't have been worried about the locks. By the time they reached Heybridge, they'd already passed eleven and she'd managed them all on her own. But she knew this one would be different. The minute they approached it, several men and women appeared from nearby houses and pubs to help her leave the safety of the canal and head onto the far more unpredictable river.

'Guess you're heading to the dry dock?' one man said as he turned the windlass on his side of the canal. The water rushed in to fill the lock. 'What's up with her? She looks in pretty good nick to me.'

'Just on a little trip,' Daisy replied. She didn't want to get into it here, not with people who probably knew a lot more about canal boats than she did. They might well say something to put her off, and that was the last thing she wanted.

Given it was high tide, it didn't take long for the lock to reach the level of the water, and let them out onto the open water.

'I've got this,' the same man said, gesturing to the gates. 'You get on her. And have a good trip.'

'Thank you,' Daisy replied, grateful she got to be aboard the *September Rose* for this part of her journey. As the gates opened, she steered them away from the canal. When she was all the way into the river, she cast a quick gaze over her shoulder and offered a wave of thanks to the man who was busy closing the gates behind her.

'Well, that's the first part done easily enough,' Yvonne said.

'It was easy, wasn't it?' Daisy replied.

Unfortunately, the momentary relief she felt at having made it off the canal so easily was followed by a sudden flood of adrenaline.

'There are so many sailing boats,' she said, the observation leaving her half aghast. 'Has everyone in Maldon got a boat?'

Before that moment, Daisy had only been vaguely aware that sailing was a popular pastime on the Essex coast. After all, she had grown up farther inland, and it wasn't like these types of vessels came up the canal to Wildflower Lock.

As the *September Rose* trundled out onto the river, Daisy was mesmerised by the sea of white sails drifting above the water. In every direction, she saw vessels of all shapes and sizes, their sails taut from the wind as they weaved one way and another across the river. Families, individuals. Boats that looked almost as long as the *September Rose* and others that could barely fit three people aboard.

'Well, it's the holidays,' Yvonne said. There was clearly a touch of disdain in her voice. 'That's what it's like now. Oh, it used to wind Harry up proper.

Not that he couldn't sail himself, mind. No, he was a wonderful sailor. One of those types, you know, could do anything once he'd been shown how. Now, you don't want to go too close to the bank. It's pretty shallow there.'

Daisy kept hold of the tiller, noting Yvonne's every slight movement. She was certainly a skilled boatman, and thankfully, the river was wide, providing plenty of room for the boats to pass. The further they travelled, the fewer and fewer of them there were.

Gradually, she settled back into a rhythm, her body relaxing onto the back of the stern. How was it she'd never taken the boat on the river like this before? she thought, as she watched the seagulls swoop in the skies. It was so different from the canal. From the view to the wind, and even the smell of salty brininess that filled the air.

As they continued on, she and Yvonne fell into an easy silence. Now and then, one of them would point out a particular bird, or something on the shoreline that the other might not have seen, but mostly they just took their time enjoying the peace and tranquillity. Little by little, the river was getting wider.

'You don't mind if I head inside and close my eyes for half an hour, do you?' Yvonne asked, just after they had spotted a heron diving into the water and emerging with a fish in his beak. 'All those locks this morning seem to have taken it out of me.'

'No, of course not,' Daisy replied with just a hint of nervousness in her voice. She hadn't been expecting Yvonne to leave her on her own quite so soon after heading onto the river, but it was quiet, and there didn't seem to be much trouble she could get herself into. Besides, like Yvonne had said, Daisy was the skipper; it was her boat.

For over an hour, Daisy did nothing but look around her as she steered around the occasional boat that still whipped down the river. The buildings were becoming sparser and flat expanses of marshland spread out on either side of them. She glanced at her watch to see how long they'd been going, then looked out in front of her to find nothing but water.

'Yvonne!' she called loudly into the boat. 'Yvonne, I think we're nearly there.'

It took a couple more minutes before Yvonne appeared, her eyeliner and make-up smudged ever so slightly from the pillows.

'I think we must be getting close to the mouth now,' Daisy said, her voice now trembling from the enormity of what she was about to do.

Yvonne's hand covered her mouth as she let out a small yawn. 'You're right. We got here quicker than I thought. Good news is we've got a perfect day for it. Barely a wave on the sea.'

15

Yvonne was right. It really was a perfect day to make the trip. The water was so still that the reflections of the clouds sparkled up at them from below.

As they reached the mouth of the river, Daisy realised she'd been holding her breath. Her lungs quivered and her knuckles whitened on the tiller as she slowly steered to her right. Beside her, she could feel Yvonne in the same state of anticipation until, as the *September Rose* broke away from the banks, they let out a collective gasp. They were doing it. They were out on open water.

'Oh, wow. I can't believe it,' Daisy said as she reached down beside her and picked up their life jackets. They weren't something she normally bothered with on the lock, but out here, it seemed dangerously naïve not to use them. 'Here.' She handed Yvonne hers.

'Well, let's put these on, and I'll get us both a little glass of bubbly to celebrate.'

'Bubbly? Now?' Daisy questioned. After all, they'd still got a way to go until they moored up.

'Only a sip,' Yvonne insisted. 'After all, if you don't celebrate the little things, you'll never appreciate the big ones when they happen.'

'I can't argue with that,' Daisy said.

Daisy couldn't believe how smoothly the morning had gone. Had she written down her perfect expectations for the day's events, it still wouldn't have gone as flawlessly as that morning. And, adding to the amazement of the day, she had another bonus. As Yvonne reappeared on the back of the boat, holding mugs filled with an inch of bubbles, Daisy spotted something else on the shorelines.

'Are those seals?' she said excitedly.

'Oh, yes, you get a lot of them out here.' There was a forced nonchalance to Yvonne's voice, like this was nothing special, but Daisy could see the excitement in her eyes too. However many fabulous things she had seen on her travels, she'd been landlocked for a long time, and seal sightings were almost a distant memory. Not any more, though.

'Just be careful; don't go too close to the bank,' Yvonne said, resuming her role as skipper. 'The ground under here is like cement. The last thing we want to do is run aground. You'll never get to Theo if that happens.'

Daisy followed her instructions, staying a fair distance out from the bank, while trying to snap photos of the seals that bathed lazily on the rocks.

Before long, the next estuary came into view.

'Look at that,' Yvonne said, tapping the little book of tide times she had used to plan the journey. 'Everything is going like clockwork.'

The nerves from earlier in the morning had subsided, only to be replaced with yet more excitement. It really had been like clockwork. No problems at all. If this was a sign of things to come, she was going to be with Theo in no time.

'Do you think we should keep going a bit longer?' she said. There was an estuary to her right – the river that led to their planned mooring for the night – but with such perfect conditions, it felt like they should keep pushing forward. 'Maybe we could keep going to Southend? The tide still looks pretty high. I'm sure we could make it?'

Yvonne offered her a deep scowl. 'Don't think you can judge what the tide is doing. It'll only get you into trouble. Besides, Burnham's a nice place. And it'll be good for you to see a bit more of the Essex countryside too.'

Accepting that Yvonne was almost certainly correct in what they should do, Daisy pushed on the tiller, steering them into the next estuary, where yet more seals basked on the mouth of the river.

'Just going to be straight up here for a while now.' Yvonne said. 'Do you want me to take over?'

Daisy briefly considered the offer. There were bound to be occasions on the trip when she had to default to Yvonne's experience, but for now, while she was doing okay, Daisy wanted to keep going.

A while later, the marshland began to thin out and a seawall appeared in the place of a riverbank. It was early afternoon and she could see the town coming into view, along with a couple more boats, too.

'We're going to head up towards the marina,' Yvonne told her. 'Then we can moor up and pour ourselves a proper glass of bubbly.'

16

'I can't believe how well we did!' Daisy was practically bouncing on her feet as she jumped from the boat and tied the stern rope to the mooring.

If she'd ever had any doubts about Yvonne's abilities with a narrowboat, they'd faded now that she'd seen how expertly she manoeuvred the boat into its mooring.

'Honestly, it was such a dream. And all those seals!' Daisy stepped back on board, this time grabbing the bowline from the front of the boat to secure it to the bollards. 'And the fact that we're here so early means I can open up the coffee shop for a couple of hours too. Honestly, if this is how the rest of the journey goes, I wish I'd done it sooner.'

'I thought you only had your propeller fixed a couple of weeks ago?' Yvonne said, though Daisy ignored the comment and set about opening up the coffee shop.

'What do you want to do while I'm working?' Daisy asked. She'd had people on the boat when she was working before – the girls, Theo – but normally they'd help, making coffees and taking money. She wasn't sure if that was something that Yvonne wanted to do.

'Do you know what, love? I might just have a nap. You don't mind, do you? I didn't get much sleep last night, and when you're my age, you need as much as you can get.'

Yvonne had already had well over an hour's nap earlier in the day but Daisy wasn't going to mention that.

'Of course. I don't blame you. I think it might be an early night for both of us, though maybe we could get dinner in the town after I've finished up here? If you fancy that.'

'That sounds lovely. Now, I'll let you get on with it. You don't want me under your feet,' Yvonne said.

A minute later, she disappeared into the cabin, leaving Daisy to get ready to open up.

It was Daisy's firm belief that she sold more coffees and teas when she had cakes on display. Even if people didn't fancy something to eat, the baked goods were the things that normally caught a passer-by's eyes and drew them in and they'd usually end up purchasing a hot or cold drink. So, wanting to get something out as quickly as possible, she whipped up a banana cake, the aromas from which, wafting into the air, brought her the first customer of the day.

'This is new,' the woman said. She was in her seventies, her arm linked with that of the man she was walking with. 'I haven't seen this before, have you, Jack?'

'I haven't, love.'

'I'm not a permanent fixture,' Daisy said, feeling the need to infiltrate herself into the conversation. 'I'm normally up at Wildflower Lock. Do you know it?'

'Oh, yes,' the woman said enthusiastically. 'Lovely place. We used to go there when we were first dating, didn't we, Jack?'

'We did indeed, love.'

'Well, I was just saying I needed a cup of tea. You do serve tea, don't you?' The lady smiled, which Daisy reciprocated warmly.

'Absolutely.'

'Fantastic. Two teas, please.'

Daisy had only served another two customers before the buzzer informed her that the banana cake was ready, though she let it cool for half an hour before she put it out to sell. That was when she got busier.

It wasn't as crazy as a weekend on Wildflower Lock, but it didn't take long for news to spread about a coffee shop on a canal boat set up near the marina. After that, there were certainly enough customers to keep Daisy busy and leave her wishing she had put two banana cakes in the oven rather than one. Everything was running so smoothly that she almost forgot that Yvonne was aboard until a little after five when she appeared out of the cabin.

'Goodness me, I really needed that sleep,' she said, stretching out her arms. 'How have you been? Plenty of customers?'

'Enough for us to get dinner,' Daisy answered with a smile.

'Well, that sounds like an offer I can't refuse,' Yvonne replied.

17

'There used to be some lovely pubs here, back in the day,' Yvonne said as they walked into the town. 'Looking out on the water. I'm sure there probably still are.'

Together, the pair wandered down by the seawall. Just like in Maldon, the river here was dotted with sailing boats, and people were out, enjoying the heat of the evening sun. Not wanting to travel too far away from the *September Rose*, they found a pub with benches outside next to the river, where Daisy enjoyed a jacket potato while Yvonne opted for a plate of chips. It hardly seemed like a sufficient evening meal, given all the pushing of locks Yvonne had done that day, but Daisy didn't want to appear pushy. After all, there was plenty of food on the *September Rose* if she wanted something later. As it was, while Daisy had nearly eaten her entire potato, Yvonne only seemed to pick at the chips and could have barely eaten a dozen.

'So, did you and Harry ever come down this way?' Daisy asked. She'd promised herself she wouldn't pressure Yvonne into revealing more about her past, but now that they were sitting here together, it seemed like a natural topic of conversation.

Yvonne, however, had other ideas.

'You know, I remember when your mum and dad came this route. On their honeymoon.'

Even Daisy could see Yvonne had played her with a perfect distraction. She could never say no to hearing about her father.

'They took this route? The exact one we're going on now?'

'More or less. They definitely came this way before heading to Southend. I know they went through London too, just like we're going to do. I'm not sure what they did when they got to the west, though. Maybe they headed to Stratford-upon-Avon for a bit. You should ask your mother. I'm sure she'll be happier to talk to you about it now.'

Yvonne placed significant stress on the word 'happier'. It was true that her mother had become more amenable to talking about her life on Wildflower Lock now that she was with Nicholas, but she was far from forthcoming. Still, part of her had to realise Daisy would want to use this chance to learn more about what her father had done.

'What was he like?' Daisy asked. 'What was my father like?' It felt ridiculous that she'd never asked such a question before. When her mother had spoken about her father, she'd painted him as a dark, unforgiving villain. So now, with the dappled clouds floating above them, and the silvery leaves of a birch tree waving in the gentle breeze, it felt like the perfect time to learn about this man who had loved boats even more than she did.

Yvonne's smile broadened. Clearly, this was a topic she was happy to discuss.

'Oh, he was larger than life,' she said with a sense of nostalgia. 'Your father never did anything by halves. No, he went the whole hog with everything he did. And he was always the centre of attention, even though I don't think he meant to be. His voice was so loud.' She chuckled lightly. 'Honestly, I don't think I've ever met a person with a voice as loud as your father's. Especially when he was laughing. I could hear him over in my boat some evenings, when you were a baby. Your dad's laugh would boom out into the night.'

Daisy reflected on these memories, and only a hint of sadness lingered. Her mother's stories of Daisy being a baby were very different. Those early years had been marked by numbness and sorrow and she spoke only of the grief and pain that she had endured. It was strange to hear such a different recollection of the same time.

'What else?' Daisy was eager to learn more. 'I know he painted. Do you know what type of art he used to do? What type of subjects he liked?'

Yvonne looked at her, a deep frown forming on her forehead. 'Oh, I'm such a fool,' she said. 'Sometimes I hate getting old.'

The comment caught Daisy by surprise, as it seemed to come from nowhere.

But Yvonne was on her feet, leaving the rest of her chips in her bowl. 'I can't believe I never showed you before.'

'Showed me what?'

'His paintings. Come on, I know I've got at least one on the boat.'

18

Daisy lowered her cutlery to the table, her heart drumming in her chest, the heat prickling behind her eyes. For a second, she was sure she must have heard Yvonne incorrectly. She stood slowly up.

'You have one of my father's paintings?' she repeated.

Yvonne's face pinched slightly.

'Well, I should confess I'm not 100 per cent sure what's in the trunk,' she said.

Daisy frowned. 'I don't understand. How can you not know what's in it? Surely you packed it?'

Yvonne's pinched expression tightened. 'Well, my clothes are in the rucksack, you see. The trunk I normally keep in my cabin. It's where I put all my precious things. Folders of birthday cards and pictures people have done for me. My grandmother's jewellery and my father's pocket watch. Little gifts, that type of thing. I just pop them in the trunk to make sure I don't lose them. But it's been a while since I last had a look through everything. If I did still have one though, that is where it would be, and I can't think why I would have given it away.'

'Do you think you can check?' Daisy said. 'Maybe this evening? If that's not too much trouble.'

Yvonne's eyes sparkled.

'I think we should get that bill now, don't you?' she said.

Daisy wished she could have sprinted back to the *September Rose*. She certainly had enough adrenaline in her body to do so. But she suspected Yvonne was only just keeping up with her at a steady marching pace. The last thing Daisy wanted to do was leave her behind, especially when she was the one who knew where the painting was.

'I told you it was a good idea to bring that trunk with me,' Yvonne said.

'Absolutely,' Daisy agreed. Never again would she complain about how difficult it had been to lug over the bridge, not if there was one of her father's paintings in it.

As they drew closer to the *September Rose*, Daisy gave herself an internal talking to. There was no point in getting her hopes up. Yvonne herself had said she couldn't remember when she had last seen it. She couldn't even remember what was in that trunk of hers. It would be perfectly understandable if she'd forgotten where she placed Johnny's work after all these years. Still, it didn't quench the bubble of excitement that flooded through her as she stepped onto the boat and followed Yvonne into her cabin.

Already, Yvonne had laid claim to the space, with various photo frames and crystals sitting on top of the dressers, though, thankfully, she hadn't burned any of her pungent incense sticks yet.

Slowly crouching, Yvonne unlocked the trunk and flipped over the lid. Daisy's heart sank as she stared at the open luggage, trying to make sense of everything that was in there. There were photos, framed and loose, fabric, jewellery, pens, letters both in their envelopes and floating around. Not to mention all the brass objects Yvonne had told her about. It was full to the brim and if there were paintings in there, Daisy had no idea what kind of state they would be in.

Feeling suddenly claustrophobic, Daisy fanned herself with her hand.

'Do you mind if I wait outside?' she said. 'I'm sure you don't want me watching over you while you go through all your belongings.'

'You do as you need, love,' Yvonne said. 'I can go through this. You're right, it might take me a while, but if I've got one in here, I'll find it for you.'

Still feeling woozy from the sudden heat that struck her, Daisy headed out onto the deck. Closing her eyes, she drew in a deep breath and tried to steady her pulse. After all, it was just a painting. Did it really matter that much if Yvonne found it?

Daisy's eyes were still closed, and her mind lost in deep thought, when a voice broke her contemplation.

'Excuse me?' Daisy opened her eyes to see a woman standing there with a large, black dog on a lead. 'Is this your boat?'

Daisy took a moment to gather her thoughts.

'It is.'

Normally, Daisy would feel a sense of pride filling her chest when someone asked if the boat was hers. Provided that person didn't look like an inspector, that was. But this time, her thoughts were too lost elsewhere.

'How funny,' the woman responded. 'It's got the same name as a narrowboat down at Wildflower Lock. That one's a coffee shop.'

At this, Daisy shook her head, struggling to believe it.

'Actually, this is the same boat,' she said. 'The *September Rose*. I'm just taking her on a trip for a few days.'

'Are you, now?' the woman said with an air of awe. 'I don't suppose that means you're opening the coffee shop, are you? I could murder a slice of cake.'

'Sorry,' Daisy said. 'I'm all sold out at the minute. I was open earlier in the day.'

'Oh, that's a shame,' the woman said. 'I've heard such lovely things about your cakes. I'll catch you next time you're back at Wildflower Lock, though. You won't be gone for too long?'

Daisy shook her head. 'No, three or four weeks.'

'Well, I hope you have fun.'

'Thank you. I'm sure I will,' Daisy said.

The woman offered one last smile before tugging on her dog's lead and turning away.

Grateful for the solitude, Daisy was about to sit down and enjoy the quiet moment she so desperately needed, but no sooner had she pulled out a chair than Yvonne's voice called her from inside.

'Guess what?' she said. 'I found it.'

19

'Sorry it took a little while,' Yvonne said as Daisy followed her back into the *September Rose*. 'I keep promising myself I'll have a proper sort through all my things, but you know what it's like. Time just runs away from you. Honestly, I'm not entirely sure where half of these things have come from.'

It was only when Daisy stepped into her cabin that she realised exactly how big a job finding her father's painting had been. The entire floor was lost beneath Yvonne's paraphernalia which included – amongst other things – a vintage Roberts Radio, a set of metal dumbbells, at least three elephant ornaments and a typewriter.

'I've had a few friends give me their paintings throughout the years,' Yvonne said, as she dusted off a large, brown folder. 'This lovely woman Fiona painted some wonderful artwork up in Glasgow, and another friend of mine, Jessica, did nude work. Very risqué stuff, not the type of thing you put up in the house. But very talented, very talented indeed.'

'And my father's paintings?' Daisy asked, finding it hard not to sound impatient. 'Is that one of his?'

Yvonne's smile widened as she handed Daisy the folder. 'Why don't you take a look at that while I make a start on this mess?'

Only then did Daisy notice how her hands were shaking. And it wasn't just her hands; her breath had grown noticeably shallower in the moments waiting for Yvonne, and her heart was drumming hard enough to crack a rib.

With the folder in her hand, she walked over to the dining room table and sat down. For a moment, she did nothing but stare at the dusty, brown cover, imagining what was inside. Every card and gift her father had tried to send her over the years, her mother had returned to sender without her even knowing. This was the closest she had ever come to having a piece of him, and she wasn't sure which emotion was stronger: excitement or terror.

Taking a deep breath, she closed her eyes and tried to imagine what she would find inside. What would his style be like? Was artistic tone part of your DNA, or something you learnt? There was no way she could know until she looked inside.

With another deep breath, she opened her eyes and pulled out the first painting.

The gasp was instant, though it wasn't caused by the painting itself but the signature on the bottom. Signed in pen, it was an elongated squiggle, yet entirely identifiable: Johnny. Not his surname, but Johnny, in bold, black pen.

With her eyes then moving from his name, Daisy took in the picture, covering her mouth as she attempted to stem her tears.

The style wasn't anything like hers. While she went for delicate, intricate details in both the characters she drew and the landscapes she painted, her father had a wholly different approach. It was like he let the water and the paint do the talking. Some parts of the picture were in perfect focus, like the flowers in the foreground, and the butterflies and birds that rested on them, but the further back you moved, the more abstract and hazier the image became. It didn't matter, though; Daisy knew in a heartbeat what she was looking at. It was the *September Rose*.

She hastily wiped at the tears sliding down her cheeks, fearful that she might damage the work. For a minute, she did nothing but stare, imagining herself lost in the moment, stood on the canal side beside her father as he sketched the image, after which she placed it to the side of the table and picked out the next.

The second painting wasn't of a narrowboat or even a lock, but a simple meadow filled with flowers. Cowslips, daisies, dog roses, poppies. She didn't know if it was an actual place or not, but it didn't matter. She stared at it, mesmerised. What would the curator at the art gallery think of this? she thought as she hovered her fingers carefully above the artwork. Not that it was derivative, that was for sure. No, the colours in this were all bolder than in real life, every flower so vibrant, it looked like it was trying to burst from the page. As far as Daisy was aware, her father hadn't gone to art school or had any formal training at all, and yet he'd been producing pieces worthy of any art gallery. By instinct, she moved it to the side of the table with the picture of the *September Rose* and opened the folder again, only to feel a sting of disappointment when she realised these were the only two in there. Still, two paintings from her father were a thousand times better than zero.

She was slipping the first back into the folder when her phone buzzed over in the kitchen. Wiping the tears from her face, she stood and answered the call, which was from Theo.

'Hey, gorgeous,' he started. 'How are you doing?'

'I am... I am...' Daisy struggled to find a word. 'Okay, I guess.'

It was a sign of how well Theo knew her that Daisy didn't need to say any more for him to know something was wrong.

'What happened?'

'Yvonne found some paintings,' she began, grateful that she had something to talk about that was straightforward. 'Paintings that my father did.'

'Oh, wow.' The silence expanded, implying that Theo knew exactly how big a deal this was. 'What are they like? Does he paint like you?'

'He uses watercolours, but that's about the only similarity. His style's not like mine at all, really.'

'Well, I can't wait to see them. Do you wanna send me pictures? Or I can see them at the weekend. It's only a couple of days away.'

'At the weekend?' Panic coursed through her. 'I thought you weren't here this weekend? You said you were going to be busy?'

'I was, but I've had a look at the rota and I think the guys should be able to manage without me, so guess what? I'm coming to Wildflower Lock.'

20

Daisy cleared her throat. 'Sorry, did you say you're coming to Wildflower Lock? This weekend?'

She tried to keep her voice as natural as possible, but even though he couldn't see her face or read her expression, she could tell that Theo knew something was up.

'What is it? Don't you want to see me?' he asked playfully.

Daisy racked her brain for something to say. If she left now, could she be back in time? Maybe, but that was assuming the tides were on their side for the lock at Heybridge. She might not manage at all, and then where would that leave her? Besides, she'd only just started this journey, and she wasn't ready to give up on it.

'You know I want to see you. It's just... It's just...' The panic rose in her chest as she tried to think of an excuse. 'I'm having time with the girls. I'm so sorry. It's a full weekend thing.'

Once she started, the lies came easily.

'Claire is bringing Amelia down in the day, and they're going to help me in the shop, then drive me back to London for a movie night at theirs. Then we're going to do an early breakfast together before Bex brings me back and stays to work with me on Sunday. I'm sorry, they just jumped into action, you know, to keep me busy whilst you're not here.'

'You're lucky to have such good friends. You know that, don't you?'

'Absolutely,' Daisy replied while thinking how she would have to fill the girls in on the lie just to help her keep track.

'And it's probably a good idea,' Theo added with a defeated sigh. 'I'd probably have spent the entire time worrying the guys here weren't doing their job properly. I guess it's best.'

Relief washed over her.

'I'm going to miss you, though,' she added, and not just because of the guilt that was filling her. 'I really miss you when you're not here. I'm thinking about buying a second boat, just to put in the *Escape*'s mooring so it doesn't feel so empty.'

Theo chuckled.

'Really? You've only just got your expenses in line. Please don't do something like that yet. Besides, these next five weeks are going to fly by, I promise you. And then I'll be able to take some time off. I'll be due so much holiday, you'll be sick of me by the end.'

'You know that could never happen.'

'I hope so.'

Daisy sensed the conversation was nearing its end, and she was grateful. Any longer and Theo would start asking how the shop was going and Daisy would be forced to lie, and that was the last thing she wanted. So she took the natural pause as a cue to end the conversation.

'I better get going. I love you,' she said.

'I love you too. I'll see you soon,' Theo replied.

21

Daisy had spent the evening baking as much as she could. Lemon muffins, along with fruit scones and chocolate-dipped shortbread, were all on a cooling rack, waiting for the morning. In getting everything prepared the night before, Daisy was going to allow herself a slight lie in, but at 5 a.m. the next day, she was staring up at the ceiling.

The entire night she had been restless. One minute, her mind had been on Theo, and the fact he might turn up at Wildflower Lock any moment to surprise her, and the next second, she would think about her father. She thought about his paintings and how many of them might be out there in the world, unbeknown to her, but she also thought about what he would think of her making this journey, and whether he had moored up at any of the places she was planning on staying. Perhaps he had stared out at the exact array of constellations as Daisy as he'd stood with his arm around her mother and thought they'd have their entire future together.

By five-twenty, Daisy had had enough. With a slight huff, she swung her legs over the side of the bed, slipped on some clothes, and headed outside.

The last of the night's stars were fading, dissolving into the pale-blue sky as the sun broke over the horizon. The world was so peaceful at this time of day, she thought, as the single melody of a bird accompanied the gentle lapping of the tide. It was hard to believe there had been a time in her life when she'd thought mornings in London were quiet. They weren't a patch on this. And given how she had time to spare, she found herself struck with the sudden urge to explore the countryside.

With no real purpose, Daisy followed the river away from the town and over the path towards the marshland. She wasn't sure how far or for how long she wanted to walk; all she knew was that she wanted to walk and take in the world around her. And, for once, she had the time and the space to do that.

It was a well-worn path, with high, brittle grasses rising along the edges of the stony terrain. On one side, the land was low. Grassy fields stretched out towards woodland, beyond which the tops of large houses could just be viewed. On the other side of the path was the river, where boats rocked lazily back and forth, the chimes of their masts a counterpoint to the birdsong. Daisy's attention, however, was stolen not by the river water, nor by the delicate tufts of clouds that floated in the sky, but by the flowers that grew in those low-lying fields.

Daisy had always loved painting flowers. Since she had learned how to sketch, she had been mesmerised by all the colours and shades that could be found in a single petal. But since moving to Wildflower Lock, that passion had developed further, as had her knowledge of foliage. As she gazed out at the grasses, it was a particular shade of purple that caught her attention.

'Please let that be what I think it is,' she said to herself as she inched towards the edge of the path to get a better look.

Daisy would never tell the girls how she had developed this geeky love for all types of fauna, but she had, and her phone was filled with photographs of flowers. Mostly, she took them to aid her paintings and help ensure she was using as accurate a palette as possible, but Daisy had also developed a love simply of taking photos. The skill of catching the light, glimmering off the petals, was very different to the skill of painting, but it gave her a deep satisfaction to get the composition of the shot just right, especially on rare flowers like the one she was staring at. The marsh orchid. She was sure that's what it was, with its trumpeted, magenta petals rising in pillars between the grasses. She had painted them before, but only from images on the internet. Never from one she'd taken herself.

Pulling out her phone, Daisy zoomed in on the flowers and tried to capture a shot.

The result was blurred and out of focus.

'Come on, what's a zoom for?' Daisy said as she stretched her phone's camera to its maximum capacity. She just needed to be a bit closer. A metre or two would do it.

Daisy considered what she was going to do next. She knew plenty of people who had picked wildflowers using the excuse that they dried and framed them as a reason to disturb nature, but she wasn't one of those people. She knew that flowers were best left in the ground where they could continue to offer joy to everyone who saw them – not to mention aid the ecosystem. But that didn't stop her from wanting to get a perfect shot of this rare specimen, and there was no way she was going to leave without taking it. The only problem was that everything off the footpath was private land.

Daisy looked around, wondering what her next move should be, but knowing that she only had two choices: not get the photo, or spend less than a minute trespassing.

22

Daisy May was not a lawbreaker. Not ordinarily, but this didn't really feel like breaking the law, and it was an exceptional circumstance. It was a marsh orchid, and while she might see one again on her journey, it was likely to be in the same situation – on private land, just out of reach.

With her pulse hitching up a notch, Daisy looked around her. A little way in the distance, there was a jogger. She admired their commitment, being out at such a time of day, but at that moment, what concerned her most was their speed. They seemed to be going relatively fast. But it wasn't like she needed long. Just enough time to race down the slope onto the field below and get a decent photo of the flower. A couple of minutes at most. She could do that, couldn't she?

Daisy took one last glance at the flowers. It was a fairly steep slope going down to them, but not steep enough that she wouldn't be able to climb back out. With one last look towards the runner, she slipped her phone back into her pocket and took her first step down towards the field.

Considering how dry the grass was everywhere else, Daisy was surprised to find the slope slightly slippery, and her front foot slid forward a short way before she regained her balance. Perhaps it would take slightly longer to get the shot than first anticipated, but did it really matter if the runner saw her? It wasn't like she was doing something that terrible. She was only taking a photo.

Daisy took another step that was far more stable than her first, although her third step once again slid forward and it wasn't so easy to regain her balance as before. She staggered forward. Then, rather than slipping again, her feet began to sink. It was almost instantaneous. They stopped moving forward and sank downwards instead. Unfortunately, her body didn't do the same. Her arms and torso continued to carry the downward momentum from the hill, and her body was still moving forward. As she tumbled towards the grasses, she realised her grave error. It was a marsh orchid. As in, it grew in *marshland*. That was why the slope had been damper than the rest of the path. With one last attempt to save herself, Daisy tried yanking one foot upwards. While her shoe stayed put, her foot flew forward with unexpected speed and force. There was nothing she could do. As if in slow motion, Daisy saw the ground growing ever closer. Then, with a squelching thud, her hands disappeared into the mud.

'Oh God,' Daisy said, feeling her knees and hands start disappearing beneath the sodden ground too. It wasn't normal mud. It was so thick and viscous, yet at the same time, it didn't seem able to support her weight. It was like quicksand. Of all the ways her morning could have gone, this was worse than anything she could have imagined.

With one shoe missing, Daisy tried to crawl back up to the slope. Mud had drenched her coat and was seeping through her trousers, while midges were pestering her eyes. Without thinking, she used the back of her hand to swipe them away, only to smear dirt across her face.

'For crying out loud! I just wanted a photo of a flower!' Daisy screamed as she lifted her head and blinked away the mud so that she could see. 'I just wanted a photo of one blooming flower.'

She wasn't expecting her comment to be answered by anyone. After all, she hadn't been shouting to some great deity. It was just frustration, that was all. Which was why her heart did a somersault when a masculine voice replied.

'Looks like you've got yourself in a bit of a mess there.'

23

A hand reached down to Daisy. A perfectly clean hand, and yet she didn't hesitate. She grabbed it fully with her mud-covered palms and fingers, although the grip wasn't enough – as the man tugged her upwards, she quickly slid back down. On the second attempt, Daisy shifted her hands up onto his forearm, plastering it in muddy handprints. When she finally had a decent hold, Daisy allowed herself to be hoisted up and back onto the dry, stable footpath, where the sandy stones and shingles promptly stuck to the mud and her bare foot.

'You appear to be without a shoe.' The voice spoke again, and this time Daisy looked up to see the speaker.

The young man appeared to be of a similar age to Daisy, with dark hair and blazing green eyes, which were currently locked on her. Rather than being embarrassed that he had found her trespassing on private property, Daisy was both relieved and horrified, but also confused. It had to be the runner. There was no one else around, but he wasn't dressed for exercise. Instead, he was wearing a pair of chinos and a polo shirt and would have looked very smart if the outfit had not been splattered with mud.

'Thank you. I have no idea how I would have got out of there without you,' Daisy said, breathless from both the exertion and the shock of the event. 'I didn't realise it was marshland.'

'I gathered as much. But you're okay now? Bar the missing shoe?' the man said.

Daisy glanced at her foot, although she couldn't make out her toes under the thick cake of mud that was covering it. Still. A shoe was replaceable. She couldn't have imagined how much worse a state she would have been in if the man hadn't come along when he did.

'I'm okay. Thank you. I can't thank you enough. I really can't. I was just trying to get a photo, that was all. A photo of a plant. A marsh orchid.' It was only when she paused to catch her breath that she saw the man wasn't actually looking at her. Instead, he was looking back down the pathway, the way he'd come.

'Do you need any more help?' he said. 'I don't mean to sound rude, I'm just incredibly pressed for time, and if you're okay—'

'I'm fine,' Daisy insisted. The last thing she wanted to do was ruin the day of a man who had just been her saviour.

'Are you sure? Do you have far to walk? Can you do it in only one shoe?' He was talking to Daisy, but his eyes were still skitting around.

'Yes, yes, I'll be fine,' Daisy said. Finally, the man looked at her again, once more fixing that bright-green gaze on her.

'In that case, I'll leave you. And try to stay on the path this time.'

A moment later, he was jogging away from Daisy, who was still dripping with mud, wondering exactly what had just happened and who the hell her knight in shining armour was.

24

Yvonne was horrified, though mostly at the quantity of mud rather than how Daisy could have been really hurt.

'You need to take all those clothes off before you come into this boat,' Yvonne said as she stood out on the stern, hands on hips. Daisy was going to respond that it was actually *her* boat, and she was the skipper and if she wanted to walk into it covered in mud, then she could. But that seemed like a pretty churlish thing to do, considering she was the one who'd have to clean it all up afterwards.

So, out in the morning sun, she stripped down to her underwear before heading straight into the shower.

'So, a handsome young man just pulled you out of the mud and then disappeared?' Yvonne said after Daisy had finished telling her what had happened.

'Pretty much. He said he had to be somewhere.'

'And you didn't even ask his name?'

Daisy shook her head. Asking his name was probably the most basic level of manners she should have shown, but she'd not even managed that. The minute he'd run off, she'd felt terrible, but there was no way she could have run after him. As it was, she'd had to limp her way home, stopping every so often to pick the stones out of her foot.

'I don't know what I would have done if he hadn't been there. Honestly, that mud was like quicksand. I've never known anything like it. I won't be heading off paths again, I can tell you that much,' she said.

Yvonne let out a slight chuckle. 'Oh, it's all part of the adventure, though, isn't it? It's one of the stories to tell the grandchildren. If you have any, that is.'

Thoughts of grandchildren and children caused Daisy's mind to flicker straight to Theo. There was no way she could tell him about this. He'd be furious if he knew she'd wandered off in the early morning, somewhere she had no idea what the terrain was like. Still, it was a lesson learned for Daisy.

'I guess I'll just stick to the internet for reference photos from now on,' she said.

* * *

While the morning had not got off to quite the start Daisy had expected, her exceptionally early walk meant it was only just gone seven when she was all cleaned up and ready to open the coffee shop. Yvonne was in charge of checking all tide times and, according to her little yellow book, high tide was around eleven o'clock. While they weren't planning on waiting until full high tide to leave, it meant they could stay moored where they were until at least nine. And if this place was anything like Wildflower Lock, then it meant the dog walkers would soon be out, offering Daisy the perfect opportunity to sell some of her cakes and coffees.

She was slightly surprised, therefore, when the entire pathway, as far as she could see, was clear. The disappointment stung, and after thirty minutes passed, Daisy still hadn't served a single customer.

'We didn't clarify this before we left,' Yvonne said, standing by her shoulder. 'But do I have to pay for your coffees? I don't mind, it's just someone my age has to budget, you know.'

'No,' Daisy said, emphatically. 'All drinks are definitely on me. Now, what would you like?'

'A cappuccino, please, but can you make it decaf? I only allow myself one cup of coffee a day, and I suspect I'm going to need it when we get going along the river.'

Daisy moved over to the coffee machine, hoping that Yvonne was being flippant. Given how stress-free the day before had been, Daisy was hoping for the same level of smooth sailing again.

After making two cappuccinos, one decaf for Yvonne and a full-caffeine, full-fat one for herself, Daisy placed the bell on the countertop – just in case a customer appeared – and sat at the dining table next to Yvonne to enjoy the drink.

'I don't know what you want for breakfast,' Daisy said. 'As it's quiet, I can cook something. Pancakes? And there's bread if you want toast.'

'No, but thank you. I'm not really a breakfast person if I'm honest. A good lunch and a light supper are all I need.' Yvonne gazed out of the window towards the sailing boats that were moored up in the marina, the soft chime of their sails singing into the air. 'It's lovely and quiet here, isn't it?'

'Yes,' Daisy agreed. 'Quieter than I expected.'

'Perhaps your knight in shining armour will run back this way?'

It was a thought Daisy had had, too. Shouting the man a coffee and cake was the least she could do, and she had been keeping a deliberate eye out, but so far there had been nothing. She wondered if perhaps he was a long-distance runner, one of those that started at dawn and didn't stop until the sun set. It would make sense as to why he was running so early, but what kind of runner wore chinos and a polo shirt? And where had he been running to or from? Both were questions Daisy wanted answers to, but for now, the horizon was clear.

'Well, what do you want to do?' Yvonne said, breaking Daisy's stream of thoughts. 'The tide's already coming in, a little earlier than expected,' she tapped the little yellow book on the table in front of her. 'We can probably head out in the next half an hour. Unless you want to keep the shop open a bit longer, serve a few more customers.'

It was all Daisy could do not to scoff at the remark. In all her days with the coffee shop, she couldn't remember a morning as bad as this one, and that included days when it was pouring with rain. At least she knew she'd made the right decision in setting up at Wildflower Lock.

Which made her even more unsure whether closing up to visit Theo was really the wisest thing to do.

'Perhaps we give it fifteen minutes more, then get ready to head out,' she suggested. Yvonne nodded in agreement.

'That sounds good to me. And just to check, do I need to pay for those lemon muffins, too?'

25

Any hope Daisy had of a sudden flurry of customers was fading with every passing second. It wasn't that the town was completely dead. She could hear cars in the distance, and even the shrieks of one or two children, but none of them came anywhere near the *September Rose*, and by the time she closed the hatch, she still hadn't had a single customer.

As she secured all the cups and milk jugs, she tried to give herself a pep talk. It didn't matter if she didn't make money every single day. Most businesses closed for at least a couple of days a week, anyway. There was nothing wrong with taking a break from work now and again, especially when things were going so well. If anything, she thought, it could well be the universe telling her it was time to slow down for a bit. To enjoy the journey, rather than just thinking about the destination.

By quarter past eight, Daisy and Yvonne were on the stern of the boat, ready to cast off.

'Are you sure you don't want to take the tiller for a bit?' Yvonne asked as she steered them away from the bank and into the middle of the river. 'It's quite lovely.'

Daisy's immediate response was going to be no. This river – the Crouch – was far narrower than the Blackwater they'd joined at Heybridge, which meant it was far easier to run aground on one of the mud banks. She wanted to spend some time getting used to the area first. Yet waiting would mean getting closer to the mouth of the estuary, which was when Yvonne would definitely need to be in charge. Which was why she changed her mind.

'Actually, yes,' she said. 'But you'll stay here, right? Just till I'm comfortable.' Controlling the boat on the narrower stretch of water was far easier than Daisy had expected. 'You never know, I might give it a go when we get out to sea,' she said with just a hint of nervousness.

'Be my guest,' Yvonne replied. 'But I'm taking no blame if something happens to you.'

Daisy laughed. With her hand still on the tiller, she breathed in a lungful of sweet, salty air. It was a different sort of relaxation, being on the river, she decided. You still had to be alert on the canals, but there was more of a safety net, what with all the moorings and people and locks to slow down the pace. Here, that safety net was gone, and the relaxation came from the openness. The vast expanse of freedom that stretched out in front of her.

Daisy had been at the tiller for quite a while and was allowing herself an indulgent gaze out at the landscape when Yvonne called out to her.

'Watch it!' she said.

Daisy barely had a chance to realise what *it* Yvonne was talking about when something whipped around the starboard side of the boat. In panic and confusion, she pulled the tiller hard towards her, and away from the object. The boat swerved towards the bank and for a split second, all Daisy could do was watch on, waiting for the impending disaster.

26

'Move!' Yvonne shouted, pushing Daisy out of the way and grabbing the tiller. The *September Rose* turned away from the bank, but it was still rocking from side to side. 'Silent buggers, aren't they?' she said with a deep breath out. 'I don't mind them so much here, where you've got a bit of room, but sometimes they're a nightmare. One time, Harry and I went up to the Norfolk Broads...'

Daisy wasn't listening. Her heart was lodged all the way up in her throat and her knuckles were white. The sailboat had passed them now, but its wake kept coming. Wave after wave hit the hull of the *September Rose*, each one causing Daisy's pulse to rise higher and higher. She gripped the side of the boat, only to glance down into the churning water. Her stomach lurched.

'Are you all right there?' Yvonne asked. 'You're not going to be sick, are you? You didn't tell me you got seasick.'

'I'll be fine,' Daisy said. 'I think I just need to sit down for a second.'

As Daisy took the steps inside the boat, her legs felt like jelly – although it wasn't just her legs, she realised, as she poured a glass of water; her hands were shaking too. After a sip of the drink, Daisy moved further into the boat, perched herself on the edge of the sofa and blew out several long breaths.

This was a mistake. How had she not seen the sailboat coming towards her? That's what she wanted to know. And why had she pulled the tiller the wrong way? It was such a rookie steering mistake to make. She'd thought she was past silly errors like that. If she wasn't, then she probably wasn't safe to have on the water.

As she took another sip of water, Daisy glanced across the boat to where her phone was charging. The urge to ring Theo was overwhelming. She needed him to reassure her. To tell her she was perfectly safe and that everyone made mistakes out on boats now and then. That's what he'd tell her, even though she was sure it wasn't true. She couldn't imagine him ever messing up like that. Besides, how could she tell him what had happened without ruining the surprise?

Daisy drew in another deep breath and held it in her lungs for a second before blowing it out with a sigh. The boat was moving steadily now, she realised. It rocked with only the slightest sway that was no greater than if she'd been in a lock. However terrifying the moment with the sailboat had felt, the *September Rose* could definitely handle it, and judging by the way Yvonne was whistling to herself, it hadn't stressed her out at all. The only weak link on the trip was Daisy.

She stared at her phone again before shaking her head. The last thing she wanted was to come across as an overly needy girlfriend, now that Theo had told her he loved her. So, trying to force down the anxiety that still bubbled away, Daisy downed the rest of the water, put the glass in the sink and walked back onto the stern with Yvonne.

'So,' Daisy said, trying to sound as confident as she had felt earlier. 'How long until the next mooring?'

* * *

It turned out that the next mooring was far closer than Daisy had expected.

'Do you fancy going for a walk?' she asked when the boat was all tied up. Since the incident with the sailboat, she'd had an undeniable urge to put her feet on dry land. 'I thought I might like to take some photos.'

'That sounds lovely,' Yvonne said. 'Although I thought I might have a mid-morning siesta. You don't mind, do you? I think it must be all this sea air making me sleepy.'

Daisy avoided glancing at her phone or frowning. At most, Yvonne had been up for four and a half hours. It seemed unlikely that she was that tired already, unless she had lied about being able to sleep the night before. Then again, it could just be that she was trying to give the pair of them space, as they still had a long way to go.

'Of course. Why don't you have a nap while I go for a walk, then afterwards, I can fix us both sandwiches for lunch?'

'That sounds just perfect,' Yvonne replied. 'You can take my binoculars too. You never know what you might spot out here.'

27

There was no need to bother getting a coat or changing into walking boots so Daisy headed off the *September Rose*. She wasn't planning on walking far. Even in summer, the marshland was a maze of muddy inlets and rushes and as beautiful as they were, she could only imagine how disorientating it could be to someone who didn't know the area – particularly with the tides going in and out. And so Daisy walked around the marina to where the boats had thinned out and found a bench with a view.

She'd promised the girls she would keep them up to date on her adventures, and her mother had sent more than one message checking in on her, yet so far a single photo from Burnham was all she'd sent. Given that she had nowhere else to be for a while, this seemed like the perfect opportunity to get in touch. She took her phone out of her pocket and was still deciding who to contact first when a scruffy brown and white collie dog bounded up towards her.

Daisy glanced in the direction the animal had come from, scouring behind it for people. If it was a good walking spot, then it could be worth opening up the cafe for a couple of hours. But other than the dog and the boats, everything was empty.

'Hello,' she said, crouching down and rubbing the animal's scruff.

'Where are your owners? Are they around here somewhere? Are they on one of the boats?'

The dog beat its tail on the ground before picking up a stone beside her and placing it by her feet.

'A stone?'

The dog looked up at her, its eyes wide and expectant.

'Is this a present? Or am I meant to throw it?'

The dog's tail wagged harder. Daisy tapped the stone a little with her foot, rolling it less than a metre away.

With its tail a near blur of excitement, the dog picked it back up in his mouth and dropped it by Daisy's feet for a second time.

'Okay, so I take it this means I'm meant to throw it.'

This time, after picking up the stone, Daisy twisted around and threw it down the path towards the boats. The collie bolted away, leaving plumes of dust in his wake, and Daisy turned her attention back to her phone. After a moment's deliberation, she selected her mother's name on the screen, only before she had even pressed the call icon, the dog reappeared. Once again, he dropped the stone back at her feet.

'I feel like this could go on for a while,' she said, trying to stifle a laugh. 'Well, I don't have anything else to do. I suppose I can keep playing until you get bored or your owners appear.'

So with the phone now pressed against her ear, Daisy continued a game of fetch, even when her mum answered the call.

'Daisy, I was getting worried. How's it going?' Her mother's relief was audible down the line. 'Is everything going all right?'

'It is now,' Daisy said. 'Though there was a bit of a hair-raising moment this morning.'

While still picking up and throwing the stone, Daisy decided not to tell her mother about getting stuck in the marshland but instead proceeded to tell her about the incident with the sailboat.

'Oh, you did well to cope with that, Daisy love,' her mother said. 'Sailboats, they're a menace. I swear, one of them nearly took the roof off the boat when I was doing that trip. Might have been on the same river, even.'

A flicker of warmth lit inside Daisy. Her mum never volunteered information about her time on the boat before – not without extreme coercion, anyway. Perhaps this trip would offer a chance to break down some of their walls and open up conversations about her past, and her time with Daisy's father, after all these years.

As Daisy talked with her mother, the dog remained fully invested in its game and his interest showed no sign of waning. Daisy's arm, on the other hand, was starting to ache.

'That's it, last one,' she said quietly, then pulled her arm back and threw the stone in the opposite direction of the *September Rose*, after which she stood up and began to walk back to the boat, assuming the dog would do the same, and head back to wherever its owners were.

There was one other thing Daisy had considered telling her mother, although until a moment ago, she hadn't been sure whether she should broach the subject. However, she now felt like she could at least test the water.

'So, Yvonne found something in her pack,' she said, trying to sound as casual as possible. 'Two paintings. By Johnny. My father.'

Silence reached Daisy's ears. Silence that made her think bringing up her dad so directly hadn't been a great idea, even though her mum had already mentioned doing this trip herself, which alluded to Johnny, even if he hadn't been mentioned by name. When the tension had grown more and more tangible, Daisy cleared her throat, ready to say something that would brush the comment away, when her mother spoke first.

'Talking about paintings, have you thought about exhibiting again?' she asked. 'You know you really should.'

'Oh, well, not at the minute,' Daisy said, a heavy weight settling in her stomach. The deliberate and sharp change in conversation was a clear sign that Johnny was not on the table for discussion.

'Well, love,' her mother continued, her voice straining slightly. 'I really shouldn't be babbling on like this. You've got lots of things to be getting on with. Send my best to Yvonne, won't you?'

'I will.' Daisy was almost as surprised by this comment as she had been by the remarks about her travels. Her mother didn't like to be reminded about her past on Wildflower Lock, of which Yvonne had been a substantial part. As far as Daisy was aware, the pair hadn't spoken in years.

'And check in soon?'

'I'll try. Love you.'

By the time she'd hung up, she was already back at the *September Rose*. She put her phone away and was about to step aboard when something stopped her – a small, grey rock rolling to her feet. Already knowing what she was about to find, she turned around to find the dog sitting right there beside her, with that same expectant look and wagging tail.

'Wow, you don't give up easily, do you?' she said, reaching down and getting the stone for what she promised was going to be the last time. 'This is it, right? You have to go home. Someone will be missing you.'

Once again, she hurled the stone away from her, this time noting with a bit more detail how unique the pattern on the dog's back was. He was mostly white but had brown fur on either side that formed a V, the points of which met on its spine, whilst an inverted shape, smaller in size, was on its forehead. It would make a great little subject for one of her paintings, she thought. She hadn't painted a dog in quite a while.

And so, with a sudden hit of motivation, she headed inside and found her paints. As she had a willing model, it seemed silly not to use him.

28

Daisy quickly learned that a moving animal who constantly wanted stones thrown for him was a less-than-ideal model.

To start with, she found it near impossible to decide what pose she wanted to draw him in. He looked so cute when he was sitting on the ground, looking up at her, eyes wide, waiting for her to throw a stone, but she liked to have a level of movement and animation in her character paintings. So, in that sense, she knew it would be far better if she painted him running. Then there was a moment when he was lying down, his head between his paws, which was utterly adorable. But given that he only did it once, it was too difficult to get the proportions rights with no reference, and so she opted for her first idea – stone in his mouth, looking up at her. She even snapped a photo of him too, so she could work on it later when the light had changed.

The light was another thing that Daisy decided to paint that night. Or at least the sunset.

As often happened when Daisy started painting, one idea led to another, and it wasn't hard to be inspired by the views outside her window and it was only when Yvonne said she'd fixed them a simple dish of pasta and cheese for dinner, did she realise how late it was. She wasn't the only one who had lost track of time, though.

Daisy had stopped throwing stones over an hour earlier so that she could concentrate on the painting. She had assumed that if she stayed strong and didn't give in to his wide, pleading eyes, the dog would get bored and go back home to his owners, but that hadn't happened and even as they sat at the table eating, Daisy could hear him padding up and down the stone path outside.

As she wolfed down her food, Daisy found herself desperate to get back to her painting. It was a tough balance. The last thing Daisy wanted was to appear rude, especially when Yvonne was the one helping her out, but normally, if she was painting like this, she wouldn't even stop for an actual meal, just picking at a few snacks as she worked instead. And that night, she really worked.

After taking several snaps of the sunset, Daisy left her unfinished painting of the dog to dry and got to work on her second piece of the day – a sunset over the marshland.

'It's like a diary,' Yvonne said, leaning over Daisy's shoulder to look at her work so far. It was a habit that used to drive Daisy mad when she was younger; her mother would always lean over her shoulder well before the paintings were finished and when she didn't want anyone to see them. And that dislike of peering hadn't gone anywhere, but rather than snapping at Yvonne the way teenage Daisy would have done, she simply sat back in her chair and looked at the painting.

'I suppose it is. Although I didn't paint anything yesterday.'

'Well, it's not too late. You could paint something from passing through Maldon. Or a seal, maybe. Then you could take photos of the paintings and post them online. It'll be a nice memory. And you never know, you might get some followers. That's what they call it, isn't it? People who like your things on the internet? Followers?'

Daisy smiled at the comment. 'Yes, I guess it is.'

Staring at the two unfinished paintings, she pondered Yvonne's suggestion. Ever since the charity auction, Daisy had promised herself she would work more on promoting her work – post pictures on social media, perhaps create an online gallery, that type of thing. But life always seemed to get in the way. There were always other jobs to do. Only tonight, there wasn't. With the coffee shop closed, there was no need to do extra baking, and as long as they were being dictated to by the tides, it seemed silly not to make the most of these quiet evenings.

'You know what, you're right,' she said. 'I'm going to do it. A diary in paintings. And I can post one a day online.'

Yvonne smiled broadly. 'Well, that sounds just fantastic. I'm sure your mother and friends will love to see all the adventures we're getting up to. Not to mention your artwork.'

The comment caused a twist of uncertainty in Daisy. Sharing her work publicly would mean that everyone had access to it, including Theo. Her turning up in Slimbridge would hardly be a surprise if he'd watched the entire journey documented in watercolours.

'Maybe it'll be best if I do it under a new account,' she said, more to herself than Yvonne. 'I could call it something like "Canvases and Canals". Or "Art Afloat".'

Her mind turned over with the various ideas as she saw the vision coming to life.

'Well, it seems like you've got lots to be getting on with,' Yvonne said, breaking Daisy's train of thought. 'Probably best if I head to bed and leave you to it.'

Daisy was about to wish her goodnight when she glanced at the clock and saw it was barely nine o'clock.

'Are you sure?' she asked, putting her paintbrush in the water and finally tearing her eyes away from her work. 'Sorry if I'm being antisocial, but please don't think you have to disappear to bed. You really don't. You can watch a film if you like?'

With a thin smile, Yvonne placed a hand on Daisy's shoulder. 'That's very sweet of you, dear, but really, I'm used to having the evenings to myself too, and I've always been one for an early night. Don't worry about me, though; I've got a Kindle full of books that'll keep me occupied for years. You have a good night, my dear, but don't be too late to bed. It's a big day tomorrow.'

'Aren't they all?' Daisy replied.

'They are. That's how you know you're living.'

29

A telephone call before bed was part of Daisy and Theo's routine, and usually it was one of Daisy's favourite parts of the day. She would hang up the phone, feeling like a teenager utterly besotted by her first crush. But that night, when Daisy had finally got to sleep, the only feeling filling her had been guilt.

She had known the telephone call wasn't going to be as easy as normal, given how much she couldn't tell him and the fact her lungs were practically bursting with the urge to recall all her adventures so far. Daisy could just imagine the way Theo would have laughed if she'd been able to tell him about being rescued from the marshes, once he'd got over being mad at her for walking off in the early hours of the morning, that was. Or how he would have comforted her after the whole tiller incident. But not telling him things was far easier than the lying she had to do.

The first lie was only a small one. She had told him she'd been painting, and he'd asked to see her work. Given that the painting was almost finished, she'd flicked the camera around to show him the artwork of the dog.

'He looks cute,' Theo said. 'Where did you see him?'

'Oh... uhm, yes... He was just around...'

Daisy cursed herself. It was a ridiculously vague response and she was sure Theo was going to question her further, but instead, he changed the conversation entirely.

'I forgot to ask you,' he said as if he'd just remembered something. 'Have you seen my watch?'

'Your watch?'

'Yeah, I've searched the *Escape* and I can't find it. I think I might have left it when I came and saw you.'

Daisy shook her head. 'No, I've not seen it. Sorry.'

'Could you check down the side of the bed? It might have slipped off the bedside table. That's the only thing I can think of.'

'Oh, sure,' Daisy said, grateful that they were no longer talking about the dog.

'Thank you. I don't suppose you could check now, could you?'

'Now?' Daisy blinked. Yvonne was already tucked up in bed and had been for quite some time. There was no way Daisy could just go rummaging around in there while she was asleep.

'It's not expensive, but it was a twenty-first birthday present and if it's not there, I need to figure out where else I could have left it,' Theo said. 'I'll be gutted if it slipped off my wrist while I was working, but I don't see how it could have done. I'm sure it has to be in your cabin somewhere.'

'Right, yes, sure...' Daisy said, still struggling to work out how she was going to do this. 'I was about to head to bed, anyway, so why don't we say goodnight and I'll message you if I find it?' Her voice sounded stoic and awkward and she was certain Theo would hear it too, but instead, he smiled gratefully. An act which only caused Daisy's guilt to deepen.

'Sure thing. Thank you. And I'll speak to you tomorrow?'

'Absolutely.'

'Love you.'

'I love you too.'

If Daisy had thought the guilt would end when she hung up the phone, she was very wrong. She then had to send a message to Theo saying she'd looked for the watch – which she hadn't – and had not been able to find it. Then, to make matters worse, when she'd finally got to check the next morning when Yvonne was up, she found it in less than a minute, meaning she had to send Theo another message. No matter how pleased she felt that she'd found the watch for him, it didn't make up for the series of lies she was now piling on top of one another, and the guilt she felt with every one. Although lying to Theo was only one of her current issues.

'What are you still doing here?' Daisy asked as she pulled back the curtain to find a now familiar brown and white face standing by the boat. The minute he heard her voice, he thumped his tail. With a slight groan, Daisy fixed herself her morning coffee before she headed outside the way she normally did. Only that morning, she had company.

'You didn't spend all night here, did you?' she said as she offered the dog a quick rub on his head. There was no sign of a collar, but in the countryside like this, she knew that didn't mean much. He could easily have an owner who wasn't that worried about him running off, although where that owner lived was another question entirely. Taking a long sip of her drink, Daisy scoured the scenery. He had to belong to one of the nearby boats, she decided. Maybe someone who worked at the marina; that would make sense.

'I'm afraid you're going to have to find someone else to throw your stones for you,' Daisy said, feeling guilty for a moment. He looked so happy every time she went to pick one up. 'We're going this morning. High tide and all that. I've got a boy I need to go and see, and he's very nice.'

Given how quiet the dog had been up until that point, his sudden bark caused Daisy to jump. For a split second, she thought that perhaps his owner had appeared, but the animal was looking directly at the *September Rose*.

A moment later, Yvonne stepped onto the stern.

'What a racket,' she said, looking at the dog and frowning. 'It's way too early for that. Go on with you.' She waved her hands wildly. 'Go. Where's your home? Go home, will you?'

The dog barked once more, but rather than leaving as Yvonne had gestured for him to do, he simply looked at Daisy.

'I think he's after a bit of company,' Daisy explained. 'He wanted to play with me yesterday, too. Though he didn't bark like that.'

'Obviously, he can tell I won't give him any treats,' Yvonne replied, looking at the dog for a moment longer before she turned her full attention to Daisy. 'We need to get going, though. They don't man the bridge all day.'

'Man the bridge?' Daisy was confused by the statement. Why did a bridge need manning? Her attention was now drawn away from the dog and back to the day ahead.

It didn't take long for her to find out. Within twenty minutes, the *September Rose* was pulling away from its mooring. Thankfully, there was no sign of the brown collie; Daisy didn't have time to worry about a dog she didn't know. She had enough of her own worries to deal with.

There were so many river names, it was hard to keep track of where they were, and at that precise moment – according to Yvonne – they were currently on a creek as opposed to a river or an estuary, although what the differences were, Daisy really wasn't sure. Perhaps, she thought, she should have ordered some sort of guide to help, but maybe she'd be able to pick one up at one the marina. With her piles and piles of notebooks and guides, however, she was sure Yvonne had enough for the both of them.

The bridge in question was long and grey and the only route between Foulness Island – which seemed unfairly named given how attractive the area was – and the mainline. It was also the first bridge Daisy had ever gone under that raised up to allow boats to pass.

'They look very serious,' Daisy commented as she waved to the man on the bridge. He might have still been a way off, but it looked like he was scowling at her.

'MOD,' Yvonne replied.

'MOD?'

'Military of Defence. All very hush-hush here. My Harry had some ideas of what went on, you know, testing… That type of thing, but never been too sure. Happens all around here.'

'Oh,' Daisy said, not sure how else to reply. Yvonne had knowingly had them stay the night at a military testing zone and had not said anything. Next time, she would ask her what exactly went on in the locations they were staying.

As they headed through to the mouth of the river, Yvonne looked at Daisy with a wide smile on her face. So wide, Daisy was almost certain she was missing something important.

'What is it?' she asked.

'I just thought you might want to get your phone out, that's all. Take a snap.'

'A snap?'

'A photo. You can paint it and put it in that diary of yours.'

Daisy looked at the view again. It was certainly pretty. Blue skies, fluffy, white clouds, an immense amount of water. Yes, it was pretty, but no prettier than any other of the views she had seen over the forty-eight hours. And she really wanted to save her paintings for the best things she saw each day.

'I think you might be missing the importance of this moment,' Yvonne said as she steered the *September Rose* out of the creek to join the far, far wider mass of water in front of them. 'This is it.'

'It?' Daisy questioned, still not sure what Yvonne was talking about.

'The Thames. This is it. The very start of the mouth of the great river. From here on, it's one straight line to London. Well, almost.'

30

It was hard to believe they were travelling through an estuary and not the sea, given how wide it was, but a quick check of the location on her phone and Daisy could see that they were well and truly in the middle of the Thames Estuary. Because of the depth of the river water, they stayed near the centre, where they didn't have to worry about the tide going in and out. In fact, they were moving at an impressive speed, and while there were plenty of sailboats out enjoying the summer sun, the fact that they were substantially more spread out than they had been the day before meant Daisy could actually enjoy the view as they passed the beachfront at Southend-on-Sea, complete with its long pier and funfair.

This was very different from the first couple of days when they were only able to travel for a couple of hours. They were moving non-stop now and didn't even have the option of mooring up most of the time. After Southend came yet more towns and villages, which grew farther and farther apart.

'I guess you should make us some lunch,' Yvonne said, a little after midday when there was absolutely no mooring in sight. 'We've still got a way to go.'

She wasn't joking. It wasn't until late afternoon, when the clouds were thickening in the sky, that Yvonne pulled out a pair of binoculars and looked off into the distance.

'This is the place I was thinking of. Glad it's still here,' she said, staring proudly at the scene in front of them.

'I thought we were heading to a marina?' Daisy asked, confused by the expanse of wide-open wilderness that spread out in front of them. 'Where are we supposed to moor up here?'

'The jetty, obviously. Don't worry, you'll see it in a minute.'

The marshland that surrounded them was dense and low and could have been an entirely different country. Although, as they kept going, Daisy could see that Yvonne was indeed correct. A single jetty stretched out from the marshland. This was going to be the most remote place she had ever moored, that was for sure.

One other boat was moored up, but as they got closer, Daisy saw the rust patches that covered its hull and the thick layers of grime coating its broken windows.

Daisy had always thought she would need someone – ideally a boyfriend – to go on adventures with. Instead, she was here, taking control of those adventures in her life, and she'd never been more excited. Perhaps she would do three entries in the painting diary that night – entering the Thames, the fairground they passed, and here in the wilderness. They would certainly all bring something different to the collection.

As Daisy tied a knot in the rope, a rustling in the grass caught her attention. She tensed. It seemed an unlikely place for people to be out wandering or walking their dogs and her immediate thought was of adders. They were found near water, weren't they? Panic struck and her pulse soared. What would happen if she got bitten by an adder somewhere as remote as this? She looked around her. There were still plenty of hours of sunlight left. Perhaps she should suggest to Yvonne they find somewhere a little more populated to moor up. Yes, she considered, as she crouched down to untie the knot. That was what they should do. Only the moment her fingers touched the rope, a loud bark shot out into the air. A moment later, the animal appeared from out of the rushes. Daisy blinked and tipped her head to the side. The dog was covered in mud, clearly having waded through marshland, but there was something incredibly familiar about it, a familiarity that deepened as it jumped onto the jetty and walked towards her, wagging its tail wildly. When it reached Daisy, it stopped and dropped a stone by her feet.

'You have to be joking?' she said.

Now she was close up, she could see just how thick the mud was. All the way up its front and back legs, and even across its face, too. And yet there beneath it all, two features were clear. Two dark Vs, one across his back, and one on his face.

31

Yvonne stood next to Daisy, the pair of them staring at the dog in absolute silence. The same way they had been doing for the last three minutes.

'Are you sure?' Yvonne finally said, asking the same question she had asked when Daisy had first called her outside.

Daisy studied the dog again. Not that she needed to. Three white feet, with the left back one reddish-brown. And those Vs. And that was before you got started on its obsession with stones. There was absolutely no mistaking it.

'I'm positive. It's definitely him.'

She had already opened up the map on her phone and calculated how long it would have taken him to go across land from their previous mooring. As the crow flies, it really wasn't that far. Easily doable and in far less time than it took them to wind around the narrow bends of the river. What Daisy wanted to know was why? Had he really followed her? That didn't make sense, did it? All she had done was throw a few stones. He couldn't have built up that much of an attachment to her in that time, could he?

Yvonne crouched down and made a kissing noise. Immediately, the dog started barking.

'Okay, it definitely sounds like it's him too,' Yvonne said.

Ignoring his barking, she picked up the stone and threw it down the jetty. As the dog bolted after it, she turned to Daisy.

'There's no collar, so either he slipped out from someone's house, or he's a stray.'

'So what do we do?' Daisy asked. 'There's no one around here.'

She looked at the dog again. At first impressions, he seemed relatively healthy, but on closer inspection, she wasn't so sure. His back legs were notably thin and there were several mats in his fur. There was also a distinct smell of marshland rising from his coat.

'If I'm honest,' Yvonne said, possibly noticing the same things as Daisy, 'I think the first thing we need to do is give him a bath.'

*　*　*

Daisy had never bathed a dog before. It wasn't that she didn't like them. She loved them. For years, she had begged her mother to let them have one. Terrier, Great Dane, she didn't care. Any dog would have done, but with her mother's work in restaurants, and the long hours, it hadn't been possible. When she moved in on her own, the idea had crossed her mind again, but her landlord had been less than keen, and given how cheaply he'd kept the rent, she'd not wanted to do anything to upset him. Now, having a cafe on the boat hardly seemed like a fitting place to have a dog either, which was why, rather than inviting him into the *September Rose*, she filled a large bucket with warm water and sat outside the stern.

'You're very well-behaved, aren't you,' Daisy said as she used the soapy water to wash the mud off his legs. She was almost certain human soap wasn't the best thing for a dog, but it was either that or leave his fur to get even more matted, so she continued to work away. The dog was entirely nonplussed. If anything, it seemed to like the attention. 'Where's your human? You must have a human somewhere, don't you? You're far too lovely not to have a human.'

It was hard not to make comparisons between cleaning the mud off the dog and the way Daisy had needed to clean herself off after the marsh orchid incident. As had frequently happened over the last couple of days, Daisy's mind wandered to her smartly dressed rescuer.

Everything about him had been an enigma. Where had he been going dressed like that so early in the morning? And jogging, too. Why had he not insisted she pay for his dry cleaning or checked if there was anyone Daisy could have rung to make sure she was okay? There were so many questions she wanted to ask him, and yet given how she didn't even get his name, or offer him a proper thank you, she didn't see how that would ever happen.

Daisy's mind was still lost in that marshland when, without warning, the dog reached forward and left a slobbering wet lick along Daisy's cheek. She squealed in shock.

'No, that's horrible!' Still, she couldn't help but laugh, causing the animal's tail to beat against the stern.

When he was washed, she dried him off with a towel she kept for drying the outside of the boat after the rain. And if she'd ever had any doubt that it was the same dog, it was gone. It was definitely him, but the questions of how and why remained.

'Should we ring someone?' Daisy asked as they sat down to eat their dinner. 'There has to be a lost dog helpline or someone we can contact.'

When the dog was washed and dried, Daisy had left him outside while she got on with cooking the meal, though as the aroma of roast chicken thighs floated into the air, she had been struck with a pang of guilt. The smell was enough to make her salivate; she could only imagine what it would be like for an animal that had walked five hours, possibly non-stop, to get here. Now he was staring at them through the window as they ate.

'I'm sure there is, but I doubt they'll come out this far this late in the day,' Yvonne replied. 'Honestly, I think we let him be, for tonight at least. He'll probably make his way home soon enough. If he's still here in the morning, I guess we'll have to rethink it then.'

Daisy nodded as she stared at the animal. Whether he'd picked his place outside the window so that he could see her or the chicken, she wasn't sure, but every time he caught her looking at him, he wagged his tail like that was all he wanted in the world. With her meal half-finished, she looked at the chicken on her plate. Guilt twisted within her. Perhaps he had followed her because he was starving. If he was, like Yvonne had said, a stray, then it was possible he hadn't eaten for days. For a second, she considered picking off a couple of pieces of meat and throwing them out the window for him. But what good would that do in the long run? He might hang around even longer and not return home to his owner. Assuming he had one. So she drew the curtains and began to paint.

Normally, Daisy knew what she was going to paint when she started to sketch, but this time, it was only when the image began to take form that she realised what it was. The elongated snout, the floppy ears. For the second time in as many days, she was drawing her new friend. But this differed greatly from her first painting of him. With the outline drawn, Daisy looked at her palette. Normally, she would have gone for realistic tones, perhaps slightly brighter here and there, but immensely detailed, with every whisker and hairline drawn in. This time, however, she decided to paint as if she were her father, splashing colour onto the page with raw abandon and making each stroke brighter and more vibrant than the last. Where the dog had brown-red fur, she gave him vivid orange. Where his eyes were a hazy green, she gave him a blazing emerald that shone out from the page. Purples and pinks. Golds and blues. All appeared on the patchwork of his body. It was only when she finished that she sat back and observed it. A smile rose on her lips.

'Well, Dad?' she asked aloud. 'What do you think?'

32

The next day, they had one simple aim – to get as far as possible. With very few scenic places they could stop en route, it should have been fairly straightforward, although they still needed to consider the practicalities of the tide. While they could, theoretically, travel while the tide was going in the opposite direction, according to Yvonne, there was very little point. Progress would be slow and it would be an inefficient use of both time and fuel. Daisy wasn't sure how true that was and – given how long Yvonne had slept the night before – she wondered if it was just a ruse for Yvonne to get a lie-in after missing her morning nap the day before. However, when Daisy's body clock woke her up at five-thirty in the morning, she was surprised to hear Yvonne already talking away.

'No, not Harry, please. You've got it wrong. It's not him. It can't be.'

Daisy hesitated. Was Yvonne on the phone? It certainly sounded that way. Yet she hadn't even seen Yvonne with a phone. And Harry? The only Harry Daisy had heard Yvonne mention was her husband. And there was something about her tone that didn't sound quite right.

Hoping she wasn't invading her privacy too greatly, Daisy pushed open the cabin door to see Yvonne there on her bed, twisting and turning, repeating her late husband's name over and over again.

'Not Harry. You have to have it wrong. It can't be Harry.'

Daisy's pulse shot upwards. Yvonne was clearly having a nightmare, and the last thing Daisy wanted was to leave her friend in such a situation. But were you meant to wake people up if they were having a nightmare? She knew you were meant to let sleepwalkers be, but was it the same if someone was having a bad dream? She didn't know, but going in and waking Yvonne up, when she was clearly going through something personal, didn't feel right. And so, Daisy turned around, closed the cabin door and put on the coffee machine, hoping it would be loud enough to do the job for her.

While waking up and hearing her boatman having a nightmare was a less-than-ideal start to the morning, there was, thankfully, one unexpectedly pleasant surprise. After fixing her drink, Daisy headed out onto the stern and scanned the horizon. A flood of relief washed through her. The dog was gone.

As grateful as Daisy was that she didn't have to deal with a stray collie, when they cast off from the riverbank an hour later, she couldn't help but feel a little sad that she hadn't got to say goodbye, or found out where he had come from.

'It's for the best,' Yvonne said as if she could read Daisy's thoughts. When Yvonne had appeared from the cabin, not long after Daisy made a coffee, she seemed perfectly chirpy, as if she had no recollection of the nightmare at all. And when Daisy had asked her how well she'd slept, Yvonne had replied with a simple 'like a baby', confirming in Daisy's mind that bringing up the nightmare would definitely not be the right thing to do. Now they were on the way, and Yvonne seemed completely fine.

'Dogs are a big commitment,' she continued. 'And you don't know anything about him. Now, why don't you take the tiller while I make breakfast? There's not much that can go wrong as long as you don't go too close to the bank.'

It wasn't the most comforting pep talk, but Daisy took good notice and made sure she was a fair distance away from the riverbank as Yvonne left her to go make breakfast.

A slight pang of sadness struck her. On the ridiculous chance that the dog was following her again, she really wanted to be close enough to spot him. Even with all the distance between her and the land, she found herself repeatedly looking across to see if there were signs of her furry, four-legged friend.

'Have you got that throttle up full?' Yvonne asked as she came back onto the stern carrying two plates of scrambled eggs and toast. She handed one to Daisy, who glanced at the lever on the side of the boat before taking it.

'Yes, the throttle's on full.'

'Huh,' she said. The comment caused a fluttering of nerves to ignite in Daisy. She waited for a further explanation, but instead of elaborating, Yvonne promptly started tucking into her food.

'Is that a good thing or a bad thing?' Daisy asked, realising she wouldn't get any more without pressing. 'Should I turn the throttle down?'

She reached over to the lever, only for Yvonne to shake her head.

'No, no, leave it where it is. We're just going a little slower than I'd have expected, that's all. It must have been further past high tide than I thought when we left.'

Once again, Daisy didn't know how to reply. It didn't sound like a particularly good thing, given that they'd been aiming to leave just before high tide each day, but Yvonne didn't sound unduly concerned.

'It's only a couple hours until we stop anyway,' she said.

The town Yvonne had mentioned stopping at was a little further away than she'd thought, and it was closer to four hours later when the jetty came into view. Along with a solid mooring, there were dozens and dozens of people and a sigh of relief passed Daisy's lips; hopefully, she would be able to do plenty of afternoon business with the coffee shop and make up for the last couple of days. Hopefully, she would be able to shift a few of the chocolate shortbreads and lemon muffins she had left too. She just needed to get opened up first.

Between them, Daisy and Yvonne had found a rhythm for mooring, which involved Yvonne steering the boat into the space while Daisy grabbed the ropes and stepped off to tie the boat up. Given how well it had worked previously, Daisy saw no reason to change the method and they didn't even bother talking as they fell into the routine, which, for the first part, worked perfectly well.

With the back rope tied, Daisy moved to fetch the front rope from the boat, only to find herself rooted to the spot. The stern of the *September Rose* was a pleasant little area that she and Theo often sat out on for an evening drink, but since Yvonne had taken her cabin this trip, Daisy hadn't been on it at all. Yet, as she passed a fleeting glance inside of it, her stomach lurched. A pair of dark-brown eyes were staring up at her from the front of the boat. The *September Rose* had its first stowaway.

33

Daisy didn't even open the hatch for the coffee shop. There was no way she would be able to focus on work with the dog to deal with. Her chest felt tight with the anxiety of it. If the dog did have a home, perhaps near one of their earlier moorings, she had just taken him even further away. So along with getting to Theo, finding the collie's owners was now her top priority.

Having looked up vets in the area, Daisy found one only fifteen minutes' walk away. She had rung them and explained the situation, and they had been more than happy for her to bring him straight in, although that meant she had another issue to contend with.

'I think he'll just follow me,' Daisy said as she stood outside on the jetty. She had already walked from one end to the other and the dog had stayed close to her heel the entire time, his tail wagging. Given how much he'd already followed her, she knew she could probably take him all the way to the vets in the same way, but it didn't feel right. Even some of the most regular visitors at Wildflower Lock, who brought their dogs almost every day, always checked with Daisy if they minded them being off their lead outside her boat. With her mind made up, she headed back into the *September Rose*, found a spare length of rope, and made a makeshift leash.

'Are you sure you don't want to come with me?' she asked Yvonne one last time. 'It's a nice-looking town. We could always have a walk around the shops?' Daisy still hadn't mentioned to Yvonne that she'd heard her having a nightmare, or calling out her late husband's name in her sleep. It wasn't a subject she was sure how, or even if, she should broach, but she couldn't help but feel that Yvonne getting out of the boat and having a walk outside might be a good idea. It would also mean she wasn't alone in taking the dog to the vets. Sadly, Yvonne shook her head.

'I'll stay here if it's all right with you,' Yvonne said. 'I need to book us into a marina for this evening, and to be honest, I'm feeling a little out of sorts. I think it's been so long since I took the *Ariadne* on the water that I've lost my sea legs.'

'I understand,' Daisy said. 'Well, hopefully, I won't be long. And I may or may not be on my own when I come back.'

Daisy kept the makeshift leash taut as she walked, but in reality, she didn't think she needed it at all. The dog stayed close, even stopping when they came to the road. It took a quick tug to make him sit down while they waited for the first set of traffic lights to change, but by the time they were on their third set, he was sitting instinctively, as if he knew what was expected.

'I don't know if you've done this before, or you're just very smart,' Daisy said, looking down at the dog. His tongue hung from his mouth as if he was smiling. A moment later, the little man on the traffic lights turned green, and the pair of them were striding across the road. Daisy was only halfway across when she spotted a man jogging on the other side of the road. His hair was jet black and there was something about him that looked remarkably similar, though it was only as he started striding away from her that she realised why that was.

'It's him!' Daisy said, more to herself than to the dog. 'It's the guy from the marsh!'

34

Daisy was sprinting, yanking the lead as she dodged past one person, then another, trying to get to the pavement before he disappeared.

'Wait! Wait!' she yelled after the figure who was still jogging away from her. All she could see was the back of him. Large headphones were firmly fixed on his black hair as he weaved in and out of the other pedestrians. Daisy never weaved. She didn't have the elegance to weave at the best of times, but it was even harder with a thirty-five-pound dog attached to a rope at the end of her arm. But she was determined the man wouldn't get away from her. Somehow, little by little, she was catching up with him.

'Please, please wait!' she yelled again, even though he was unlikely to hear her with his headphones on. Her legs were tiring and once again, the man was gaining a distance between them. Daisy was about to give up altogether when she noticed a crossroads in front of them and the set of traffic lights that were about to turn red for all the pedestrians. If she could just reach there, while it was still red, she would have him.

With every bit of energy she could muster, Daisy sprinted towards the traffic lights. The cars were moving again, and the man had been forced to stop with everyone else, though he was jogging on the spot and she knew he wouldn't be there for long.

'Sorry, sorry!' Daisy apologised as she squeezed her way past one person, then another until she was finally only inches away from him. The traffic lights were about to change again, though, turning red for the cars and green for the people, and Daisy could see the man poised, ready to start running. She needed to grab him now.

It was a leap. That was the only way she could describe it. An outright leap off the pavement and into the air with her arm outstretched. She reached forward, her eyes half on the traffic lights, half on the shoulder in front of her. And then, somehow, she had it. She had the fabric in her hand.

Relief flooded through her. She had found her man. She had found the man she needed to thank for saving her from the marsh.

'I'm sorry, I just didn't think I'd—'

The man turned around on the spot, glaring at her with his deep-brown eyes.

'What the hell are you doing?' he said.

'It's me, it's the woman you—'

Daisy stopped. The man's brown eyes were still narrowed on her, and that was the problem. She recalled with perfect clarity the way she had locked on to those bright irises when they had pulled her out of the mud. Bright *green* irises. Not brown.

'I'm sorry,' she said. 'I think I've made a mistake.'

The man shook his head and muttered. A moment later, he was sprinting across the road, leaving Daisy and the dog alone once again.

35

The incident left Daisy feeling altogether shaky. She had been so sure it was the man from the marsh. So sure she had chased down a complete stranger on a street. What was wrong with her? Obviously, the impending trip was causing her far more stress than she had realised, so much so that she was imagining people, although it was a reasonable mistake to make. Both men were of similar age, build and hair colour. If only she'd actually thanked the man properly, then maybe she wouldn't have felt this constant urge to find him again.

The detour to race after a runner had taken them in the opposite direction to the vets, and as such, they arrived only a minute before their appointment time.

With a deep breath in, Daisy stood outside the door. She had wanted this to be a trip of firsts for her but hadn't expected her first trip to a vet to be on that list.

'Come on,' she said, looking down at the dog with a feeling of trepidation filling her. 'Let's see if we can find your owner, shall we?'

A small bell jangled above the door as Daisy and the dog stepped into the vets and headed to the white desk.

'Good morning,' Daisy said to the woman sitting behind a computer. 'My name's Daisy May. I rang earlier. I've had a dog following me for a couple of days. I think he's a stray, and I wanted to get him checked out. See if he's chipped and hopefully reunite him with his owners.'

The woman looked down at the amiable dog, its tail still wagging. 'No worries. If you'd just like to take a seat, I will call you as soon as the vet is free.' The woman gestured to a row of seats on the other side of the room. After another word of thanks, Daisy headed over and took a spot between a large bull-mastiff, who was wearing a cone of shame and trying to scratch unsuccessfully, and a cat who was whining incessantly in its cage while the owner was desperately plying it with treats as they tried to make it stop.

'Aren't you a lovely-looking chap,' the mastiff owner said. He reached out a hand to stroke the collie. Immediately, the dog began barking. Daisy pulled tightly on his lead.

'Shh,' she said, before turning to the gentleman. 'Sorry, he's just loud. He barks a lot around strangers. But it's mostly just noise.'

'No worries. I should have kept my distance. I forget they're not all as soft as this one.' With a wide grin, he reached down and rubbed the mastiff's belly. The dog's tongue flopped out of the side of his mouth as its tail whacked the ground. While the owner carried on lavishing attention on his dog, Daisy looked back at the collie. Was it mostly noise? she wondered, thinking about what she had said only seconds before. She had certainly never seen the dog do anything other than be totally friendly, but perhaps she would need to be a little more cautious. After all, she knew next to nothing about him.

After close to fifteen minutes, Daisy was finally called in to see the vet.

'Daisy, isn't it?' the vet said. She was a young woman, with dark hair plaited down her back, and a pair of glasses hanging from a chain around her neck which she put on as she looked at the computer screen. 'And this is the stray you've brought in?'

She frowned as she looked at the dog, pulling her glasses off to reach out a hand. Once again, the barking started.

'Shh! Stop it,' Daisy said sharply. 'You don't need to behave like that, do you?' Immediately, he fell silent.

The vet looked at her, confused.

'Sorry, I misunderstood. I thought he was still a stray. I didn't realise you'd already adopted him?'

'Adopted?' Daisy's pulse rose. 'Oh, no. I haven't. At least, not deliberately. He's been following me for a couple of days now. Well, following my boat, then stowing away.'

'Following your boat?'

Daisy didn't want to go into all the details. It sounded completely insane to believe a dog would follow her just because she'd spent half an hour throwing a stone for him. But then, didn't you hear stories about cats that travelled miles from war zones to be reunited with their owners? Only she wasn't his owner. Definitely not.

'He's very friendly. I'm not entirely sure he is a stray.' Daisy said.

'Well, he certainly seems to respond very well to you. Let me get him up on the table and see if we can find a chip. We can have a look at the rest of him while he's there, too.'

The vet's scan was thorough. Along with weight, temperature and checking for signs of fleas or skin conditions, she checked several areas multiple times where chips were normally placed, just to be sure. However, five minutes later, she was certain.

'So, he's definitely not got a chip.'

'Definitely?' Daisy replied, even though she'd watched every part of the check-up.

'Definitely. And he's not that old. From his teeth, I would guess he's about a year at most.'

'Okay... So does that mean he's a stray, or he's just not chipped?' Daisy asked.

At this, the vet pressed her lips together before letting out a sigh.

'To be honest with you, if someone is going to have a dog and not chip it, they're not the type of people that should be dog owners. It's illegal, to start with. They certainly don't deserve someone as lovely as this young man.'

Daisy looked down at her four-legged friend, who was currently lapping up the vet's attention. His behaviour had been the same with her as it was with Yvonne: a series of barks before he relaxed. He was good with people. Surely a dog like that must have had a human at some point, so what had happened? Had an owner taken him in then changed their mind, deciding he wasn't worth the stress? And how old could the dog have been when that had happened? The thought made her feel physically sick. Right now, though, she didn't have time to think about that. There was one far more pressing issue that needed to be dealt with.

'So, if he's not chipped,' she said, drawing the vet's attention away from the dog and back to her, 'what happens now?'

36

Daisy had found herself in several unexpected situations over the last couple of days, from facing her first sailing boat in the middle of a river to being stuck in marshland. But this, asking a vet what she was meant to do with an unchipped, apparently stray dog that had become undeniably attached to her, felt like it was the strangest.

'Well, you have a couple of options,' the vet said. 'You could put out notices on local social media around the area where you found him. An owner might pick up on it that way, but I'll be honest with you, it looks like it's been a long time since he's had a good meal and the fact that there's no dog of his description appearing on one of the missing pet databases is a pretty sure sign that whoever had him isn't that concerned. I could be wrong, of course – you sometimes get people who don't know about using social media for lost animals, particularly old people. He might still have someone out there.'

'And if he doesn't?' Daisy asked, already sensing the answer.

'Well, then it's up to you. There are plenty of dogs' homes around, and he's friendly enough, although often people want puppies or at least an animal with a history, so they know if they can have them around other pets and children. But he's young enough. I'm sure he would be in with a chance of being re-homed.'

A chance of being re-homed.

'So I would put him into a dogs' home and hope he finds someone?' Daisy said, more to herself than the vet.

'That would be my suggestion. We do have room in our kennels at the moment. If you want to leave him here, I can get in touch with the local dogs' home? They are normally fairly prompt with pickups.'

Daisy looked down at her feet. The dog was staring up at her, his eyes wide, almost pleading. As if he'd understood exactly what the vet had said and desperately didn't want to be left there.

'You'd be okay, wouldn't you?' the vet said as she reached across to stroke the dog. Only rather than letting her, he ducked behind Daisy and let out a loud bark.

The vet straightened up.

'Well, he's certainly got some character, though I'm not sure if that will help him find somewhere to live or not.'

Daisy's mind was whirring. Could she really do this? He had followed her for days, let her wash him, and had looked at her with nothing but love and devotion since they had first met. Could she really just pass him off to grow older and older in a cage, praying that someday someone might take him home? And what if he did have an owner? What if he belonged to someone who had loved him dearly? Who hadn't known about getting him chipped? Or who had planned on doing it just before he went missing? There were just too many unknowns.

'You know what?' Daisy said, pushing her shoulders back and taking the lead in her hand. 'I'll take him back with me for now. I'll put up a notice myself. If I don't have any luck, then I can take him to a dogs' home afterwards.'

The vet nodded, just the slightest smile twitching at the corner of her lips.

'Given how fond he seems of you, I think that's a wonderful idea,' she said. 'Only, if you are going to take him, we really need to chip him. It's easy enough to swap over when you find the original owner, or when you find someone who wants to take him on permanently, but for now, he'll need to be registered to you. That won't be a problem, will it?'

Daisy looked at the dog by her ankle. Did all dogs look at people like this? she wondered. Like they knew absolutely everything that was going on in a situation, not to mention everything she was thinking. Maybe they did. Maybe that's why they were known as man's best friend.

'I guess you'll have to,' she said.

The vet's smile widened.

'Brilliant. Well, with that sorted, how are you paying?'

37

It could have been Daisy's imagination, but she was sure as she walked back towards the *September Rose* that the dog's tail was wagging with an even more pronounced vigour.

'This isn't permanent, you know,' she said, looking down at him. 'We'll find your owners, and if we don't, I'll look for someone who can take you in. But first, I guess I better get you some food.'

Given that the dog was a stray, the vet had kindly subsidised the cost of getting him chipped and treated for fleas, but Daisy still had to pay for the worming tablets herself, and now she was looking at another fifteen pounds for dog food. The vet had also made some comment about them selling actual leads and collars, with a nod to Daisy's homemade leash, and so, while settling the bill, Daisy had also purchased those extras, too. Owning a dog wasn't cheap, and she didn't even own him.

Back at the *September Rose*, Daisy found Yvonne was outside the boat. A look of bemusement flashed on her face as she saw Daisy approaching, the collie walking perfectly to heel with his new collar and lead.

'I thought you were taking him to the vet and leaving him there?'

'It turned out there was a change of plans.'

Until that moment, Daisy hadn't thought about how Yvonne would feel with a dog on the boat. Daisy knew she wasn't allergic to them, of course – that much was obvious from the way Yvonne had stroked him. But there was a difference between not being allergic to an animal and sharing your cabin space with them for the foreseeable future. A ripple of guilt fluttered within.

'It's not permanent,' she said. 'I'm going to look for his owner on the internet tonight. Post up some pictures on lost pet sites. And if we can't find them, I'll find him a home.'

Yvonne raised an eyebrow.

'It's fine by me. It's your boat and you can do what you like. But if I were you, I'd have him sleeping out on the stern. You don't know if he's house-trained. That's your decision, though. We need to get going. I've booked us a mooring for tonight, but it's a good four hours of travel ahead of us. I hope your dog can handle boat life.'

As it turned out, he could. The minute the engine rumbled into life, his tail wagged excitedly. He perked up at the boat's gentle movement and leaned into the rush of cold air, looking for all the world like he was smiling. Daisy couldn't help but laugh. There was something so refreshing about the energy he brought to the boat.

While Yvonne took the tiller, Daisy used the time to check lost pet sites for potential matches, but two hours later, despite her efforts, she was no closer than when she'd started.

'He could've come off a boat, perhaps?' she pondered aloud. The heat of the day had subdued into a lovely evening warmth. 'Perhaps someone came travelling from the continent, where the dog wouldn't need to be chipped. Is that possible?'

'I guess so,' Yvonne replied. 'So I assume you haven't had any luck?'

Daisy shook her head. 'No, nothing at all. I'm going to post a photo of him online.'

Realising she needed a picture, Daisy pulled out her phone and snapped an image. He looked perfectly at ease, gazing out over the water, and she couldn't help but wonder if the comment about coming off a boat was really that far-fetched. He certainly looked used to being on the water.

Before Daisy could upload it to any of the sites, her phone began buzzing – Theo on a video call.

'I'd better take this,' Daisy said. 'You don't mind, do you?'

'Of course not. Just maybe keep an ear out. I'll yell if I need you.'

Inside the *September Rose*, Daisy sat on the sofa and was about to open the call when she realised the view behind her was definitely not Wildflower Lock, but a passing vista of factories. Hurriedly, she closed the curtains.

'Hi, you,' she said, trying to make her voice sound as natural as possible.

'Hey. You know, you're a tough woman to get hold of.' Theo's face was grinning back at her, his picture-perfect smile causing a fluttering in her chest. 'Did you not see my missed calls this morning?'

'Sorry, yes – I've been crazily busy. I'm so sorry.'

'Well, I guess it's a good thing the girls were there to help. How did they get on?'

Daisy frowned, trying to work out what Theo was on about. 'The girls?'

'They've come down to help you, right? Isn't that why I couldn't come down and see you?'

Daisy gulped. There was no point in closing the curtains if she couldn't remember the simplest of lies she'd told Theo to keep this journey a secret.

'Yes, yes. Sorry. They were. They are. It's been good. Really good. Busy. Sorry, I'm not quite with it. You know what it's like after a crazy day.'

'Well, make sure you don't stay up partying all night,' he said, before squinting at his screen. 'Have you got plans for this evening?'

'Oh, you know, the usual. Just a couple of bottles of wine, nothing special.'

Daisy could feel her pulse getting faster and faster as she desperately searched for a way out of the lie that wasn't just more lies.

'Sorry, Theo. They are all waiting for me. We're going for an evening walk. Can I ring you tonight?'

'Sure thing. Though don't worry if you don't have time. You enjoy the evening with the girls.'

'Thank you. I love you.' A flood of relief rushed through her as she drew to the end of the conversation. It had been a long way from smooth, but she had got through it. All that was left was for him to say goodbye. And his lips were already moving.

'Love you t—' Before he could finish the sentence, his words were cut short by a blasting horn so loud, it shook the *September Rose*.

38

Daisy jumped upwards, only doing so wasn't as easy as she'd hoped. The *September Rose* was rocking back and forth.

'Daisy, what was that? Are you okay?' Theo was staring at her on the screen, his eyes wide.

'Yes, yes...' She looked towards the stern, where she could make out Yvonne's feet still standing by the tiller. Yvonne had said she would yell if something was wrong, so she must have had the situation under control, although the way the *September Rose* continued to rock made Daisy think otherwise.

'What was that?' Theo said. 'It sounded like a barge horn.'

Her cheeks reddened. Barges? Were they sailing through barges now? If that was the case, she wanted to be on the stern now, with both hers and Yvonne's life jackets on. Only she couldn't say as much to Theo.

'It's just some kids playing pranks, that's all. Probably a holiday boat?'

'Really? It looked like the *September Rose* was moving a lot.'

Daisy shook her head. 'No, no. It's all fine. Honestly. I'm just balancing a lot of things in my hand, that's all. Look, I better go. Love you.'

'Love you—'

This time, she was the reason he didn't get to finish his sentence.

Out on the stern, Yvonne was happily whistling away, while their newest crew member was still standing with his head off the edge of the boat, ears flapping in the wind.

'What was that noise?' Daisy said, handing Yvonne her life jacket only to realise her question was superfluous. Theo had been right. Barges. Massive barges.

'Blooming things think they own the water,' Yvonne said with a sniff. 'But we were fine, weren't we?' She was looking at the dog, rather than Daisy, when she spoke. 'Handled it like a pro. Although I think if he's going to be a permanent fixture, we should think about getting him a life jacket.'

'A life jacket?' Daisy replied, before realising there was a more pointed part of Yvonne's comment that needed addressing. 'He's not a permanent fixture. I'm going to find out who he belongs to now.'

Throughout the rest of the day, Daisy continued to search for the dog's owner, determined she wouldn't start researching other options until she was certain he didn't have one. So far, though, she'd had no luck, and so a new home was looking like the most likely outcome.

'Tomorrow is the big one,' Yvonne said when, according to her, they had less than thirty minutes to go to the marina, meaning they would be moored up well before sunset. 'It'll be a long day, and by the end, we'll be in Central London. Are you ready?'

'No, but I don't think I've really been ready for any of this, if I'm honest,' Daisy admitted. 'There's just so much to think about, you know. I thought it would be a case of getting on the boat, getting past the sea bit, and then plain sailing to Theo, so to speak. I hadn't even thought about things like booking moorings or tidal changes. I'm so glad you're here to take care of that.'

'Well, once we're through London, we're back on the canal, so you don't need to worry about the tides then,' Yvonne said. 'The water is deep enough that we can travel whether it's high or low. Now, I fancy going inside and getting myself a cuppa. I'm sure it's my turn. Are you okay with holding the line for a bit?'

'Well, I'm not exactly on my own,' Daisy said as she looked down at her canine companion. Yes, she really needed to think of a name for him, even if he wouldn't be with her much longer. Thinking of him solely as *the dog* didn't seem particularly fair, but she didn't want to get attached either, and that was far more likely to happen if she gave him a name, wasn't it? Not that it was difficult to get attached to an animal like him. Not given how far he'd travelled to be with her, and how easily he had adapted to life on the water.

'You're a good boy, aren't you?' she said, making sure the tiller was completely straight as she bent down to stroke him. Her hand had just touched the scruff of his neck when a loud clatter came from inside the boat, causing Daisy to jump up in shock.

'Yvonne!' For a split second, Daisy forgot that she was on the *September Rose*, in the middle of one of the busiest rivers in the world, with barges and speed-boats and every other type of vessel on it. In her state of concern and surprise, she let go of the tiller. Her grip was off the metal bar for barely a second, but that split second was all it took for the tide to yank around to the side and send them right into the path of an oncoming barge.

39

Daisy couldn't breathe. She couldn't move. All she could do was yank the tiller back as far as it would go, hold it there, and pray.

Just as quickly as the *September Rose* had veered off course, it was back straight again. The whole incident couldn't have lasted more than a minute, and yet Daisy's pulse pounded as she gasped for breath. She could have hit the barge. She could have hit the barge and crashed the boat and drowned.

As the adrenaline dropped and her pulse slowed, she remembered the entire reason she had let go of the tiller in the first place.

'Yvonne?' she called into the boat, not daring to let go again. 'Yvonne? What happened? Are you all right?'

'I'm okay,' Yvonne's voice called back before her head appeared out the door. 'I'm sorry, love, I broke one of your mugs. Dropped it on my damn toe. Didn't frighten you too much, did I?'

Daisy glanced at the barge, which was now serenely gliding past, a distance of at least three *September Rose*s between them. Once again, time felt as though it had been distorted.

'Yes, yes, I'm fine,' she said after a moment. 'What about you? Is your toe all right? It sounded like you hurt yourself.'

Yvonne brushed off the concern with a wave of her hand. 'Oh, don't worry about me. I was just being a silly old woman. Yes, I'm fine.' She gazed outwards as she spoke, using her hand to shield her eyes from the sun. 'Though I'm afraid I didn't make us those teas. Perhaps we should just wait until we're moored up.'

'Sounds like a good idea,' Daisy agreed.

By the time they were enjoying their cups of tea, along with a light dinner of carrot soup, the sun was low on the horizon, with wisps of clouds criss-crossing across the pale-blue sky. Even with the unexpected trip to the vets, they had made good time. If it carried on this way, Yvonne was certain Daisy would be on schedule to see Theo soon. Which was great, because it would mean no more lying to him.

Despite having promised she would ring later that evening, Daisy didn't feel like she had it in her. There was so much she wanted to tell him, from the sailboats and barges to the dog and her watercolour diary of the events. She just didn't know how she would keep herself from spilling the beans. Not when she was as tired as she was. What she wanted was to curl up in bed and read her book with a glass of wine.

However, as Yvonne disappeared inside to get ready for the night, Daisy faced a new problem. One that was sitting right by her feet.

'I hadn't really thought through the sleeping arrangements,' she admitted to the dog, recalling what Yvonne had said about him not being house-trained. Well, not that they knew of and there hadn't been any accidents yet. 'I think it's best if you sleep out here for tonight.'

The dog tilted its head to the side as if understanding her.

'Don't look at me like that. I can't have you inside the boat. I can't. I have to cook in here. I know we're travelling all day tomorrow, but after that, I'm planning on opening up again. I can't have you in there when I'm doing that.'

His head tilted further still, his eyes growing wider and wider.

'No, stop it. I won't feel guilty. You've been sleeping outside in the grass before now.'

The dog continued to stare at her, without even the slightest hint of a blink, but Daisy wasn't giving in. She'd not gone through all the rigmarole of getting the licence for the coffee shop, and the propeller fixed, to lose everything for a stray animal that she wasn't even going to adopt.

'Wait here,' she said, clenching her jaw as she headed back into the boat. 'I'll get you some blankets. Nice, soft blankets.'

Finally, he dropped to the floor with a slight huff. Annoyed at herself for feeling so guilty, and at the dog for making her feel even more so, Daisy headed into the *September Rose*. 'Sorry, I need to grab something from your cabin,' she said, knocking on Yvonne's door. It was funny how long it had taken for her mind to shift perspectives. Less than a week in and she wasn't even thinking of it as her space any more.

When there was no reply, Daisy knocked again, this time pushing the door open a little as she did.

'Sorry, Yvonne. Do you mind if I come and grab something from one of the cupboards? A blanket for the—'

Daisy stopped. She peered inside to where Yvonne was sitting on the bed. Her legs were crossed and her swollen toe was on full display.

'Yvonne, is that what you did with a mug?' Daisy stepped inward for a closer look. Yvonne's big toe was entirely purple, with one large cut going across right on the knuckle. 'Why didn't you tell me? It must be agony.'

Yvonne shook her head, brushing off Daisy's concern.

'It's not that bad, really. Honestly, it looks a lot worse than it is. When you get to my age, you bruise a bit more easily. That's all. I might just put a bit of ice on it.'

'You should have put ice on it straight away,' Daisy responded.

'Well, it wasn't a very convenient time. Stop fussing. Honestly, a bit of ice will have it right as rain. Do you have some?'

'Yes. Don't you move,' Daisy said sternly. 'I'll get it.'

Back in the kitchen, she emptied an ice tray into a plastic Ziploc bag, then covered it in a tea towel before taking it back to Yvonne.

'I really wish you'd said something,' Daisy said. 'You might need to see a doctor.'

'For a bruised toe? Don't be ridiculous. It's fine. Now, what did you want? You came in saying you needed something. For the dog, was it?'

'Oh, yes.' Daisy blinked, recalling the reason she had come to

Yvonne's room. 'I need to grab some towels. I think I've got some blankets and pillows. Things left in the cupboard.'

'Well, it's your home, not mine. Help yourself.'

As Daisy rummaged in the cupboard to find what she was looking for, she couldn't help but glance at Yvonne, trying to get another look at her toe, but the ice was now covering it. How she could have carried on through mooring the boat and throughout dinner like nothing was wrong was a mystery. Daisy would have been bawling her eyes out. But maybe that said more about her than Yvonne.

When Daisy walked back out on the stern, the dog stood up and wagged his tail. She dropped two large pillows, which had been in the boat since she found it, with an old picnic blanket and placed them in the corner by the door.

'The weather forecast is absolutely fine,' she said, once again feeling the guilt rising within her. 'Better than fine; it's a heatwave. You're the lucky one being out here, trust me. It's a lot nicer than in there. You've got a proper breeze.'

Still, the eyes stared back at her. It was as if he knew the exact look to give to tug at her heartstrings.

'Look, if the forecast says it's going to rain before we find you a home, then we'll talk about this. But for now, you're fine out here.'

She looked at the stern rope tied against the mooring, keeping the *September Rose* locked in place. Perhaps, she realised, she needed to do something similar for the dog. After all, he was registered to her now, and the last thing she needed was him running off and causing a load of trouble in her name.

After adding an extra length of rope to the lead to make it a little longer, she fixed him to a hold on the boat. There was plenty of room for him to get up and move around the stern, but not jump out onto the jetty.

With that sorted, she headed back to fixing his food. While she'd remembered to buy dog food, a dog bowl had slipped her mind entirely, so he'd eaten his previous meal out of a plastic dish she normally put fruit in. It was as good as anything, she thought, as she filled it up with biscuits, then put another bowl down for his water.

Given how hot the night was, she meant what she said about the cool breeze and was slightly jealous of him getting to spend the night outside.

'That's it,' she said, scratching under his chin. 'I need a good night's sleep. We're going through London tomorrow. That's gonna be busy. And I don't want you keeping me up barking. Have you got it?'

40

'I've changed my mind.'

Those were the first words out of Daisy's mouth on the Monday morning. Her alarm had only just gone off at six-thirty and before she'd even sat up or fully opened her eyes, Yvonne had appeared in the living area, dressed in a silk dressing gown and matching negligée.

'Ready?' Yvonne asked. 'We're about to go through Central London.'

That was the moment it hit her. 'I've changed my mind,' she said.

Yvonne let out a short chuckle, though Daisy couldn't see anything funny about the situation. Sitting up, she discovered the nerves went past her belly and all the way up to her throat, which was already tight with fear. 'This is ridiculous. We can't take the *September Rose* on the Thames. We can't.'

Yvonne laughed. 'You know we were on the Thames all day yesterday, don't you? And most of the day before.'

'Of course, I know that,' Daisy said, exasperated. 'But this is different. This is *the Thames* Thames. This is London Bridge, Tower Bridge, all the bridges. You know they have hot tub boats on the Thames? Hot tub boats? It's going to be so busy. No, I don't think we can do it.'

The feeling of overwhelm was almost too much to bear. As she stood up, she instinctively moved to the coffee machine, only to change her mind. Was caffeine really what she needed on a day like today? She was already a mass of jitters.

'There are a lot of bridges,' Yvonne agreed, 'and a lot of other boats, but a lot of incredible things to see, too. Come on, where is your sense of adventure? Trust me, this is a good place to be. They've got lifeboats everywhere. Any crash and people are going to see it and come racing to our rescue. Much safer here than when we were out on the sea. That was definitely the worst part. Or on that little creek after the Crouch. Now that's a type of place you definitely don't want to have an accident.'

Daisy wasn't sure if the comment was meant to comfort her or not. Or if it had. Still, Yvonne was right. Being at sea was the part Daisy had worried about the most, but it hadn't been half as dramatic as she'd expected. From now on, it should be smooth sailing – quite literally.

'Okay, what time do you want to get going?' Daisy asked Yvonne, who was once again studying her pamphlet of tide times, though the page she was currently open on was not only torn at the corner but stained with what looked like coffee too. Daisy only hoped there wasn't anything they needed on that part of the page.

'The sooner, the better,' Yvonne said, abruptly closing the book. 'Why don't you fix our drinks, and—'

A bout of barking from the dog drowned out her words. Yvonne scowled slightly as she looked at Daisy.

'Actually, change of plans. I'll fetch the drinks. You can feed the newest crew member.'

Outside, a wagging tail was waiting for Daisy, along with plenty of licks.

'Wow, looks like you're a morning person,' she said, placing a handful of food into his bowl. 'So, what do you say, ready to see the Houses of Parliament?'

After a couple of minutes' attention, Daisy went into the boat to find her phone buzzing away on the table. Her first thought was Theo, but instead it was the word 'Mum' flashing on the screen.

'Hi, Mum. Is everything all right?'

It wasn't unheard of for Daisy to hear from her mother before work, but normally that meant around 8 a.m. She couldn't remember ever hearing from her before seven. Therefore, it was unsurprising that she assumed there was something wrong.

'What's happened?' she added, hearing the panic in her voice.

'Oh, nothing, darling. Nothing. I was just thinking that today's probably the day, isn't it? When you go through London on the *Rose*?'

Daisy was stunned to near silence. Her mother never discussed the boat with Daisy, even though she now had a boyfriend who lived on the same canal as she had once done. Trying to get her mum to engage in a conversation about the *September Rose* was normally like asking her to walk across hot coals. And yet now she had brought her up as if it were normal, casual conversation. The *Rose*? Was that what her father had called the boat?

Daisy's mind was so busy whirring with the unexpectedness of the situation, it was only when her mother cleared her throat and spoke again that Daisy remembered she was on the phone.

'Did I get it wrong?' her mother asked. 'I thought you'd want to get there as fast as possible. Nic calculated that you'd be starting the main part of the Thames today.'

'No, no, you're right,' Daisy said. 'It's today. We're going to leave in a bit. I just need to get dressed and then we're casting off.'

'Oh, well. That's good. Take care, won't you? Of yourself. And Yvonne too.'

There was a tone to her voice that made Daisy think perhaps she wasn't so concerned about anything happening to the *September Rose*. Even so, to ring up and mention the boat was more than Daisy would have expected. Maybe at some point, her mother would be able to say Johnny's name, too.

'Sure. Yes, of course. And I'll ring you when I'm onto the canals.'

'Only if you've got time, love.'

'I'm sure I will. Love you.'

'Love you too.'

When Daisy hung up, she found herself lost in a stunned silence. Was it an omen, her mother's blessing on this part of the journey? Maybe she didn't need to be so worried after all.

41

Daisy didn't know where to look. It was one thing being on the Thames, surrounded by factories and waterworks and other large, nondescript buildings, but she was in London town now. The heart of England. The picture-perfect vista with the Houses of Parliament and Big Ben, which featured on postcards and television shows around the world. First, though, they were coming in through the dockland, past the O2 arena with its white canopy and bright-yellow posts and towards the famous Canary Wharf.

'So, is it what you imagined?' Yvonne asked as she sat next to Daisy. They hadn't spoken for at least half an hour; not because Daisy didn't want to, but because she felt like if she started, she wouldn't stop, and there was so much she wanted to take in. To soak up.

'It doesn't feel real,' she admitted. 'None of it. Not me being here. Us being here. Him being here.' She gestured to the dog. 'It feels like some part of a dream.'

'A good one, I'm assuming?'

'Absolutely.'

Yvonne was holding on to the tiller, keeping them to the right and a comfortable distance from both the bank and boats coming the other way, when Daisy spotted something to make her heart leap.

'Look, other canal boats! Over there.'

This wasn't the first time they had seen other boats like the *September Rose* on their journey, but Daisy struggled to remember where the last one had been. And this was different. She could already feel a camaraderie buzzing between herself and these other boats. They weren't living life in the slow lane, sticking to the quiet, controlled canals and laid-back lifestyles. They, like her, were adventurers out on the Thames. And she was heading straight towards them, with a desperate urge to wave as wildly as she could.

'Oh, yes, that'll be the Limehouse Lock,' Yvonne said, shrugging nonchalantly. 'It leads onto the Regent's Canal that takes you all the way through London. You get lots of narrowboats there.'

It was only when they had passed them and Daisy's arm was starting to ache from all the waving that she realised what Yvonne had just said.

'The canal entrance? Isn't that where we should be going?'

Again, Yvonne offered the same shrug. 'We could, but it'll hardly be as exciting. We'll miss all the best sights if we do that. Don't worry, we'll get onto the Grand Union at Brentford. It's much more fun that way. It's what my Harry and I used to do.'

Daisy opened her mouth to say something, only to change her mind. Yvonne hadn't let her down yet. If she said this was the best way to go, then Daisy would believe her. Besides, they could always come through the canal route on the way back.

'Daisy, love, I'm feeling a bit tired – probably that early morning and everything. You don't mind if I have a quick lie down, do you? Just on the sofa. You can call me if you need me.'

Daisy looked at the view ahead of her. The twists and turns that appeared so tightly coiled on a map of London snaked much more gently in real life, and while there were countless boats of all shapes and sizes, they were all sticking to their side, giving each other plenty of room.

'Of course, you go rest. We'll be all right here, won't we, Furball?'

The dog barked, somewhat indignantly. Apparently, Furball wasn't its choice of name. But it was as close as she was going to get to giving him one. That would be someone else's job. His owner, when she finally found them.

After checking her life jacket was completely secure, Daisy took the tiller from Yvonne before perching herself on the back of the boat. A moment later, she and the dog were alone.

Daisy had lived in London for so much of her adult life that she considered herself an expert on the city. She knew the quickest Tube routes to get you across the city depending on the time of day. She knew which restaurants were always packed on the weekend and when and where all the different congestion zones were. She had seen every landmark from Trafalgar Square to the Tate Museum at least a dozen times, but she had never seen it like this.

As carefully as she could, she pulled her phone out of her pocket and opened up the video camera. It didn't matter that she was going to do this same route on the way back in just a couple of weeks, or that she and Theo were likely to do it a dozen more times together during their relationship. She wanted to remember this. This first trip, when she took the *September Rose* under Tower Bridge with a random dog at the helm. This was the type of life she had only ever dreamed of. And now it was hers.

The closer she got to the centre of the city, the more densely packed the bridges became. Initially, Daisy had thought she would want Yvonne on hand to help her with them, but as she approached, she changed her mind. Every now and then, the soft rattle of a snore made it over the rumbling of the engines and the water. It was clear that Yvonne needed her sleep, especially if her nightmares were commonplace. And it wasn't like these bridges were difficult. There were boats twice the height of the *September Rose* gliding beneath them, and three times as wide. And so, Daisy decided, she would go it alone.

'Go us!' Daisy shouted with excitement as she emerged from the other side of Tower Bridge. London Bridge was the next one along and already in sight. Still, she expected it to take a little while to get there, which was why Daisy was surprised when, only a few minutes later, she was once again under the shadow of a bridge.

'Is it me, or did we take that one a bit speedily?' Daisy said to herself as much as the dog, though he didn't bother replying. He was currently pacing from one side of the boat to the other, as if he couldn't decide where it was he wanted to stay.

Deciding that she wanted to take the next bridge a bit slower, and get a couple of videos too, Daisy pulled back on the throttle. Of course, she wanted to get to Theo, but she'd regret it if she didn't take her time enjoying the journey. And evidence it. After all, if the plan had just been to get there as quickly as possible, she could've just driven.

A few minutes later and the speed didn't seem to have decreased at all. Daisy checked on the throttle, preparing to pull it back further, only to find it was as low as it could go, and yet she was still speeding past the other boats and landmarks faster than at any other point. She was already encroaching on the next bridge, and now she was aware of the speed issue, it felt like she was going even faster.

'Yvonne!'

She didn't pull in the tiller. The last thing she needed was to collide with someone at this speed. Her heart rate was now increasing as fast as the boat.

'Yvonne! I need you to come out here. I think something is wrong with the engine.'

The moment she spoke, the speed surged again, and this time, she felt it. The boat was hurtling forward, cutting through the river, causing a wake the likes of which the *September Rose* had never produced before. And she wasn't the only one. Ahead of her, a massive barge was blocking the view of the river, and just to her right, a speedboat was set to overtake, its crew and passengers bouncing around as they hit one wake and then another.

'Yvonne!' This time Daisy couldn't hide the fear in her voice. 'Yvonne! Something's wrong! Something's wrong with the boat!'

42

Whenever someone asked if Daisy liked her lifestyle change, she would always tell them that canal boating was a peaceful way of spending one's life. There was a limit to how fast one could go in a narrowboat, and it wasn't much faster than walking.

Only at that precise moment, it was. At that precise moment, they were soaring down the Thames through Central London, and there was nothing Daisy could do to stop it.

'Yvonne!' Daisy screamed. Her lungs burned with the taste of the water as she yelled as loudly as she could.

A moment later, the dog disappeared into the boat.

'What are you doing now?' Daisy called after him.

The fact that Daisy didn't want the dog inside was now irrelevant. She didn't feel like she was in a boat at all now. She had lost control of the *September Rose* and it felt like they were in a hollowed-out tree trunk, about to go cascading down water rapids, the way you saw in children's cartoons. Only this wasn't a cartoon.

'Yvonne! Dog! Will you both get out here? Please!'

A moment later, Yvonne stumbled out, limping, partially from her foot but also because the dog was pulling the bottom of her cardigan. If it hadn't been the most terrifying moment of Daisy's life, she may well have thanked him, or at least laughed at the situation, but that wasn't possible.

'Yvonne, something's gone wrong.' The warble in her voice made it clear that she was about to burst into tears, though from the pace at which Yvonne acted, it was like she couldn't tell at all.

With a slight twist of her neck, she scanned the scene from port to starboard before nodding.

'Well, we've picked up some speed, haven't we?' The way she spoke made it sound as if it was the most natural thing in the world. Flying through the Thames. Hurtling faster and faster with every second.

'Walking pace, isn't that what we're supposed to be doing?' Daisy stressed.

If walking pace was how she normally drove the *September Rose*, then this was the hundred-metre sprint. Usain Bolt would have had difficulty keeping up with the *September Rose* the way it was currently moving. Still, Yvonne didn't seem that concerned at all.

'I don't get what's going on?' Daisy said, unable to hide the panic in her voice. Yvonne had got her out of all the stressful situations so far and she needed to do the same now, but she wasn't doing anything other than looking at her watch and checking the yellow notebook with all the tide times in. 'The throttle is all the way back.' Daisy carried on talking, hoping Yvonne might realise the issue and jump in and save them. 'I think it must've jammed somehow. I think there's too much fuel getting to the engine.'

Yvonne pressed her lips together tightly, looking over the edge of the boat as she went back to the notebook. When she finally looked back at Daisy, her cheeks were decidedly pink.

'I think I must have got the tide time slightly wrong,' she said.

Daisy frowned. 'What do you mean? I didn't think it mattered when we went out. We can travel on high and low tide.'

'That is true, technically, yes...' The way Yvonne was slowing her tone and avoiding making eye contact made Daisy feel like this really wasn't a good thing.

'Yvonne?'

'It's fine... Really, it's fine. We're just going in with the tide, that's all. Tends to make things a bit faster.'

'A bit faster?'

Daisy's hair blew behind her with a gust of wind, stressing her point. 'This can't be safe.'

'Don't be silly. My Harry used to love coming in like this. Wouldn't travel any other way. And it'll save us a bit of time getting to our mooring. You might be able to open up the coffee shop for a bit too. And it saves on fuel. Positives all around, if you ask me.'

Daisy didn't reply. Her eyes were still on the barge in front of her. The distance between them had shrunk, only marginally, but still. If she kept going in such a manner, she could well collide with the back of it.

'Just steer around it, the way you would any boat,' Yvonne said, obviously reading Daisy's concern. 'Honestly, I thought the incident with the sailboats would've calmed you down a bit.'

Daisy couldn't reply. Her heart was hammering in her chest and she longed to return to the mild panic she had felt when swarmed by sailboats on the River Crouch. After all, those boats had been tiny. It wouldn't have been good for the people on board if they collided with the *September Rose*, but as selfish as it was, Daisy and her boat would've likely received little more than a scratch on the paintwork. This was a whole different matter. She was nothing to these massive barges. An insignificant ant that could be crushed with the slightest sideways swerve.

I was calm until this happened. Daisy wanted to respond to Yvonne's comment. *I was calm when I was steering my boat at a sensible pace and didn't think I was going to crash.* But her throat was closed shut with fear.

'What if I put her in reverse?' she said, voicing her thoughts aloud, hoping they might spark an idea that could get her out of this catastrophic situation. She looked at Yvonne. 'Would that work? If I put the boat in reverse, that would slow us against the tide, wouldn't it?'

'You can try, but it'll be a waste of fuel,' Yvonne said with a shrug of her shoulders. 'Honestly, this is what it's like on the tidal Thames. Obviously, not all the time, but we were bound to pick up a bit of speed while we were on here. What else did you expect?'

Daisy pondered the question for a moment. She hadn't really thought about it long enough to know what she expected.

She'd envisioned moving along the water at a leisurely pace, like on Wildflower Lock, just with more tourists to wave at on the banks of the Thames. She'd envisioned being able to wave up at dog walkers and children and catch wafts of the burgers cooking on Southbank. That was what she expected. Not this.

She looked at her fuel gauge. Did she want to risk using it up to slow down when Yvonne thought they were perfectly fine? Daisy wasn't sure what it would do to the engine, pushing back against such a powerful tide with the current pulling it forward. It didn't seem like a sensible thing to do. But the throttle was already as low as it could go. Which meant there was only one other thing she could do to slow them down and give her enough time to manoeuvre around the barge.

She passed her idea to Yvonne, who gave a nonplussed nod. It was as close to an agreement as Daisy thought she was going to get. So, holding her breath, Daisy took the key and switched the engine off.

43

Experiencing the Thames from aboard the *September Rose*, hurtling along at an unexpected speed, was an experience like no other. Without the familiar hum of the engine filling her ears, Daisy found herself in a new state of heightened awareness. Until that point, she hadn't appreciated just how accustomed she had become to the background soundtrack of the previous part of the journey – the engine, the birds and seagulls squawking, the occasional chatter of passers-by or cars and lorries from nearby roads. All these sounds had blended together, forming a symphony that, to Daisy, was as comforting as a hot chocolate or watching a horror film under a blanket on a cosy night. Now, however, the absence of the engine's drone felt like an all-consuming silence. A void. Had she made the right call?

They had slowed slightly. However, the gap between the *September Rose* and the barge in front was still decreasing.

'I don't think I'm allowed to pass him, am I?' Daisy said. She'd been learning the rules on the canals by Wildflower Lock as she went, but this was a commercial river. There were other rules to remember, and right now, she wasn't sure she could stick to them.

'What choice do you have? Either you pass him, or you hit him,' Yvonne replied unhelpfully.

Daisy could feel her breath growing shallower and shallower. Yvonne was right; it was either break the rules of the river or crash. When put like that, it was a fairly easy decision.

'I think you should steer,' Daisy suggested, her hand trembling on the tiller. 'You'll handle this better.'

But Yvonne only shook her head. 'No, it's fine. My arms have been a bit achy this morning. You go ahead. I'll go fetch us a cup of tea.'

'A cup of tea?' The mere thought made Daisy feel nauseous, but she knew this technique of Yvonne's. It was a ploy. A ruse to convince Daisy she was capable of doing things by herself. Well, she didn't need to play any games. What she needed was Yvonne's support.

Just then, the dog barked at her feet. When she looked down, he was staring straight at her. His gaze was intent, not hostile or frightened, but steady. There was reassurance in his eyes. She could do this. She *had* to do this. Determined, she shook her hand out, letting go of the tiller with her right hand for a moment before swapping it for her left. She then grasped the throttle, preparing herself for the moment. All she needed to do was speed up and pass the barge as quickly as possible, just like she would when overtaking a car on the road.

'I think it's probably best if you stay here,' Daisy said to Yvonne, newfound confidence seeping into her voice. 'Things might get choppy. I'd hate it if you broke another of my mugs. Or another of your toes, for that matter.'

A slight smile rose at the corner of Yvonne's lips.

'Come on, then, skipper. Let's see what you've got.'

With a deep breath, Daisy removed her hand from the throttle, placed it on the horn and let out one long blast. When she let go, she restarted the engine and replaced her hand on the throttle. The *September Rose* surged in response, the gap between her and the encroaching barge rapidly decreasing. This was just like any other vehicle on the canal, she reminded herself, as she prepared to steer the boat to the left. She would leave herself plenty of room, and everything would be fine.

With another deep breath, she pulled out and pushed down on the throttle, but just as she adjusted her course, a Thames cruiser zipped past her. The wake splashed against the side of the *September Rose*. The cold spray doused both Daisy and the dog, but somehow missed Yvonne, who had jumped to the other side of the stern.

'Idiots!' Daisy yelled after them. The distraction had, unfortunately, allowed the *September Rose* to drift uncomfortably close to the barge.

'You don't want to get too close to that thing,' Yvonne advised, sounding annoyingly nonchalant. 'It could squash us in an instant.'

Grinding her teeth, Daisy tried to block out Yvonne's comment. All she could focus on was the river and her boat.

Another barge was coming up on the other side, albeit much, much slower. That would be okay; she would pass this one first, and then she could deal with the second one. She just needed to maintain her nerve. And she did, expertly navigating the *September Rose* parallel to the enormous barge. The ant analogy had been spot on, she realised, as they were lost in the shadow of the gargantuan vessel, which was full of bright-yellow stacked containers.

'You're doing well,' Yvonne said, her desperate need for tea forgotten, though Daisy wasn't sure whether there was a question mark at the end of her sentence or a hint of surprise. Either way, she didn't have time to decipher it. She was too focused on moving past the barge as quickly as she could. Her hair splayed out behind her as she drew level with the trawler. A crew of three were upfront and offered her a brief wave as she passed, but she didn't respond. She wasn't being rude; she just couldn't let anything break her concentration.

With the tugboat slipping behind them, Daisy carried on. The last thing she wanted to do was underestimate the barge's speed and slip back in front of it too soon. Not when she had come this far. And so she continued on further.

Finally, she looked over her shoulder and saw the trawler well behind them. Relief washed over her and she turned to Yvonne, a wide grin spreading across her face.

'Wow!' The flood of adrenaline was enough to make her breathless. 'That was crazy. I mean, really crazy, wasn't it? God, I should have got you to film it. Theo is never going to believe I did that. Maybe if we need to overtake one again, you can video it?' Her cheeks were aching, and she was so excited, she'd almost forgotten about the crazy speed they were going at.

Remembering what Yvonne said about saving fuel, Daisy cut the engine, only then realising that Yvonne still hadn't spoken, although the dog had resumed its strange side-to-side pacing.

'Yvonne? What is it? Are you okay? Is it your foot? Are you in pain?'

The fact that Yvonne was significantly paler than she had been only a few moments before was what led Daisy to this conclusion, but still, Yvonne didn't reply. Instead, she rifled through her bag for her binoculars. When she found them, she looked back towards the barge they had only just passed.

'What? What is it?' Daisy asked, her gaze darting around.

The dog was still beside her. There were no other boats in sight. Nothing seemed broken. She couldn't fathom what was causing Yvonne's distress.

'What is it?' Daisy repeated, looking back at the older woman. Yvonne bit her lip, a pained expression on her face, and an inexplicable icy chill ran down Daisy's spine.

'I think we might have missed our turning,' she finally said.

44

Daisy stared at Yvonne, not sure that she'd heard her correctly. She had cut the engine, but they were still racing down the Thames, though Daisy wasn't really looking at where she was going. It was only when a speedboat beeped its horn that she realised she'd drifted too far over. She pulled hard on the tiller, readjusting her trajectory before she spoke.

'What do you mean, "missed the turning"? How do we miss a turning?'

'Well.' Yvonne swallowed hard. 'I got my timings a little wrong, that's all. That nap I had was obviously longer than I thought and I didn't realise the speed we'd been going. Besides, I based the calculation on the book, you see. And... and...'

'And?'

'And I guess it might be a little out of date.'

Daisy looked at the yellow booklet from which Yvonne had gathered all the information on boating the tidal Thames. She pulled it out of Yvonne's hand and stared at the cover. It was the first time she'd looked at it properly and it made her light-headed.

'Yvonne, this is from 1993!' she said, unable to stop her jaw from hanging open.

'Of course it is. That's the last time I did this trip. I didn't think they'd change things that often.'

'The tides? You didn't think the tides would change that often?'

Yvonne pouted. 'It was perfectly fine for the first couple of days. I'd thought if there was a problem, we'd have noticed when we left Maldon. As that wasn't the case, I assumed it all matched up nicely.'

Daisy took a deep breath in and tried to steady her building anxiety.

'Take the tiller,' she said, opening up the booklet herself. As luck would have it, it flopped open to the page she needed – the Thames Lock at Brentford, which, according to this, was marked with three yellow oil drums. Daisy stared at it in disbelief before glaring at Yvonne. 'You were looking for three yellow oil drums, marking the turning we needed?'

Yvonne pushed her shoulders back indignantly.

'I don't know why you're speaking like that. If it ain't broke, why fix it?'

Daisy was drawing in deep breaths, trying to steady her heart rate. Now that the trawler was a safe distance behind them she had cut the throttle, but the speed was still fast, and she was racing away from the turning she hadn't seen. She glanced back at the map in the pamphlet. Yvonne had been wrong about the tide times, so maybe she'd been wrong about the position of the canal too. If that was the case, they might not have even passed it yet, though a quick check of the map and her surrounding location quickly put paid to that idea. They were already past the King's Observatory, meaning the canal was, without doubt, behind them. And as much as Daisy hated to put all her eggs in Yvonne's basket so soon after such a major issue, she knew she had no other choice.

'What do we do?' she said, making no attempt to hide the disdain in her voice, though her anger was equally directed at herself. She should have taken more responsibility for this trip from the start, then they would never have got into this mess. 'Is there another turning somewhere else we can get onto the canal?'

She began to flick through the pages, only for Yvonne's snort to cut her off.

'It's not the M4,' Yvonne replied. 'No, it's fine. We'll do what we always do. These things happen. It's not the end of the world. We'll just do a U-turn.'

Of all the ridiculous things Daisy had seen and heard that day, this one had to be the most absurd.

'You're joking?' she said, assuming this was another of Yvonne's peculiar jokes.

'Of course I'm not joking. How else are we going to get back down to the turning? Honestly, what are you worried about? We've got plenty of room.'

Daisy shook her head, wanting to believe Yvonne was having her on. 'It's not about the room!' she said. 'It's about the fact that there are all these other boats coming up and down. I saw a speed-boat a minute ago, for crying out loud.'

'Well, they'll just have to be careful, won't they? Really, you're not the first person this has happened to. Stop making such a fuss. We need to do it soon, though. We'll be going against the tide on the way back. Look, it's clear enough now. Give me the tiller.'

Daisy wanted to refuse, but before she could, Yvonne was pulling the metal bar full lock to the right. The *September Rose* turned sharply, the dog yelped beside Daisy and a series of clatters that sounded horribly like glass smashing rang out from inside the boat. Daisy winced at the thought of her paintings falling from the walls, the broken pieces of glass spearing hours of work, but there was nothing she could do.

'Yvonne, I don't think—'

'It's fine, just hold on.'

The tiller remained on full lock, but they were going so fast that the boat lifted to an angle and its flat bottom, which was absolutely not created for water like this, was clearly exposed.

We're going to sink, Daisy thought, somehow keeping the words in her mind as the left side of the boat dipped precariously close to the water. She was going to capsize on the Thames. This was it. Theo would learn of her grand gesture by seeing the *September Rose* on the front page of the news along with its possibly deceased crew. Though the dog would probably survive. Wasn't that what usually happened in these situations?

'Nearly there,' Yvonne said, although the comment seemed near delusional to Daisy. They were smack bang in the centre of the River Thames, the boat perpendicular to all the streams of metal coming at them from both directions. If they didn't capsize, they could be hit by something instead.

Unable to bear it any longer, Daisy closed her eyes. She had to. Whatever was going to hit her, she'd rather she didn't see it coming.

She remained like that, with her eyes scrunched closed, for what felt like an eternity. A minute later, her heart was pounding just as hard against her ribs, but something felt different. She opened one eye just a smidgen, still squinting. Then she opened them fully and looked around. She was back, parallel to the bank of the River Thames, the way they should be.

'We did it?' she said, disbelief hitching her voice. 'You actually did it. We didn't capsize in the middle of the River Thames.'

'You say that like I've never done it before,' Yvonne said with a roll of her eyes.

'*Have* you done it before?'

Yvonne's lips twitched. 'I've *seen* it done before. Does that count?' Her smile stretched broader. 'Harry and I didn't miss a turning, though. No, we did it for fun. Three times the same day, would you believe, though the river was quieter back then, mind. Didn't stop the feeling, though. That rush. That hasn't changed.'

Daisy wasn't sure it was a rush she wanted to repeat anytime soon, but she couldn't deny the feeling of elation as she reached around and squeezed the old woman so hard, she was pretty sure she heard a bone click, but she still couldn't stop. Of all the things they had done and seen, she knew now there was nothing on the journey they couldn't achieve. And hopefully, nothing that would be quite as terrifying or exhilarating. After a moment, Daisy let go of Yvonne, only to have the dog bark at her.

'Yes, you were very brave too,' Daisy said, reaching down and stroking his head. 'And I promise, if we don't find you an owner and you ever end up back on the river, you'll have a life jacket, too.'

As she finished speaking, the dog jumped up, placed both his paws on her chest and gave Daisy the most slobbery, wet lick across her cheek, but she didn't care. She was alive and on the Thames, though they were still a long way from Theo.

'Okay, so we need to keep an eye out.' Daisy put her mind back on the present moment. 'I'll get my phone too, see if I can find out what signs there are for this canal turning. Preferably ones that have been placed there this decade. We don't want to miss it.'

'Oh, I wouldn't worry about rushing, love. We've got ages to get there yet.'

Daisy looked at her friend. It had been less than five minutes since Yvonne informed her they'd missed the turning and in that time, they'd also completed the successful, if somewhat miraculous, U-turn. Five minutes in Daisy's book didn't feel like very long. But then she realised why Yvonne had made the comment. The throttle of the *September Rose* was pushed all the way forward, the engine pumping out as much power as it could, yet the boat looked as if it was barely moving.

Ahead of them, a restaurant was fixed to a jetty. It couldn't have been more than fifty metres away, yet they didn't seem to be getting any closer to it.

This wasn't walking pace; this was one step forward, one step back pace.

'This is why we always try to go with the tide,' Yvonne informed her.

45

The movement was worryingly slow. The engine of the *September Rose* was giving everything it had, yet they were going nowhere fast. If it kept struggling like this for too long, it would surely end up overheating. Daisy cursed herself. How irresponsible could she be? Taking a trip this long should not have been a spur-of-the-moment decision. Her mother was right. This was a trip you spent months planning. This was a trip you had your engine triple-checked for, so that you knew everything was up to working standards, and didn't just rely on the word of some man who gave the boat a quick once over when he fitted your new propeller. This wasn't a trip you did with an old woman who had a manual from 1993, and an engine that hadn't gone over ten miles on a round trip since she'd had it.

Daisy was an idiot, and she knew it. At this rate, she was going to have to have the *September Rose* lifted on a crane back to Wildflower Lock. She could practically hear the money leaking out of the boat as it growled forward.

'Have you got that phone of yours?' Yvonne asked as they carried on at their snail-like pace. 'You said you wanted to check it. We don't want to miss the turning again.'

At the pace they were going, Daisy didn't think that was likely. Still, she didn't say as much.

'My phone is in the boat. I'll just go get it.'

As Daisy stuck her head inside the *September Rose*, she let out a long groan. She had been right in thinking there had been clattering, and correct in assuming that glass had broken. Thankfully, it wasn't any of her pictures, as she had feared. Clearly, they were fixed to the walls better than she had expected. Instead, it was several jars that had tumbled out of cupboards. Some had landed on the worktops and in the sink, but a jar of sun-dried tomatoes had smashed straight onto the floor. Yellow oil was spreading out with little flecks of red in it, like part of a crime scene.

At least the sofa was spared the broken glass, unlike when the window had smashed before. It was a good job, too; there would have been no way she could afford to replace that.

As she headed inside, the dog went to follow her.

'No, absolutely no way,' she said to it. 'You've already cost me enough in *one* vet's bill. I can't pay for another. Stay.'

Seemingly understanding what she was saying, the dog promptly sat down and turned his head so that it was looking up at Yvonne on the tiller.

Daisy would have loved to have dealt with the mess then and there, but she had more pressing priorities. Mainly finding out where the hell the turning onto the canal was. However, when she picked up her phone, the canal turning slipped from her mind, as four missed calls from Theo glared at her on the screen.

'Crap,' she said to herself. There were also three messages.

> I take it you're busy, that's good news. Ring me when you can.

That was the first one. The second message read:

> I've got a lunch break in a minute. Give me a call if you can.

She didn't even read the third message. It would only increase her feelings of guilt, and that wasn't something she wanted to deal with.

Now, more than ever, she was regretting the decision not to tell him. Perhaps it would be best if she did, she thought, only to shake the thought away. There was nothing he could do now. They needed to get off the main Thames, onto the canal, and then she could think about ringing Theo, or at least send him a quick text.

With her phone in her hand, Daisy stepped back onto the stern, typing into a search engine as she did so.

'This website looks like it might have some answers,' she said, looking up at Yvonne. The old woman was hurriedly brushing something off her cheeks.

'Yvonne, is everything okay?' she asked. 'You're not hurt, are you?'

A tight smile twisted Yvonne's lips, though it didn't reach her eyes, which, to Daisy, looked as though they were filling with tears.

'No, not hurt. No more than normal, anyway. No dear, I was just thinking.'

'About Harry?' Daisy didn't want to intrude, but if Yvonne wanted to talk, then she wanted to give her that opportunity.

Yvonne glanced down at the book in her hand, drawing a breath into her lungs, which she held there for a moment before realising it into a long sigh.

'They tell you that life moves faster the older you get, and you never really believe it. But this—' she lifted the yellow booklet and waved it slightly '—this was the last time we did this journey. 1993. Thirty years ago. I don't understand where the time's gone. It feels like yesterday in some ways. I think it's even worse if you have children, isn't it? People always say the years fly by then. One day, you're holding a tiny baby in your arms and the next, they're asking if you want to be called Nanny or Grandma. But Harry and I weren't that lucky. Not that we weren't lucky in plenty of other ways, mind. We had lots of luck of our own.'

Daisy had always wondered whether Yvonne had any children or relatives, but had never asked out of fear of prying. It had crossed her mind to ask her mother once or twice, just in passing conversation, but unless the topic revolved around Nicholas or the coffee shop, her mum was not one for talking about Wildflower Lock, which included Yvonne. But it made sense. It wasn't like Daisy ever saw her have any visitors. It also explained why she relied on Theo so heavily to help with the *Ariadne*.

'It must be hard,' she said, not sure how else she could reply, but wanting to fill the silence that was building around them. 'You two were obviously very much in love.'

'We were. We were. And not all the years go fast, mind,' Yvonne said wistfully. 'The years after I lost him. Those ones, where I could hardly leave the boat for fear... No, those ones dragged. Every hour dragged. When you lose someone, it takes part of you. All those memories you had, the laughter, the joy, it's tainted now. You can't remember the happiness, because you're so consumed in the injustice of it all. Losing him like that, so suddenly. We didn't even get a chance to say goodbye. I didn't think I'd ever be able to face the world again.'

Daisy recalled the words Yvonne had been uttering through her nightmare. How she had been talking to someone. *Not Harry*. Wasn't that what she had said? There were a thousand possibilities for what could have happened, though. It could have even been a boating accident.

Daisy pushed the thought from her mind and focused on the moment. Even with all the chaos, there had been no melancholy on the boat, and Daisy wanted to keep it that way.

'But you are facing the world,' she said softly. 'Some people never leave their homes at all after something happens to a loved one. And you're out here, doing U-turns in the middle of the freaking Thames! I bet Harry would love to know how well you're doing.'

Yvonne raised her eyebrows and nodded, though she offered only a fleeting smile.

'Yes. He would be proud of me for the last couple of days. Let's be honest, though, this is a little different from my average day. But you're right. He wouldn't have wanted me to hide away, that's for sure. No, he would want me to be out there, living my life. And I've tried. Perhaps not as hard as I should've done. Not as hard as he would have liked me to. But I have tried.'

A pause spanned between them. This was by far the most Yvonne had shared. In that moment, Daisy felt that something had passed between them. Something special and sacred, and she wanted to acknowledge it, even if it was just with a touch of her hand. But as she moved, she caught sight of something on the other side of the riverbank.

'It's there!' she shouted while pointing wildly. 'The turning! It's there!'

All the advances in technology, from solar power to smart phones, and the turning to the canal was still marked with three rusted, yellow oil drums. It really was a funny old world.

46

Whether it was luck, skill or some form of divine intervention, Daisy didn't know, but somehow, they arrived at the mooring right on schedule. They were in London. Actually in London. People were milling about on the canal side in suits, with their phones pressed to their ears, or little Bluetooth earbuds bulging out the sides of their heads. It was crazy to think that she had been one of these people not so long ago. Moving from day to day, merely in a state of existence. Not really living, the way she had been doing these past few months. And the heat of work clothes? Ties and buttoned-up collars. There were even some women in tights. How were people doing it? Daisy was struggling in just shorts and a T-shirt. Yes, no matter how chaotic today had been, there was no way she wanted to go back to that old way of life.

Daisy knew exactly what painting she was going to do for her watercolour diary that evening, although painting would have to wait until later, as it was only as she tied and hitched up the boat that she realised they hadn't eaten anything since breakfast. Apparently, Yvonne was thinking the same thing.

'I thought I'd cook tonight,' she said. 'You know, say thank you for bringing me along with you. And apologise, you know, for the slight miscalculation.'

'You don't need to apologise, really, Yvonne,' Daisy assured her. 'It's my fault. I shouldn't have put so much on you. Not when I was calling myself the skipper. If anyone needs to apologise, it should be me.'

'Well, why don't I cook us dinner tonight, and we'll call it quits. It'll make up for all the shortbread I've eaten, too.'

It was clear Yvonne wanted to cook a meal, and truthfully, Daisy was more than happy to let her. She was exhausted and wanted nothing more than to curl up and sleep. Probably all the way through until the next morning. And yet someone had a different idea.

The dog was once again pacing back and forth, but this wasn't like he'd been doing earlier. For the first time Daisy had known, he was whining. High-pitched and sorrowful sounding.

'What's wrong with you?' Daisy asked. 'Are you hungry too? Well, I'll get you some food in a minute.'

'I think you'll find it's something else he needs,' Yvonne said subtly. 'Poor thing's been on the boat all day, and he's not used the bathroom once. I think you need to give him a walk.'

Daisy groaned. Of course she did. How on earth could she have forgotten something like that? Dogs needed walks and toilet breaks, though the fact he hadn't gone all day only confirmed in her mind that he had to have been properly house-trained before.

'You're right,' she said, realising her nap was going to have to wait. 'Come on, let's go. Walky times.'

The moment the dog stepped off the *September Rose*, he yanked on the lead. A second later, he relived himself against the edge of a signpost. Daisy looked around, embarrassed. She'd seen hundreds of dogs cock their legs in Wildflower Lock, sometimes – and upsettingly – against the *September Rose*, but she'd never been on this side of it before. Surrounded by passers-by in their suits. What she needed was to get to a park. Get to places where they could have a proper walk. After the distance he'd been running previously, following the boat along the riverside, he probably had a ton of energy ready to burn off. A quick search on her phone told Daisy there was a park only four minutes away.

'Well, I guess that's where we're going,' she said to the dog at her side

'Although I'm going to need to make a phone call on the way, so make sure you behave, okay?'

47

'I'm so sorry, it's been a crazy, busy day.' Daisy apologised the moment Theo picked up the phone. It wasn't the easiest, trying to speak to her boyfriend while negotiating the pavement as they walked towards the park. The dog had decided it would tug at the lead, and today, she didn't have the energy to deal with it. Sweat poured down her back. It had to be the hottest day of the year. Perfect timing for her first official dog walk.

'You know, I'm starting to think you're avoiding me,' Theo said. 'Is everything all right?'

'Yes, yes, everything's good.'

'I take it business is booming with the heatwave?'

'Business?' Daisy said. Yvonne had suggested Daisy open the cafe when they moored, but she couldn't think of anything worse than standing still next to the coffee machine, steam rising round her and not so much as a hint of a breeze. 'Business is exactly what you'd expect,' she said, trying to keep her lies to a minimum.

'You don't sound too happy about that? If it's too much, why don't you ask your mum to help you? She's down at the lock most of the time now, anyway, isn't she?'

'Yes, it's just... it's just...' Daisy wasn't sure what she was going to say. She'd thought it would be fun keeping this big secret from Theo and dropping little hints as to what she was up to. Not enough for him to guess what she was doing, of course, but just enough for him to know she had something planned. That wasn't what had happened at all. Right now, all it was doing was adding an extra layer of stress to her day. Still, before she could even think of a response, a fit of barking erupted from further up the pavement. Two large Labradors on leads were staring at her dog and making a racket. And before Daisy had time to tug on the lead, her own canine companion started barking back. Loudly.

'Please don't do that,' she pleaded. 'Come on, we're nearly there. Then you can have a run.'

'Daisy?' Theo said. 'Where are you. What are you doing?'

She closed her eyes and let out a slight moan. Not being able to video call Theo and see his face was hard enough. She might as well tell him the truth about this. Or at least as close as she could come to it.

'So there's a dog,' she said, not sure where to go after that.

'I heard as much,' Theo replied. 'Whose is it?'

'Well, that's the problem. I don't know. It's not chipped, or at least it wasn't, and it's kind of attached itself to me. I've tried looking for its owner, but I've had no luck. I think I'm going to have to change plans and try to get him adopted. But right now, he's living with me.'

'Living with you? On the *September Rose*?'

'Well, he slept outside last night. It's warm enough. And I'm sure I will have found him a place by the time the bad weather comes.'

'I hope so,' Theo replied. 'You know you can't really have it in the boat, not with you cooking food for the cafe.'

'I know,' Daisy said.

She couldn't really blame Theo for the lecture. After the mess of the licence – that wasn't her fault – she was double and triple-checking all the legalities.

'Why don't you see if one of the people on the lock wants to take it? At least until you find something permanent. I know Francis on the *Georgianna* is always rescuing birds and wildlife. You could see if she wants to take it in. Or Yvonne? You know, I've been thinking for a while that a dog might be a good idea for her. Force her to get out of the boat a bit more. You know.'

'Oh, she's getting out plenty at the minute,' Daisy muttered under her breath, although it wasn't quite quiet enough for Theo not to hear.

'Really? Why's that?'

Daisy cursed herself for not keeping her mouth shut. Now she was going to have to make up another lie to cover her tracks.

'Oh, well, she came with me to the vets... to see about the chip. But she doesn't really get on with him that well. Like I said, he seems to have attached himself to me.'

'Well, could I at least see the little guy that's causing you so much stress?'

Daisy's heart raced. They had reached the park. Inside, people were sunbathing in bikini tops or lying in the shade of trees trying to keep cool. There were two ice cream vans and at least half a dozen football matches going on. There was no way she could show Theo where she was.

'I would love to show you, but my video camera's been playing up.' Her teeth ground together as she cursed herself for yet another lie. 'It fell off the counter the other day. That's why I didn't video call.'

'Sounds like you could do with me there.'

'I could. I really could do with you here. I think today might have been a lot easier with you here,' she admitted.

There was no denying she would have loved to have had Theo by her side tackling the river that afternoon, but this wasn't the last time she was going to make the trip. After all the stress and terror she'd been through, it had to be more than a one-off event.

'It sounds like you're missing me nearly as much as I'm missing you,' Theo said.

'I am. Believe me, I definitely am.' Daisy took a left, and there in front of her was a large expanse of green, where dog walkers convened in their masses. At the end of the lead, the border collie tugged forcefully. 'Okay, I get it. You want to run,' she said to the dog. 'Sorry, Theo, I have to go. I need to take the dog for a bit more of a walk. But we can speak later tonight, right?'

'I will be waiting for you to ring. And maybe you could send me a photo? If your camera still works.'

'Sure. I'll try, but not sure how well it will come out. I love you.'

'I love you too. I just wish I could see more of you.'

'Soon,' Daisy said. 'I'll see you soon.'

As she hung up, she had to remind herself that she was doing all of this to be with Theo. That was the purpose of this crazy trip, and if he was missing her half as much as she was missing him, then he would be incredibly grateful for the effort she had gone to. The guilt she'd been feeling only a few minutes before was beginning to lessen.

And so what if she couldn't tell him all the crazy tales that she had got up to so far? They had years ahead of them for her to recount it all.

But for now, Daisy had a more immediate issue to deal with.

Reaching down, she unclipped the leash from the dog's collar. 'Do not run off,' she said as she looked down at the dog.

She always had been good at offering famous last words.

48

Daisy should have known. Never work with small children or animals, wasn't that the saying? And while she wasn't working with the dog, the same rule applied; it was bound to do exactly the thing she didn't want it to do, and at that exact moment, the second she untied the leash from the dog, in a busy park full of people, in an area of London she wasn't familiar with, he bolted.

'Hey! What did I say!' Daisy yelled, waving her arms as the animal sprinted away from her. 'Get back here!'

Daisy didn't run. While many women her age had caught the running bug and could be seen out in their high-vis at all times of the year, listening to music as they ran along the towpath, Daisy had not once been tempted to join them. She'd hated running at school. Not all sports – she'd liked netball and hockey, things that involved a team and a ball – but not running. She just couldn't see the point in exerting that amount of effort for no outcome. No goals, no tries, no baskets. Nothing. Just moving your legs until you ended up in the exact same place you started. It just didn't make sense.

Only now she wasn't running without reason. She had a very definite goal – to get to the dog.

'Stop! Stop, will you!' she shouted in between countless apologies.

She cut across a football match, then jumped over a family picnic. And the entire time, she could see all the heads shaking at her – everyone was tutting at the woman who had lost control of her dog. But he *wasn't* her dog – that was what she wanted to yell at these people. She was just a good person, doing a good deed. Or trying to.

The fugitive dog was now running towards two men playing badminton, and for one horrifying moment, Daisy assumed he was going to jump up and steal their shuttlecock mid-air. But he didn't. Instead, he swerved around them and directly towards another man who was striding across the park. Daisy waited for the dog to swerve again, trying to anticipate what direction he was going to go, but he didn't alter his path. Even when he was only a few feet away from the man, he was still going full pelt.

'Watch out!' Daisy yelled, envisioning a collision that would send the man flying. But instead, the dog slowed just in time. Rather than swerving or bolting again, like he had done before, he jumped up and began licking the man.

By the time Daisy reached them, the dog was on the ground, with his belly in the air, lapping up all the attention he could get.

'I am so, so sorry,' Daisy said to the man who was currently mid tummy rub. 'I... I really don't know what got into him. I'm so sorry.'

'Don't worry, I'm a dog person,' the man said, looking up at her.

He was wearing a comic book T-shirt and shorts, though it was his face that held her attention the most, his dark hair and blazing green eyes that were locked straight on hers. 'You look a little lost. Are you lost? Maybe I can help.'

Daisy shook her head, the words falling from her lips.

'It's you,' she said. 'You're the man who saved me in the marsh.'

49

Daisy stood up, her heart drumming in her chest. She had thought about him time and time again since that incident in the marshland. Even chased down a man that she thought was him. But this time, there was no denying it. Not the way his eyes locked on her. A look of clarity dawned on him.

'Mud Girl?'

'Yes,' she said. 'Mud Girl would fit. For you, at least. I can't believe it's actually you.'

'Me neither. Small world.' Daisy wasn't sure if he sounded pleased by this or not, but before she could comment, he was speaking again. 'What are you doing here? You looked lost.'

'Oh, no, I'm not lost. Thank you, though. I'm just not much of a dog owner. Though in my defence, I'm not technically his owner, except in a legal sense, I suppose. I still can't believe it's actually you.'

She knew she wasn't making much sense, but this entire situation didn't feel like it made sense. There was a strong chance Daisy would have carried on staring and babbling for a lot longer, had a loud snuffling sound not drawn her attention. The dog, having realised that tummy rubs were over, was now on his feet again and sniffing at the man's satchel.

'I'm so sorry,' Daisy said, clipping the dog's leash back to his collar. 'I don't know what's wrong with him.'

The man smiled. 'I reckon you smell something good in there, don't you,' he said. 'Let's have a look what we've got, shall we?'

As he finished speaking, he shifted the large leather satchel around his body. The man was dressed very differently from the last time Daisy saw him, in his T-shirt and torn cargo shorts. The outfit would have been far better suited to running in than the chinos she had seen him in before, although the bag was strangely out of place. It was boxy and formal and looked more like the type of thing a wealthy commuter would carry a laptop in than something someone would take on a stroll through the park.

Although, what did Daisy know? Maybe that was just the way more fashionable people worked, pairing something completely out of sync with the rest of the outfit as a statement piece. Maybe running in chinos was something people did too. It wasn't like she was a runner.

'Now I think I've found the culprit. Look at what we've got here.'

With a wide smile on his face, the man proceeded to pull out a large packet of dog treats from the satchel. 'You don't mind if he has some, do you?' he asked.

'Be my guest.'

A moment later, the dog was sitting perfectly next to the man's feet, and offering his paw in exchange for a biscuit.

'Sorry about this. And thank you, again,' Daisy said, feeling the need to speak.

'Really, it's no problem. He's a cute dog. What's his name?'

Daisy looked down at the animal. It was getting ridiculous. It was one thing for her and Yvonne to refer to him as 'the dog,' but even she had started to find this odd. After all, if she'd given him a name from the start, there was a small chance he could have come back when she'd yelled at him. And now someone was directly asking her.

Daisy sifted through her mind, racking her brain for something fitting. She thought back to when she first found him. Perhaps something water-related. Marshland. Marshall? Her mind was coming up blank.

How was she going to explain to a stranger that she didn't know the name of the dog she had brought aboard the *September Rose*?

That was when the name struck her. The *September Rose* wasn't only hers; it was her father's. He was the one who had made her and named her. So, in a strange way, it made sense that he named the dog too.

'Johnny,' she said without hesitation. 'His name is Johnny.'

50

It was hard for Daisy not to consider how much her life had changed in the last year. Not so long ago, she couldn't even think about her father without the taste of bile stinging the back of her throat. After all, he had abandoned her – or so she thought. But that wasn't the case and now she was naming a pet, a real, living thing after that same man. Almost in honour of him. Not that the dog was hers, she reminded herself. Whoever gave him a home would probably want to rename him. But for now, he was Johnny. Johnny Dog. And though Daisy knew little to nothing about her canine's namesake, she had a sneaking suspicion her father would have liked animals.

While Daisy was pondering her choice of name, the dark-haired man was crouching down.

'Well, hello, Johnny,' he said.

'He really likes you.' Daisy was unable to hide the surprise in her voice.

'I'm a dog person,' the man said, before standing up and stretching out his hand to Daisy. 'Shaun.'

'Shaun,' Daisy repeated. It was like being able to breathe, finally having a name she could call her marshland rescuer.

'And do you have a name?' Shaun said. 'Or are you happy just to be known as Mud Girl?'

Daisy let out a short laugh that sounded far more strained than she felt.

'Sorry, yes. I'm Daisy,' she said as they shook hands.

'Well, it's nice to meet you, Daisy and Johnny,' Shaun said, already back to stroking the dog. 'So, what are you two doing here? Or should I assume here is home for you? You can't get into as much trouble on this type of grass.'

'You're right, marshlands aren't my normal habitat,' she said. 'But you already figured that out. I used to be from London, but we're just visiting for a bit. Well, a night. We're off on a mammoth trip. Burnham was actually the first stop.'

'And you wanted to make it as memorable as possible?' Shaun joked. He had a sweet smile, Daisy thought. And an ability to quickly make people feel at ease in his presence.

'Something like that.'

She had started walking again, back in the direction she had come from, and Shaun had fallen naturally into pace with her.

'So, you're on a trip. Funny that. I'm a bit of a traveller myself. I've actually just been on a campervan trip around the south coast. Only got back a week ago to pick up a few bits and pieces before I go off again. I'm planning on doing a complete loop this time, I hope. Up to Scotland, down through the Peak District and Wales. Eight months' travelling. I've got the bug now. There's no way I could go back to real life.'

Daisy knew how that felt. The freedom of living on Wildflower Lock was unlike anything she'd ever experienced before. She could only imagine how that would change even more if she gave up the fixed mooring. To be able to travel anywhere at any time... Maybe it was something she and Theo could talk about doing, although that probably depended on his job. It was unlikely they'd give him that long off, given that he'd only just started.

'A campervan,' Daisy said, pushing thoughts of Theo and the flaws in their relationship to the back of her mind and focusing on the person in front of her. 'That's amazing. Though I can't imagine eight months in such a small space and that's from someone who lives on a narrowboat.'

Shaun's eyes widened. 'Really? That's incredible. Is it tied up here, in the canal? There's a proper term for it, isn't there? You don't say tied up.'

'Moored,' Daisy said with a chuckle. It was nice speaking to someone who knew less about boats than she did. Since moving to Wildflower Lock, she always felt like the least knowledgeable boat owner there.

'I know it's really cheeky of me,' Shaun said, his eyes sparkling with a grin, 'but I've never actually been on a narrowboat before. I don't suppose I could come and see, could I? Maybe you could give me a tour.'

Giving tours of the *September Rose* was one of Daisy's favourite things to do, especially when she got to point out all the different things that she had fixed or made herself. That pride had only increased since she could refer to the things *her boyfriend* had done, too. It sounded far better than saying 'boat neighbour'. And it would be nice for Yvonne to have someone else to talk to as well.

'That sounds great,' Daisy said, before glancing down at her hand. 'And while we're walking, you can tell me why on earth you were running in chinos?'

51

They walked back through the park at a leisurely pace. While Johnny wasn't tugging on the lead anywhere near as much as he'd been doing on the way there, he wasn't being the easiest to walk, either. He kept twisting around on the lead, trying to get in between Daisy and Shaun, even when Daisy switched which hand the lead was in and tried to swap sides.

'It was ridiculous. I don't know what I was thinking. It was for this photography shoot.'

'Photography shoot, as in modelling?' Daisy said, reading between the lines, although, as it happened, incorrectly.

'I'm on the marketing side of things, but I'm flattered,' he said. A smile twisted up on his lips. Clearly, he was a flirt, but Daisy wasn't going to hold that against him. Not when he'd already done so much for her.

'I got the address wrong. Places like Burnham don't have much in the way of taxis at five-thirty in the morning, and according to my phone, the quickest route to get where I wanted was along the seawall.'

'What about the campervan?'

Shaun looked at her, his lips remaining parted for just a fraction longer than normal before he spoke.

'The garage. Typical, right? Of all the days, but hey, I got there okay.'

'Only covered in mud?' Daisy said, the guilt she had felt from the event returning.

'Don't worry, I told them I was rescuing some damsel in distress. It got me lots of Brownie points.'

Daisy laughed. 'I promise I'm not normally the type of person who gets stuck in marshes.'

'No, well, why don't you tell me a bit about yourself? If you're only here for one night, where are you off to?' Shaun asked.

'Like I said, I'm on a bit of a journey, too. Not for months like yours, just across to the Cotswolds to see my boyfriend.'

'Wow, and you're doing it all by yourself.'

'Not exactly. I've got a friend. An older lady who lives on the same stretch of canal as me back in Essex. She used to do lots of adventures like this when she was younger. I think she's enjoying it. Apparently, I'm the skipper, because it's my boat and everything, but she's very much in charge. Honestly, I would have turned back at least a dozen times without her.'

'Sounds like a great woman. I can't wait to meet her.'

'She is,' Daisy said, feeling a warmth of gratitude at having Yvonne with her on this trip, though she was fully aware that her adventure had so far dominated the conversation. 'So, where have you been so far on your travels?'

'*So* many places,' Shaun said. 'I went down south first, straight to Cornwall. The Minack, the Eden Project, I did all that. I know people don't think the scenery is great in winter, but I wanted to do it all before it got too touristy. You know? Try to see the real beauty of the place without it being obscured by swarms of people.'

Daisy nodded. She'd learned that Shaun was several years younger than her, and yet, he seemed to carry a much greater wisdom. The type of wisdom belonging to someone who travelled, even if it was within their native country.

'And then what?' Daisy asked. 'What's your plan after that? Where are you going after London?'

'Well, I'm kind of zigzagging. Honestly, this country is so beautiful. I was sleeping in the New Forest with wild ponies one night and then on the Isle of White less than a week later. I mean, we've had the summer for it, right? This weather. It's been perfect, sleeping with the doors open, seeing the stars in the sky, the smell of the forest and the sea.'

'Sounds amazing.'

'Oh, it has been. Like I said, there's no way I want to go back to living in some shared house, where no one wants to clean the bathroom after them and you spend half the time worrying that someone's going to steal your food out of the fridge the minute you go out for the evening.'

Daisy nodded in agreement, though she didn't have much experience of such a life. Her stint as a student had been short. One term at art school, after which she'd dropped out and set up home by herself in her little flat. Not that she regretted it. Not any more, at least. Her life was going well. It seemed silly to have regrets when she was so happy with where she was.

As they reached the marina, Daisy pulled Johnny in on a shorter leash. He seemed to be much happier being right up close to her, though Daisy kept worrying she was going to step on him.

'I love the names of boats, don't you?' Shaun said as they walked by the water towards the *September Rose*. 'I make a list in my head every time I see them. I might use one when I have my own. How did you decide on yours? It does have a cool name, right?'

'It's kind of normal,' Daisy admitted. 'It's called the *September Rose*.'

'That's quaint,' Shaun replied. 'Does it mean something?'

'It was my dad's choice. She was his before I inherited it, and I didn't want to change it. My boyfriend's boat is called the *Narrow Escape*. I like that. Because it's a narrowboat, and you get to escape the world out on the canal.'

Shaun smiled. 'So he has a boat too? Did you meet him boating on the canals?'

'Would you believe it, he actually had the mooring next to me when I first got the *September Rose*.'

'Wow, talk about fate.'

'Yes, I suppose,' Daisy said.

There was no way she was going to get into the intricacies of how disastrous their relationship had been at the beginning and how they struggled to get together, especially not to some guy she'd just met. It was much nicer just to think of it as fate. But if fate really had played a part in her life so far, then what did it mean that Shaun was the one who saved her from the mud in the marsh, and again in the park? Their meetings definitely felt like they had a tinge of fate to them, too.

'Well,' Daisy said, coming to a stop just in front of the duck-egg-blue vessel. 'This is me. Still fancy a tour?'

52

It was only when Daisy stepped onto the stern that she realised she probably should have messaged Yvonne first, to make sure she didn't mind having someone on the boat.

'Be careful, it's a bit slippy,' Daisy said, encouraging Shaun to take his time getting onto the boat, although the water wasn't the biggest problem Shaun had to face. Johnny was standing right in his way, jumping up and down as he wagged his tail, making it near impossible for Shaun to come aboard.

'Johnny,' Daisy said, tugging the lead when he didn't move at his name. It took Daisy a split second to realise that he probably didn't know what his name was, given that she'd only given it to him half an hour beforehand. Changing tactics, she crouched down and made a soft sound with her lips.

'Johnny, come here. That's it, Johnny. Come here, give Shaun room to come on board.'

A second later, the dog was sitting with his paws up on Daisy's knees, lapping up the attention. Only when Shaun was safely on the stern did Daisy stand up and tie Johnny's leash to the back of the boat.

'I'll get us some cold drinks to have out here before I show you inside, if you're okay with that?' Daisy asked. 'I meant to open up all the windows before I went out to give the place an air. It gets pretty stuffy.'

Daisy glanced at her watch. Somehow, it was gone five and yet it felt as hot and sticky as if it was midday in the tropics. With a passing thought, she considered how long it had been since it had last rained, only to push the thought from her mind. Thinking about the rain might put a curse on the perfect weather they'd had so far, and there was no way she wanted that. There was still a long journey to go, even if it was on canals.

'Can I come inside? Just to have a quick look?' Shaun said. 'Like I said, I'm a sucker for travelling. Maybe this will be my next option after the campervan. Trust me, it can't possibly get as stuffy as the campervan does.'

'Sure,' Daisy said. 'But mind the mess, there was an incident with a jar of sun-dried tomatoes earlier.'

As it happened, the oily mess was entirely gone, and she felt another deep pang of gratitude toward Yvonne. Unfortunately, the clean floor was short-lived.

How Daisy had trodden mud inside when it had been so dry at the park was a mystery, but it was a constant plague of boating life, and several footsteps marked the ground where she had stepped. And her footprints weren't the only ones.

'Oh, I'm so sorry, I'm making a mess,' Shaun said, looking down at the ground. The tread of his shoes was clearly distinguishable from Daisy's, with a large, coiled snake pattern appearing in the mud. 'Do you have a mop? I can clear it up.'

'Don't worry, I'll sort it in a bit. Honestly, the amount of leaves and dirt that get trodden into the boat is ridiculous. Even on days when I don't go outside. No one tells you that you'll spend half your time cleaning when you own one of these things.'

'I guess it's even worse after you've spent your morning crawling around in a mud pit,' Shaun grinned.

'I was not crawling around,' Daisy said, but she couldn't help but grin back. After realising they had been smiling at each other with their eyes locked, in a manner that could be considered somewhat intimate, Daisy's throat suddenly felt unusually dry. Swallowing hard, she called out into the boat.

'Yvonne? Are you here?'

A minute later, Yvonne appeared out of the cabin, her face crumpled.

'Sorry, love, I just fell asleep.' She glanced at her hand before letting out a groan. 'And I meant to go to the shops to get some food. I'm sorry, dear, I'll do that now.'

'Don't be silly. We've got things we can have tonight. Besides, we've got a special guest. Guess what?' Shaun was standing just a fraction behind Daisy, but in Yvonne's groggy state, she hadn't yet noticed.

'What?' Yvonne said, still looking like she was half asleep.

'I found him,' Daisy said. 'I found the man from the marshes.'

53

Yvonne's expression was everything Daisy had known it would be. Complete and utter disbelief.

'How?' she said.

'Would you believe it? The dog ran straight to him in the park. If Shaun wasn't there, I might have lost him altogether.'

'What are the chances?' Yvonne said. 'Goodness me.'

'Shaun, this is Yvonne,' Daisy said, stepping back to do a better introduction. 'She's the person who actually knows how to drive this boat properly.'

'Don't be so hard on yourself,' Yvonne said, though her focus was firmly on Shaun as she stepped forward and shook his hand. 'So you're the one who saved Daisy in the marsh?'

'I think "saved" is a bit of a strong word,' Shaun said humbly. 'I just pulled her out of the mud.'

'Trust me, you saved me,' Daisy said. 'Ask Yvonne. I've spent the last few days wondering how I could get hold of you and there you were, ready to save me again in the park.'

'Almost like fate.'

His smile twisted, and Daisy couldn't help but feel a swell of butterflies in her. It wasn't because of Shaun, per se. Not that he wasn't good-looking, but he was a bit too clean-cut for her. The butterflies were about something more than that. They were about the idea of fate and not just because she had found Shaun. She was doing the journey her father had done, in his boat, with one of his old friends who even possessed two paintings of his. Fate, it seemed, was all around her.

'This is beautiful,' Shaun said, shifting the attention away from himself as he took a step towards a painting hanging on the wall. It was the one she'd painted after being rejected by an art gallery, and other than her recent dog portrait – which had been inspired by her father's work – it was the most vivid and abstract piece of art she'd ever created. She'd thought about putting it into the auction to raise money for the boat licence and propeller, but it didn't fit in with the theme of the others, and so for a long time, she'd wondered what to do with it. She even toyed with the idea of giving it away, assuming that by hanging it on her wall, she would constantly be reminded of her failures. But that hadn't happened at all and while Daisy often thought of the snobby art curator when she looked at it, it didn't make her feel like a failure. Instead, it reminded her what she was capable of, and how to never let a person derail her dreams again. When she looked at it like that, there was no way she could get rid of it.

'I absolutely love it,' Shaun continued, lifting his fingers up to the glass. 'Who's the artist?'

Other than having people ask to see the *September Rose*, there was one question that Daisy loved above all others. She loved the way answering it made her feel, and – hopefully – the look of awe that appeared on people's faces when she responded.

A look she was hoping to see when she smiled at Shaun and said, 'Me. I'm the artist.'

54

Shaun's look was everything Daisy could have hoped for. His jaw dropped slightly, his eyes widened, and a quiet gasp left his lips.

'Seriously, you painted this?'

'I painted all the artwork in here,' Daisy said, nodding to a couple of other pictures hanging on the walls. None of them were in the same style as the one Shaun had noticed. There was one of her characters, the type she wanted to turn into a children's book. It was a heron, based on one she'd seen standing perfectly for almost an hour as it waited patiently for fish on the canal back home. Another was a watercolour of Wildflower Lock itself, and the last was of the *September Rose*. There were a couple more she had framed in her bedroom too, but given that Yvonne's belongings were in there, Daisy didn't think it was appropriate to show Shaun those.

'So, you're an artist?' he said, his voice still filled with awe. 'That's incredible. Do you have any paintings anywhere I would know? The Tate Modern? Whitechapel? The ICA?'

Daisy laughed. 'No, it's just a hobby, that's all,' she said, only for Yvonne to scoff at the comment.

'It's hardly a hobby,' Yvonne replied, looking at Shaun. 'She recently sold one of her paintings for over two thousand pounds.'

Shaun looked as though his eyes were going to bug from their sockets. 'Two thousand pounds?'

'Technically, it was two thousand five hundred,' Daisy said, suddenly feeling embarrassed by the way Shaun was looking at her. 'But it wasn't a normal situation. It was for charity. Well, sort of charity – it was fundraising for the boat. And the person who paid that amount of money, he was... he was...' Daisy struggled to work out how to finish that sentence. She didn't want to say her ex-boyfriend as that made it sound like her art didn't have any worth by itself, and she didn't think that was true. Besides, it wasn't like she could actually count Christian as a boyfriend the amount of time they'd been together. 'He was very wealthy. Used to spending that amount of money on paintings. Most of them went for quite a lot less.'

'Still, that's incredible. I wish I were that talented. Is that what you're doing on the way to see your boyfriend? Getting more paintings for the next sale?'

Daisy thought about the comment. She hadn't considered selling her current works, but perhaps, when she'd completed the diary of her trip, she could think about it.

'Maybe,' Daisy said. 'I've done a few paintings. Like a visual diary, but I haven't decided if I'm going to sell them yet. Or whether I should. Whether they're just personal.'

'Can I see those too?' Shaun asked eagerly. 'I mean, I love this, your entire journey. I think it's incredible. How long did you say you're going to be travelling for?'

'Well, it depends on the amount of hours we can keep moving each day,' Daisy said while gesturing to Yvonne. In terms of days and travelling hours, she was the one who knew the details better – assuming there weren't any more hiccups, but now they were back on the canals, that seemed much less likely.

'Fingers crossed, we'll be there in nine days,' Yvonne said. 'I suppose it depends how much Daisy wants to open the coffee shop.'

'The coffee shop?' Shaun said.

Another smile crept across Daisy's face as she gestured towards the hatch and the large machine at the corner of the boat.

'It's a coffee shop,' she said. 'The boat is. A takeaway one, at least. And I serve a few cakes and things. I have a pretty good set-up at Wildflower Lock, where we're normally moored, but I've had a couple of good days on the trip too. I guess it will depend on whether I need the money. I'd rather get to Theo as quickly as possible and maybe open up for a couple of days while I'm there. I have to travel back before the weather changes, you see. I can't take her out onto the sea if the weather's that bad.'

'Or the river,' Yvonne interjected.

Daisy turned to look at her.

'Sorry?'

'You can't take them on the river when it's that bad either. It runs too fast. And after today's adventures, you can imagine how bad that would be.'

Daisy felt her throat drying. If that was the case, she may not get as long to spend with Theo as she'd first hoped, though she didn't want to think about that at the moment. She still wasn't sure how she was going to keep up this charade of lying to him for the next nine days. Forcing a smile back onto her face, she looked at Shaun.

'Well, that's enough about me. I want to hear about you. About your travels. Why don't we head onto the stern and grab a cold drink?'

'Sounds perfect,' Shaun replied with a grin. 'But don't forget to bring the rest of your paintings. I want to see them all.'

55

Daisy had hoped the evening might have brought with it some cold air, but so far, that wasn't the case. If anything, it was getting closer and stickier. Yet it was still clear skies and, as such, the three of them enjoyed their drinks outside.

'So, what do you do?' Daisy asked. 'You said it was something to do with photography? Marketing? You must have a great job if you can travel so much.' She didn't mean to sound condescending, but Shaun looked younger than her, and although his age and the way he dressed meant he could easily have passed as a student, something about the way he spoke made Daisy believe that wasn't the case.

'I do okay,' he said with a shrug, reaching down and stroking Johnny on the head. For a stowaway dog, he looked utterly at home, relaxing outside with people who were happy to offer him quick strokes whenever he lifted his head in their direction.

'What line of work are you in?' Daisy said, still no wiser as to what her new friend did.

'I work remotely, but it's difficult to classify. I freelance a lot. Take whatever comes up. A bit of social media management. A bit of data entry. Anything really, as long as I don't have to give up my way of life.'

'Wow,' Daisy said. 'Do you never get worried, not having a fixed job?'

At this, Shaun crinkled his nose.

'No, I prefer it that way. No ties. No people to answer to. And something always comes up. I've been in a couple of sticky situations before, you know, where I've nearly run out of petrol and I've only got ten quid left in the bank. But somehow, something always comes through. I don't bother stressing about it now. There are plenty of ways to earn money if you keep your options open.'

Daisy was impressed, although she was hardly opposed to going with the flow. After all, shutting up the coffee shop with mooring fees expected soon, and the cost of fuel on the rise, wasn't exactly the sensible thing to do. Especially now she was going to have to factor dog food into the mix, at least in the short term.

As Daisy sipped on her drink, her stomach growled loud enough for both Yvonne and Shaun to hear.

'Sorry,' she said. 'Yvonne and I have had a pretty hectic day. We've not had any time to stop and eat.'

'Oh, and I just invited myself on board,' Shaun said. 'I'm so sorry. Look, why don't I take you out for something? To say thank you for letting me invade your evening.'

'Don't be silly,' Daisy replied. 'I enjoy showing people the boat. And we've got plenty of things on board. I can whip us up a quick salad. You're welcome to stay.'

'Only if I'm not intruding? Any more than I already have,' he added.

'Of course not,' Daisy said. 'You don't mind, do you, Yvonne?'

Yvonne shook her head.

'Thank you,' Shaun said. 'I take it you don't mind if I stay for food either, do you, Johnny?' At this, the dog barked, although not in the way he had done with Yvonne. It was almost as if he was agreeing with Shaun.

'Johnny?' Yvonne said in confusion. Daisy nodded her head towards the dog that had been lying peacefully beneath her chair since they had come outside. 'Johnny,' Yvonne repeated, this time a smile broadening on her lips as she understood. 'Perfect. Just perfect.'

'Sorry,' Shaun said, an expression of confusion crumpling his face as he looked between Daisy and Yvonne and back again. 'You make it sound like you've only just given the dog a name? I thought he was yours?'

'Well, it's a bit more complicated than that,' Daisy said. 'Let me make a salad and I'll come back and tell you all about it.'

56

Fifty minutes later, Daisy was sitting outside with Yvonne and Shaun, eating bean salad, having recounted the tale of Johnny and how he came onto the boat, even admitting that she'd only named him when Shaun put her on the spot and asked what he was called in the park.

'You don't like a dull life, do you?' Shaun said as he scratched behind Johnny's ears, causing the dog's tail to thump loudly on the deck. 'You just take on a random dog? That's crazy. And really generous of you. So you just paid the vet bill for a dog that wasn't even yours? I wish I had the type of spare cash where I could do that.'

'I don't think I'd say it was spare cash,' Daisy said, grimacing at the memory of the money leaving her account. 'But there wasn't a lot else I felt I could do. And the vets paid for a bit too.'

'And so now you're just keeping him?'

Daisy shook her head.

'No, absolutely not. It's not possible. Not with the coffee shop. I've posted online with photos, asking if anyone recognises him, and so far, there's been nothing, but I can't believe he doesn't have an owner somewhere. You wouldn't believe it from today, but honestly, he's been so good, walking beside me, sleeping out here.'

'Well, he's obviously attached to you,' Shaun replied. 'And by the sound of things, you're pretty attached to him, too.'

With a slight ache in her chest, Daisy looked down to where Johnny was lying with his head on a pillow, while his body fitted perfectly under Shaun's chair. As she rubbed her fingers into his scalp, his eyes closed and he let out a long yawn.

'I just want to make sure he finds a home, that's all. Someone to love him properly. I think he deserves that. I don't suppose I can tempt you?' Daisy said hopefully.

Shaun let out a short chuckle. 'I'm not sure my lifestyle would quite suit a dog.'

'I wouldn't discount it entirely,' Daisy pressed. 'He loves being on the move.'

'You're really trying to sell this, aren't you?' Shaun laughed.

'Maybe.' Daisy didn't want to push the idea, but Johnny had taken to Shaun ever so quickly. She could just imagine the collie with his head hanging out the window, ears flapping in the wind as Shaun drove them around the winding paths of undulating hills or dramatic coastal paths. Although she had to admit part of her wanted to find the dog a home with someone on a boat. He obviously loved being on the water, and if he could do the Thames without any issues, he could probably do anywhere.

'Well, that food was amazing,' Shaun said, placing his knife and fork together in the middle of his plate. 'Why don't I take you guys for a glass of wine to say thank you? There are a couple of really nice bars around here. And I'd love to repay your hospitality.'

'Really, you have to stop saying that. There is nothing to repay,' Daisy insisted. 'After all, if it wasn't for you, I could have been chasing him around that park all night.'

'I guess it's just a good thing there were those dog treats in my bag.'

Daisy tilted her head in curiosity. 'Why did you have them on you, anyway? You don't already have a dog you're keeping secret from me so I can't persuade you to take Johnny as extra company for it, do you?'

Once more, Shaun's light chuckle reverberated around them.

'No, I promise. But I did tell you I was a dog person, right? I did some sitting a couple of weeks ago.'

'Sitting?' Daisy said, not sure she understood.

'Dog sitting. Well, dog, cat, goldfish. I do a couple of house-sits every now and then, when I need a break from the van or fancy a bit of four-legged company.'

He reached down and stroked Johnny, who let out a satisfied groan.

'That's a thing?' Yvonne said, clearly as curious as Daisy about this style of life that seemed even more unconventional than their own.

'It's a big thing,' Shaun assured them. 'People would much rather have someone trustworthy in their homes, so their pets can stick to their normal routines, than shove them in cramped kennels for weeks on end. It's a win-win for everyone. I must have done at least twenty houses over the last couple of years. There's even one now in Catalan I've been considering. Three weeks in a house with a pool and four Great Danes. The only thing I'd need to pay for is the flight.'

'Wow,' Daisy said, genuinely surprised by the insight into a world she knew nothing about, although having not yet got used to looking after Johnny, she couldn't imagine how she would cope with four Great Danes.

'It's pretty cool,' Shaun said nonchalantly. 'But I haven't got any booked in at the moment, so you're more than welcome to the treats.'

'Thank you,' Daisy said. 'I really mean that.'

Across the table, Yvonne let out a deep yawn. She covered her mouth halfway through the process, but it was too late. Daisy's brain had already taken notice and before she could stop herself, she could feel an involuntary yawn stretching her own mouth.

'I'm so sorry,' she said. 'It's been a crazy day. I think I might have to head to bed soon. You don't mind, do you? It's been lovely to meet you.'

'You too,' Shaun said. 'I think it's definitely the first time I've invited myself to a famous artist's home.'

Daisy let out a chuckle while shaking her head.

'Definitely not famous.'

'Yet,' Shaun finished for her. 'One day I'm going to dine out on this story. But really, Daisy, it's been so lovely to meet you. Maybe I'll bump into you later on on your journey. I think we're travelling the same route for a bit.'

'That would be really lovely,' Daisy said, leaning in and offering her new friend a hug.

'Nice to meet you too, Yvonne,' Shaun said, going in for a quick kiss on the cheek. 'And Johnny, be good for Daisy, okay?'

From his position on the ground, Johnny looked up and wagged his tail. He really was the strangest of dogs, Daisy thought.

57

It was only when Yvonne had gone to bed and Daisy refilled Johnny's water bowl she realised she hadn't sent Theo a photo of the dog yet. It took several attempts to angle her phone properly so that only the boat and Johnny were in the photo, and only when she was certain she could see no trace of their location did she fire it off to Theo.

He looks at home

was the reply that pinged straight back.

It's only temporary

she replied, though the text caused an unease to float around inside her. It had been two days, and apart from a few comments about how cute he was, there was nothing. No one had said he looked even vaguely familiar. Which meant it was probably time she moved on from looking for his old owners and found him a new home. However, as she opened up her phone to an animal adoption site, she yawned yet again.

It could wait until the morning, she decided. What she needed first was sleep.

* * *

Daisy lay in bed, listening to the sound of rain drumming on the roof above her, keeping her eyes closed. A slight smell filled the air. A clean, crisp aroma. Rain. It was raining. Which meant she didn't have to get up straight away and open the coffee shop for all the early-morning walkers. A feeling of peace settled in her stomach.

At the beginning of her business venture, rain had been the worst outcome for a morning, and waking to the sound would be enough to make her insides twist in knots. She had so many bills waiting for her that closing, even for a few hours, was a massive setback. But now, weeks later, Daisy couldn't remember the last time she'd had a lie-in. A bit of rainfall meant she might get a little rest, or at least a slower stream of customers. It was a shame that Theo wasn't with her, though. Having Theo with her on a rainy day would make it perfect.

The realisation landed with a mixture of emotions. While the rain might stop her from opening up the coffee shop, a lazy day wasn't going to be possible. If they didn't keep moving, then they would fall well behind and there was no way she wanted that to happen. As she drew back the curtain and looked at the dark, thunderous clouds that filled the sky, the door to the cabin opened and Yvonne stepped out, this time wearing a bright-turquoise dressing gown. The array of nightwear she had really was spectacular.

'That was some storm last night,' she said as she moved across to the kitchen and poured a glass of water from the tap. 'I don't think I'll ever tire of hearing the thunder on the water. All the storms I've heard and no two have ever been the same.' She filled her glass and took a sip.

'I didn't hear it,' Daisy admitted, sitting up. 'I can't believe how tired I was. Honestly, I was out like a light.'

'Well, if that didn't wake you, I can't imagine that anything would,' Yvonne said, before pausing. Her glass hovered in her hand as her eyes narrowed. She looked slowly around the boat, then scanned it for a second time, far more quickly, before finally looking back at Daisy.

'Where's Johnny?' she said.

'Johnny?' It took Daisy a second to realise who she meant. The name was still so fresh. 'Well, he's outside, of course.'

'And he's been out all night?' Yvonne said, her eyes widening by the second.

That was when it hit her.

58

'I'm so sorry. I'm so, so sorry,' Daisy said, as she scooped the dog up in her arms and carried him into the boat. Pools of water were forming at her feet as it streamed from his shivering body.

She had found him under the small table. The same one he had been sitting under when Daisy, Yvonne, and Shaun had been eating their salads the night before. It was the only smidge of shelter he could reach, given how she had his leash short enough to mean he couldn't set a foot off the boat. She had done this. She had done this to him.

'Here, I've got a towel,' Yvonne said, throwing one across to Daisy, who placed the dog on the rug by the sofa and hastily tried to dry his fur. His ribs stuck out beneath his fur and every part of him was trembling from cold.

Guilt filled the pit of Daisy's stomach. She had done this to him. She had left him out in the middle of a storm. So much for thinking she didn't want an animal. She didn't deserve one.

'Can you get him some food? Something warm?' Daisy suggested. She didn't know whether you were meant to feed dogs warm food or not, but she was willing to try anything to help warm him up.

'What about porridge?' Yvonne suggested. 'Or scrambled egg? Do you think he'd like either of those?'

'Make them both,' Daisy replied. Whatever he wanted to eat, he could have. That was the way she felt as he continued to lie there, eyes closed, body shaking.

'It's okay, Johnny. I'm going to get you warm and dry. You're going to be just fine. I promise, you're going to be just fine.' As Daisy looked down at the dog, his left eye opened ever so slightly and he beat his tail on the ground. The flood of guilt intensified as it washed through her.

In barely a minute, the towel was already soaked through, but Johnny's fur was a long way from dry and the shivering still hadn't stopped. Daisy needed to get him dry fast. The thought had barely formed when an idea struck.

'I'll be back in one second,' she said, then stood up, not even bothering to ask Yvonne as she dashed into her cabin. It was crazy how much a place could change, she considered, as she looked around her former bedroom. There were no incense sticks, but several large crystals sat on the windowsill and bedside tables and Yvonne had even brought her own lampshade, which she had placed on a small lamp. Daisy wondered momentarily where all her belongings had gone, only to dismiss the thought. She didn't have time to worry about things like that now.

With her heart pounding, she opened the top drawer of her cabinet and pulled out the hairdryer.

She was in the doorway, ready to start drying Johnny, when something caught her eye and caused her to stop. Or rather, several things did. Several small cardboard packages and several plastic bottles, too. Medication. Was Yvonne ill?

Her concerns for Johnny were pushed from her mind. There were certainly quite a few tablets there for someone who seemed as healthy as Yvonne. Then again, she knew her mother was on several medications for everything from acid reflux to analgesics for back-ache. Yvonne was a good couple of decades older than her mum. It was probably normal for someone of her age to need to take one or two tablets.

Brushing the worry from her mind, Daisy went back into the living room, plugged in the hairdryer, and got to work on Johnny.

59

It appeared Johnny liked a blow-dry. While he was perturbed by the initial noise of the hairdryer, it didn't take long for him to relax, and though his eyes remained closed for much of the drying, it was in a chilled-out, peaceful manner, rather than because he couldn't open them. By the time he was dry, his tail was thumping on the ground and the only time he barked was when Daisy turned the dryer off.

'Food's ready when he is,' Yvonne said, coming into the living area. 'Where do you want me to put it? It's still raining pretty hard outside.'

Daisy looked out of the window, though there was really no need; the sound was more than enough to confirm the weather. But it didn't help her work out what to do. The kitchen was the closest place to the back of the boat, and while it probably made sense to feed him in there, it was also the area she cooked in for the coffee shop and she wanted to keep it entirely dog-free. The same for the area around the hatch. That meant the options were Yvonne's cabin, her small bunk, the bathroom, or where they were now in the living and dining area. Looked at in that way, there was really only one option.

'I guess you should just place it down here,' she said to Yvonne while nodding to the space in front of her. 'Though maybe not on the rug. I don't fancy getting scrambled egg out of that if he spills it everywhere.'

Nodding in agreement, Yvonne placed the two bowls down by the table. Immediately, Johnny looked up at Daisy, his whole body tense and poised. He was clearly starving. She'd expected him to run straight for the food, but instead, he waited.

'Okay, you can eat. It's for you. It's for Johnny.'

He didn't need telling twice. The eggs went first, in a matter of mouthfuls, and though the porridge took slightly longer and involved a lot of lapping with his tongue, he polished the entire thing off, including the few drops that he sprayed on the floor.

'Do you think we should make him some more?' Daisy asked as Johnny sat back and looked at her, his tail wagging. It was incredible to think this was the same dirty dog that had shown up on her boat all those days ago. He was still thin and could do with putting on a bit of weight, but his fur was already looking glossier, which had to be a good sign.

'I'd wait a bit. You know what dogs are like: eyes bigger than their bellies.'

Daisy was inclined to agree. She might not know much about dogs, but she knew she didn't want him eating so much that he made himself sick.

'So, what's the plan now?' Yvonne asked. 'The weather forecast says this is meant to clear up in an hour.'

Daisy wasn't one to believe weather forecasts. Not after a freak storm had swept into Wildflower Lock on the first day she was supposed to open the coffee shop. But it wasn't like she had much of a choice. Standing by the tiller in the rain wasn't pleasant in any situation and it wasn't like an hour would make that much difference in the long run.

'I might get up to date on my paintings,' Daisy said, thinking aloud. 'I was too tired yesterday to do one and I guess that would be a productive way to spend the time.'

'Sounds good. Do you know what you're going to paint?' Yvonne asked. 'You've got a lot to pick from with all the bridges.'

Daisy pondered the idea. There really were a hundred different things she could have made a subject from the day before, from the bridges and cruisers to the yellow oil drums that marked the entrance to the canal, but she had one memory that stuck out more than the others. One thing she had known in the moment she wanted to paint.

'Actually, it is rather different,' she said, unable to stop the smile creeping onto her face. 'Very different.'

60

Daisy wasn't a portrait artist. She never had been. During A-level art, she'd had to practice drawing faces and limbs and she'd done it well enough, but her teacher had always said the same thing – there wasn't enough expression in her work. At the time, she had thought the comment was ridiculous. After all, how did you get expression into a picture of a hand? Now she was older, she knew how ignorant she'd been. A good artist could get emotion into everything, just the way she could do it with a stormy sky or even a field of flowers. Even so, she'd treated portraits and life drawing almost as an invisible nemesis to her artistic self. She'd dropped out of art college before they started the life-modelling modules and she'd been relieved that she'd saved herself the constant criticism of her work there too. But this was different. Because Daisy didn't want to draw just any face, and she knew exactly what emotions she wanted to convey because she had been there in the moment. She had seen it all with her eyes, and now she wanted to capture it with her paint. She wanted to draw Yvonne.

'Are you planning on staying out here, or are you going to head into the cabin and read?' Daisy said with a hint of pointedness. Normally, she was fine having Yvonne in the living room while she worked, but this time, she wanted to hold off sharing the painting until it was done. Particularly as she had no idea how it was going to turn out.

'Well, I was going to make us some breakfast, if that's okay?' Yvonne said. 'But it can wait. I can make a cup of tea and head into my room and read if that's what you'd prefer.'

Daisy chewed on the inside of her mouth. There was no way she could reply that yes, she'd rather be left on her own. So she nodded.

'I'm sure this rain isn't going anywhere for a while. Why don't I fix us both some toast, then I can get on with my painting afterwards.'

It was a full twenty minutes before breakfast was made, eaten and washed up and Daisy finally sat down, ready to paint. Johnny had fallen asleep under the table and she didn't have the heart to disturb him. But there wasn't any need. It wasn't like he was in the way.

The rain was also continuing to pelt down, although there were some hints of blue sky streaking between the clouds – a sign the rain probably wouldn't last forever. They would need to get moving as soon as it was good to go, which meant that she was on a deadline. At least to get the painting started.

The moment from the day before was seared into Daisy's memory. The far-off gaze in Yvonne's eyes as she mused over the last few years of her life. All the things she had done and not done. The way everything had changed after Harry's death. That was what Daisy wanted to convey in her art, and as her pencil scraped across the paper, she found it was coming to life bit by bit.

Colour was paramount to Daisy's paintings. The greys and purples of a storm. The yellows and oranges of a sunrise. Colour allowed her to express the warmth or chill of a landscape as if she were there in the moment. It also added a vibrancy to her animal characters which art of that type needed. But as the sketch took a deeper and deeper form, Daisy found herself sticking to pencils and staying clear of her trusty watercolour palette. Even Yvonne's pink hair she implied only with simple waves in deepening shades of grey. It would be near impossible to find the exact shades she wanted, anyway. Doing it like this, she didn't need to. Besides, it hadn't been a moment full of colour. It had been a moment full of greyness and sadness.

Ninety minutes later, Daisy sat back in her chair to see the first portrait she had done in seven years there on the paper in front of her.

Pressing her lips together, she tilted her head and considered the drawing in a little more detail. It was far from perfect. Daisy knew she'd not got the angle of Yvonne's nose right, or her chin. But with a bit of work, and maybe a couple of photos to act as guidance, and she would get there.

'Looks like the rain's stopped.'

Daisy jumped on the spot, banging her knees on the underside of the table and causing Johnny to bark in surprise.

'Sorry,' Yvonne said, standing in the doorway to the cabin. 'I didn't know if you'd noticed or not. The rain has just about stopped, which means we should probably get going. If you're ready, that is? I don't mind hanging on for a bit if you'd rather, but the locks can get busy here.'

Daisy nodded, glancing quickly at the picture in front of her before slipping it under another piece of paper so it was no longer visible.

'No, you're right, we should get going now,' she said, standing up and smiling. She would show Yvonne the picture at some point. But not yet. She wasn't ready for it yet.

61

Given how desperate Daisy was to get back to her picture, she hoped that once they were happily trundling away, she could leave Yvonne manning the tiller and could carry on working on the portrait, but first they had to get out of their mooring – a task that proved harder than anticipated. By the time she had untied both ropes and stepped back onboard, Daisy was surprised to find the engine still off.

'What's happened?' she said, wondering if the old woman had double-checked her times again to realise she'd made a mistake.

'We're out of fuel,' Yvonne replied.

'Out of fuel?' Daisy squinted at the gauge. That didn't make sense. She'd had half a tank yesterday. More, even.

'It was going against that blasted tide,' Yvonne explained. 'That's what used it up.'

'Crap,' Daisy muttered. 'What do we do now?'

Yvonne surveyed their surroundings.

'It looks like quite a few people are milling about. Why don't you open up and I'll head down to the marina office, find out where their refuelling points are. We'll likely have to tow her there, though. There's not enough fuel to even get her started. And don't forget you need to let that dog of yours out. He looks like he needs the loo.'

'He's not my dog!' Daisy tried to emphasise, but Yvonne just smiled.

Yvonne had been right about both matters. First, enough people were milling around to make opening the coffee shop for twenty minutes worthwhile – even with no cakes to sell – and second, they had to pull the *September Rose* to the refuelling point. Daisy took control, leading the boat forwards from the bow rope and keeping the pace slow so that the momentum didn't cause her to lose control of the situation. Still, once or twice, she relied on Yvonne's quick thinking to hold the *September Rose* back from the stern and stop a collision from taking place. Meanwhile, Johnny trotted along beside her, with his tail wagging. Thankfully, the refuelling point was conveniently close and thirty minutes later, they were leaving, although they now faced a backlog of other boats and they were moving so slowly, it almost felt pointless.

'Are you okay if I go inside while it's like this?' Daisy said. 'I just want to do a bit more work on my drawing.'

'A drawing? Are you not painting?'

'Not this one,' she replied, hoping Yvonne wouldn't ask any more questions. She really wanted to keep the picture a secret until it was finished. Thankfully, Yvonne took the tiller without a second thought.

'No problem. I'm sure Johnny will stay out here and keep me company, won't you?' she said optimistically, only for Johnny to stand up the moment Daisy stepped through the stern door, after which, he dutifully followed her to his spot underneath the table.

'Just yell for me when we're approaching a lock,' Daisy called, before sitting down and adjusting her seat slightly so she could still see Yvonne out on the stern. Yvonne was in almost the exact position she had been the day before, though the light was very different, and she was wearing her hair down around her shoulders rather than tied back in a messy bun the way she had been, but that wasn't a problem. The aim of that morning was to get all the shapes and angles correct – chin, nose, neck and shoulders. Constantly lifting her head to reference the real-life subject, Daisy scribbled away, using her rubber as sparingly as she could to get the correct shapes to lift out of the page.

And it was working. Gradually, Daisy could see the image on her paper shifting from just a random woman to her friend, and there was emotion in the eyes, too. It certainly wouldn't win a place in any famous portrait gallery, but hopefully, it would be a lovely gift at the end of the trip to thank Yvonne for all her help.

Daisy was working on the details of Yvonne's hair when Yvonne called for her to come outside. Slipping the drawing back under her papers just in case Yvonne came in, Daisy stood up and headed onto the stern, with Johnny hot on her heels.

Having ignored him for the entire time she'd been drawing, Daisy was about to reach down and stroke him when she stopped, frozen by the sight in front of her.

'That can't be a lock,' she said, disbelief and fear causing a lump to stick in her throat.

'Oh, it is,' Yvonne replied, a now all too familiar smirk on her lips. 'Come on, it's not nearly as bad as it looks. I promise.'

Despite her initial comment, and even with her limited knowledge of canal networks, Daisy could tell she was staring at some sort of lock with paddles and gates and everything else she was used to. But it was the size that stunned her.

Normally, the locks she used fitted one boat neatly inside. Small boats tended to have plenty of room while it was more of a snug fit for a large, wide beam like hers. There were some canals, like those around Oxford, that wide beams weren't even allowed on because they couldn't get through. But this lock wasn't small. This one was humongous. So big that there were already three boats inside and it wasn't even full. She glanced behind to see another canal boat also waiting for the lock. It was smaller than hers and freshly painted with a logo on the side, which she assumed meant it was a hire boat of some sort.

'There's room for them to come in after us,' Yvonne said, reading Daisy's mind. 'But let's be quick about it. We don't want to keep people waiting.'

62

The challenge with locks as large as this was that the boats had a lot of room to move, which wasn't what you wanted to happen. As the person standing on the towpath, Daisy was responsible for securing the boat by wrapping a rope loosely around a bollard, then letting it out slowly as the water in the lock decreased. Neglecting to do so could spell disaster. But she had seen Theo do it and had practised under his guidance. The catalogue of skills she had mastered was growing longer and longer with every passing day on this trip, and with it, so was her confidence. This was something simple, which she knew she could handle. After all, a lock was a lock.

'I'd better get off,' Daisy said, as Yvonne steered towards the bank of the canal. A crew of two wasn't ideal in a situation like this, even when those people were relatively experienced. The boat needed to be held in place, which was much easier to do if you had two people holding ropes at both the bow and the stern. It stopped the boat moving around and meant whoever was onboard could focus much more. But with no extra crew members, Daisy had a single rope from the centre that she had to hold instead. Still, she knew what she was doing.

'You're doing a good job there, all by yourself.'

It took Daisy a second to realise she was being spoken to until she turned to her left and saw a smartly dressed, middle-aged gentleman in a light-blue polo shirt – sporting the type of plastic sailor's cap you would buy at a fancy dress shop – striding towards her.

'Oh, well, thank you,' Daisy said, not sure how else she was supposed to reply to the undoubtedly patronising comment.

'Looks like you're making life a bit hard for yourself, though,' he carried on. 'I'd just tie it off if I were you. A quick *hitch* should do it.'

Daisy fought the urge to comment. From the way the man leaned on the word *hitch*, it was obvious he was trying to look as though he knew what he was talking about, a fact he doubled down on when he spoke next.

'You know, I can do it for you, if you're not sure.'

At this, Daisy let out a light chuckle. 'It's fine. I'm quite happy, thanks. And a hitch is never something to do with a mid-rope,' she said, feeling the need to impress that she had no desire for any more mansplaining. 'It doesn't add the stability you want. Besides, tying off at a lock is risky as it is. I'm fine doing things this way.'

The man's eyes narrowed as if he wasn't sure if Daisy was pulling his leg or not.

'Risky, you say?'

'You know what happens when the water drops? If it's tied?'

The man looked as if he were going to say something more when the horn on his boat blasted behind them. Daisy flinched. She'd had to beep her horn a couple of times in the past, but that had been different. They had been on the water, away from people. There was absolutely no reason to use the horn in a public place like they were in when calling out would be perfectly good enough.

When she looked over at the man's boat, she saw two young children waving wildly.

He offered a short wave back before returning his attention to Daisy.

'I just wanted to ask, are you the boat I saw doing a U-turn in the Thames yesterday?'

Daisy's stomach knotted and she was sure she felt her cheeks going red. Still, she tilted her head to the side.

'No, not me,' she responded. She'd already taken her measure of this polo-shirt-clad man. The last thing she wanted was for him to be firing instructions at her while she was trying to focus on letting the boat out.

He raised an eyebrow in a manner that suggested he probably didn't believe her.

'Oh, I guess there are a few of us about, then. Have you done one of these trips before? Hired this type of boat? I have to say, it's a brave thing for you to be doing with your mum like this. Very adventurous.'

He glanced at Yvonne as he spoke, and Daisy felt her jaw tighten as she forced a smile.

'Actually,' Daisy slowed her speech, ensuring her enunciation was as precise as possible. 'She's not my mother. She's my friend and she's had narrowboats for over twenty years. And this isn't a hire boat. It's mine.'

'Oh,' he said, his eyes widening a fraction. 'Well, that's good then, isn't it? Brilliant. Well, I will let you get on. I think they're opening the thing up there.'

'Sluice gate?' Daisy offered with more than a hint of satisfaction.

'Yes, yes, that's it, of course. Slipped my mind. I think I'll go and have a look, actually. And see if I can be of any help.'

'What about your boat?' Daisy questioned, but he was already striding away from her, his hands outstretched towards the other boat captains.

Daisy turned and looked at his boat, which was tightly knotted via a mooring pin on the ground. He wasn't actually going to leave it, was he? She thought about saying something for a moment, only to dismiss the idea. She had told him it was dangerous. And the hire company was bound to have said the same thing when he collected the boat. He'd probably just left a really long length in the rope, meaning it would be harder for the person onboard to deal with. Besides, she had her own issues to deal with.

Johnny climbed out of the *September Rose* and dutifully did his business right beside her.

'Oh, this boating life is so glamorous.' Daisy sighed.

63

It was another ten minutes before everyone was in place and the paddles were opened, allowing the water to drain out so that it could lower the boats down to the same level as the next part of the canal.

After relieving himself, Johnny stayed next to Daisy on the bank. She wasn't thrilled by this. She needed to be able to focus on the boat, and the fact she had to hold and let out the rope meant she couldn't hold Johnny's leash. So instead, she placed it beneath her foot and trod on it, although, after a couple of minutes, that seemed pointless. He wasn't going anywhere. Even when a flock of pigeons landed next to him, a quick sniff was the most interest he showed, before refocusing his attention on the draining water. Much the same way as Daisy was doing.

'I do wish you could talk,' Daisy said as she glanced down at the animal by her side. 'I'm sure you've seen some amazing things, haven't you? It would definitely be easier to find out where you came from if you could just tell me, wouldn't it?'

She was looking at Johnny as if he might speak when her phone started buzzing in her pocket.

'Argh!' she groaned to herself, knowing exactly who it would be.

She had sent Theo a couple of voice messages that morning, hoping that he might reply with the same so that she could at least hear his voice a little. That was what she was missing about this. Hearing his voice and seeing his expressions as he told her about all the things he had been up to at work each day. She missed showing him the birds out of her window or the cakes she had made for the coffee shop. But it would be worth it, she reminded herself. She was doing this for him. There'd been no doubting how she felt for him when he saw she'd gone to all this effort to get there. It would be fine. Absolutely fine.

'Everything all right there, Daisy?' Yvonne called from the stern.

Daisy lifted her hand and offered a short wave in response.

One of the best things about life on a canal boat was how much time it gave Daisy to think, but sometimes, that could be the worst thing, too. After all, it gave her a chance to think how much money she could have been earning if she'd just stayed in Wildflower Lock. Money that could have gone on her and Theo having a weekend away. Or she could have invested in new art gear. After all, the bits and pieces she'd found of her father's wouldn't last forever, certainly not how she was using them up. And art gear wasn't cheap. Even paper cost more than an arm and a leg. And here she was, spending money on copious quantities of fuel when she had just started making ends meet. No, being lost in your thoughts wasn't always a great thing.

She drew in a long breath and was considering how she could speak to Theo that night so that she could actually see him, without him knowing something was wrong, when a horn blasted into the air. Daisy grimaced. She knew without turning that it was going to be the same man and his family again, only this time, it wasn't one blast. It was several. And it was followed by screaming.

'Help! Help!'

Daisy twisted on the spot, only for her jaw to drop.

The man had tied the boat up, exactly as he'd said was going to do, but rather than using a decent length of rope, he had kept it taut and short. When the water dropped, the boat had been unable to lower with it and was now hanging near vertically by the ropes. With two children inside.

64

'Stop! Stop!' Daisy dropped the rope she was holding and ran towards the front of the lock.

'Daisy!' Yvonne called after her. 'What are you doing?'

It wasn't the best idea to leave the boat without her guiding the rope down, but Yvonne knew what she was doing, and the *September Rose* was safe. Unlike the other boat at the back of the lock. By the looks of things, it was already at a forty-five-degree angle. If they didn't sort it now, it could be hanging down vertically in a matter of minutes and she had no idea how much weight those ropes could hold. Or the knots, either.

'Stop. Close the paddles! Close the paddles!' Daisy yelled, waving her arms as Johnny chased behind her, barking loudly.

'What's going on?'

The woman was dressed in cargo trousers and a long-sleeved top that seemed ridiculously hot for the weather, but she looked like she knew what she was doing.

'He's hitched his boat,' Daisy said, breathless. 'The lines are too short. Please, there are children onboard. You need to stop draining the lock. We need to refill it. Now!'

The woman nodded. She didn't question Daisy or ask to see for herself. She yelled at the man with her, 'You heard her! Sort it. Close that now.' She turned to face Daisy. 'Can you go do the other end? Open up the paddles there?'

Daisy nodded. 'I'm on it,' she said as she turned and raced back towards the *September Rose*. Johnny was once again on her heels.

'Yvonne, pass me the windlass!' she yelled. Yvonne also didn't need telling twice. Without hesitation, she passed Daisy the long, metal key that was used to open and close the locks. Even if it took the other end some time to get the paddles closed, extra water coming in would slow the drop of the hire boat.

Next to the tilted boat, the father was standing on the towpath, pale-faced, shaking as he reached for the knots, only to change his mind and try to reach for his children instead.

'Get them in the boat!' Daisy yelled at him as she sprinted past. 'Somewhere things aren't falling out. If they fall in the water, it will be even worse.'

She didn't wait to see if he'd listened to her or not.

When she reached the gate, two men were already there, letting the water in.

'Bloody idiots,' one said, shaking his head. 'Honestly, we've had one of them every week this summer.'

'You work here?' Daisy said, standing back. He was already doing a great job himself and the last thing she wanted to do was get in his way and slow it down.

'No. Well, I work in the restaurant just there.' He nodded a little further up the bank. 'But I feel like I should get paid for this now. I boat myself. Saw this one coming.'

'Well, I'm grateful you did,' Daisy said, feeling a flicker of guilt as she spoke. After all, polo-shirt man had told her what he was doing, but she hadn't taken it seriously. If she had, the poor children could have been spared all this terror.

'That's it. I think we're filling up again now,' the restaurant worker said. Daisy looked down at the water and nodded in agreement. It was slow, but the level was definitely rising.

In only a couple of minutes – that probably felt like several hours to all the people aboard – the hire boat righted itself. A flood of relief filled

Daisy as she headed back to the *September Rose*, where Yvonne had dropped some extra fenders onto the sides, ensuring the boat didn't hit the wall too hard. Yet before she could speak, polo-shirt man grabbed her hand.

'Thank you. Thank you,' he said. 'I didn't... I thought...'

Daisy could feel her teeth grinding together. People who didn't know what they were doing shouldn't be allowed boats, she thought, before swallowing the sentiment back down and forcing herself to take a deep breath in. If that was the case, then she wouldn't have ever been allowed to live the life she had now. Learning about canal boats and life on the river was a journey, and you needed people to help you along it, just like she had.

'Now you know,' Daisy said as kindly as she could manage. 'But next time, perhaps you should try listening to people.'

With that, she walked away to where Yvonne was standing on the stern with a bemused expression on her face.

'Perhaps we could try to have an afternoon with a little less entertainment?' she said.

65

Daisy was back in her element. Or at least in her comfort zone. The massive locks were behind them, and though they had tackled a couple which were far larger than Wildflower Lock, there were so many people to help, it was almost like an event. Sometimes even, Daisy and Yvonne could both stay aboard the *September Rose*. Children, enjoying the dry now that the rain had stopped, were there at almost every lock, helping to push them open when the water had filled, while parents took charge of the ropes.

Mid-afternoon, they had to change canal systems. That was where Daisy finally felt like she was home. They were still in the city and the sounds of cars and vehicles were far louder than she had ever encountered at Wildflower Lock, but there were hints of the countryside too, sneaking in on the towpath hedges with birds that flitted between the rushes and songs that drifted into the skies.

The three of them had got into a rhythm that involved Johnny jumping off the boat every time Daisy did. Sometimes, he stood with her while she was turning the windlass and opening up the lock, but other times, he did his business then sat by it, so Daisy knew exactly where she had to clean up when she was done. It was a strange relationship and the more time she spent with Johnny, the more Daisy believed he had been on a boat at some point. Doing trips like this before. But no owner had come forward, which meant she definitely had to put him up on an adoption site. But it didn't feel like something she could do until she was in a fixed location, which wouldn't happen for at least another week. Besides, another week with him wouldn't be that arduous and she could tell the new owners far more about him this way too, like his favourite foods and what he was like with other dogs.

To make up for the rain, they had been travelling non-stop. It had been nearly nine hours when Yvonne and Daisy finally decided it was time to call it a day. There was still a couple of hours of sunlight remaining, but the place they were in looked popular with locals and visitors alike. While Daisy didn't have it in her to open the coffee shop – and doubted many people would want a caffeine hit at 7 p.m. – she wanted to get some baking done. That way – weather provided – she could wake up early and do a couple of hours of trading before they carried on the journey. That was the plan, at least. Only twenty minutes after the mooring, when Daisy was busy weighing out ingredients, there was a knock on the cabin door.

'This place is okay for guest moorings, isn't it?' Daisy said to Yvonne, assuming that it was someone local.

Yvonne was sitting on the sofa reading. It had been a very up-and-down day, and Daisy knew Yvonne had struggled with it. Thankfully, she'd got a few hours of napping in between later locks, but Daisy suspected she would have liked more. Was the tiredness from the nightmares? Daisy wanted to ask. She'd heard Yvonne having the same one several times during her naps, but given that Daisy had been managing the boat and in charge of the tiller, with no one else to help her, she couldn't go in and wake Yvonne up. Instead, she'd just had to leave her. There was one time, though, when Yvonne had been crying out so loudly as she dozed that Daisy let out a short sharp blast on the horn. It definitely wasn't one of the authorised reasons to use the boat horn, but Daisy had known it would wake Yvonne up and she hadn't wanted her to suffer in her dreams any longer.

But now, they were both awake, looking at the door with confusion.

'I'm sure it is all right for us to moor here,' Yvonne said. 'There was a sign. Remember, it said it was free? At least, that's what I thought it said.'

Daisy twisted her head to the door before reaching over to the table and grabbing her wallet. Hopefully, they just had to pay a couple of quid. It would certainly be better than having to cast off and find another place to stay.

Practising her apology line in her head, Daisy opened the door.

'Hi, I'm—' She stopped short, tipping her head to the side in confusion as she looked at the person in front of her. It wasn't someone expecting payment for the mooring at all. Instead, it was a familiar face. Relatively familiar, at least.

'Surprise!' Shaun said.

66

'What are you doing here?' Daisy said, stepping up onto the stern to give her friend a hug. 'I thought you were off on your campervan adventures to Wales, or was it the Peak District?'

'It was both,' Shaun said. 'And I still am. I didn't leave until this morning, though. Well, late afternoon, actually. And then I was driving and I glanced to the side of the road and saw the canal. I was like, what are the chances? And I just had a feeling. So I thought I'd have a look. A quick walk. And what do you know, there you were!'

'I can't believe it,' Daisy said. 'What are the chances?'

She was about to offer Shaun a drink when Johnny bounded out from under the table, jumping up so that his front paws landed squarely on Shaun's chest.

'Well, somebody is very pleased to see me,' he laughed, throwing Daisy a quick smile. His eyes flashed and Daisy couldn't help but wonder if it really had been a coincidence that he saw the canal, or whether he had sought them out deliberately. But why would he want to see her again? As nice as he was, she had made it very clear she had a boyfriend.

'And I'm just as happy to see you,' Shaun said, rubbing Johnny's tummy. 'Still hanging around, are you? You know what, I think you want to stay here, on this boat, don't you?'

'Well, unfortunately, that's not an option,' Daisy said. 'Perhaps you bumping into us is a sign you should take him?'

Shaun laughed. 'You're not going to drop this, are you?'

'Not just yet.'

After one final tummy rub, Shaun straightened up and looked at Daisy.

'I'm so glad I bumped into you. I wanted to say thank you again. For yesterday. For dinner and showing me your home and your amazing paintings. It really was a lovely night.'

'You really don't have to thank me. I'm the one who owed you, remember? Besides, it's nice to have different people to talk to. I'm sure Yvonne's sick of talking to me.'

Daisy let out a slight chuckle, which Shaun dutifully reciprocated.

'No, honestly, I had such a lovely evening yesterday. It's so nice chatting to people who get what it's like to live a slower-paced life.'

Daisy thought back to the incident that morning at the lock. 'I'm not sure I'd call today slower-paced,' she said. 'But I know what you mean.'

'Shaun, lovely to see you again,' Yvonne said, appearing in the doorway, but not able to come any further due to Johnny having flopped down and blocked the route.

'Lovely to see you too, Yvonne. So, I was just about to say to Daisy, there's a lovely pub just a little walk up the road,' Shaun continued. 'It's got a really nice beer garden. I was hoping I could buy you both a drink. Just to thank you for dinner last night. And hear about today's adventures, if you're okay with that?'

Daisy looked at Yvonne. Given how tired she'd been recently, she didn't know if heading to a busy beer garden was something Yvonne would want to do, but Daisy didn't want to leave her on her own unless she was okay with that.

'What do you say?' she asked Yvonne. 'We could just go for one, though we can't be that long. I need to come back and do the baking for tomorrow morning.'

Yvonne's mouth pursed slightly and for a second, Daisy was certain she was going to refuse, but then her eyes glimmered and a smile curved at the corner of her lips.

'Let me just put a bit of lippy on,' she said.

67

The walk to the pub, which Shaun had described as 'just down the road,' was a fair bit further than Daisy had imagined, and the morning rain had created several muddy puddles, though the longer trip provided Johnny with a much-needed chance to stretch his legs. When they reached the beer garden, Daisy and Yvonne took a seat on a bench with a dog bowl underneath it, while Shaun went inside to fetch them each a glass of white wine. That was the plan, at least. Only when he returned a few minutes later, it was with a bottle.

'You didn't have to get that,' Daisy said as Shaun filled their glasses. 'Honestly, a glass would have been fine.'

'Well, I wanted to say thank you properly. Plus, you know what these places are like. It's normally cheaper to get the bottle, anyway. So what happened today? By the sounds of it, it was pretty stressful.'

For the next few minutes, the conversation was dominated by Daisy's rundown of the day.

'I can't believe it,' Shaun said in disbelief when Daisy finished the story about the lock and polo-shirt man. 'His entire boat? On the side?'

'Well, it wasn't exactly vertical, but his poor family. I have no idea how they are ever going to cope with another lock again. If I were them, I would have wanted to pack up and never see another boat again in my life.'

'In his defence, locks have always looked pretty complicated to me,' Shaun said.

'I thought that too,' Daisy replied. 'But they are so simple. And the mechanisms behind them are amazing. To think it's the same technology that was used in the seventeen hundreds blows my mind.'

She blushed a little as she spoke. Daisy never considered herself a 'lock geek' before, but it was hard not to be when you saw how they worked day in and day out. Particularly ones the size of today's.

'What about you?' Shaun said, turning his attention to Yvonne. 'Do you have any boat horror stories? Perhaps from before... You know, when health and safety wasn't such a thing.'

Daisy's stomach churned. She hadn't yet got to the root of what happened to Harry and, with a sickening unease, she wondered if perhaps it had been a boating accident. Yet Yvonne offered a slight chuckle.

'Oh, I've got plenty. You know, when I first went out on boats, it was with my grandad, donkey's years ago, and you didn't have proper toilets back then. Just a bucket, and more than once, it got knocked over inside.'

Shaun gagged. Daisy had to agree. It would probably be pretty horrific. One side of boating that no one ever talked about was emptying the toilets, and though the modern system she used was a long way from the bucket of Yvonne's past, it could still be a thoroughly unpleasant experience.

'What about falling in the water? Have you ever done that?' Daisy said, having realised there were questions she wanted to know from Yvonne too.

'Oh, yes, but mostly when I was a child, and it was always my fault. Not paying attention, you know. Most of the time, it was fine, but there was this one winter when I was an adult and I fell in. It was freezing, and I don't mean that figuratively. It was absolutely freezing. Ice on the canal and everything. I can't remember what I was doing now. Bringing shopping in, I think. Or maybe more wood for the burner. Anyway, I slipped on some ice and went straight off the towpath and into the canal. I couldn't have been in the water for more than thirty seconds before Harry jumped in after me and pulled me out, but honestly, I didn't think I'd ever get warm again. We sat there, right next to the log burner, the door closed so that the whole boat was filled with the smoke and heat and we were still shivering. Looking back, we probably should have called an ambulance, or at least taken ourselves in for a check-up, but people didn't do that back then. And it was all right in the end. We snuggled together under one big blanket, totally starkers, trying to use each other's warmth.'

Her eyes drifted off with the memory and Daisy knew that she was back there, in that smoke-filled canal boat, with her husband's arms wrapped around her. The love of her life.

A sadness was seeping into the air and into Daisy, so she cleared her throat, hoping to say something to break the tension, when Shaun's phone rang on the table.

Jumping up, he offered them both a broad smile.

'Sorry,' he said. 'I need to get this.'

68

As Shaun walked away from the table, pressing his phone to her ear, Daisy looked at Yvonne, desperate to say something that could ease the moment. Yvonne's face had glowed so brightly when she'd recalled the memory of her and Harry, but now that had gone and all it left was the shadowy chill of his ghost.

'Are you okay?' she asked. Their wines were barely touched, and she felt a definite drying in her throat.

As if reading her mind, Yvonne reached out and took a long sip from her own glass before letting out a sigh.

'Yes, yes. I am. It's hard. Some days, it's harder than others, but then I just have to remind myself that we may not have had as long together as some couples, but we had more adventures in that time than some people would have in twenty lives. And it wasn't as if we did bad, either. Twenty-seven years. It's hardly something to sniff at.'

Daisy nodded, her chest still swelling in an ache for her friend.

'But I guess in some ways that must make it harder, if he was the one you always had adventures with,' she said.

'Perhaps,' Yvonne agreed. 'But it doesn't have to be that way, does it?' Daisy could see the way Yvonne forced herself to smile, and it only made the ache in her chest more pronounced. 'I just wish I'd done this sooner. Got out and seen the world again before... before...'

She let her words linger in the air.

Daisy frowned, wondering exactly what it was she meant. Probably before she'd got old. That was the most likely thing. Before she'd needed to take numerous naps each day. This trip had already taught Daisy hundreds of things, but not waiting for life to start had to be one of the greatest. Somehow, she thought that was something Yvonne would like to hear, and she was about to say as much when Shaun came striding towards them, his forehead crinkled in a frown.

'Is everything all right?' Daisy asked, noting the way Shaun hovered above his seat without sitting back down.

'Not exactly. It's my brother. A whole lot of stuff you don't want to hear, trust me. But basically, it means I've got to go. I'm really sorry.'

Daisy stood up. 'Don't apologise. Although I feel terrible that you bought a bottle of wine and you've not even had half a glass.'

'I know. What can I say? My family has perfect timing. Honestly, though, I need to leave now or it'll just be more stress.'

'Well, then, we'll come with you?' Daisy suggested.

Shaun shook his head. 'I'll just be more upset if you don't finish the wine. Besides, I'm in the opposite direction. It's typical. I love hearing about all your adventures.'

Whatever was going on, Shaun clearly wanted to deal with it as swiftly as possible, without any fuss, though before he could turn around and leave, Johnny jumped up and grabbed him by the bottom of his shirt. Of all the strange things Daisy had seen Johnny do over the last few days, this was definitely the oddest. His teeth were clamped on to the fabric as he pulled backwards, as if he were trying to get Shaun to sit back down.

'Johnny, stop it. Stop it now!' Daisy tugged on his leash so that he dropped back into a sitting position, but there was a strange look in his eyes as he continued to stare at Shaun. Daisy couldn't help but think how odd it was that out of all those people in the park, Johnny had run to Shaun, and now he was looking visibly upset at Shaun leaving. She knew that she and the dog had built up a fairly close relationship over the last couple of days, but they had been spending all their time together. This bond Johnny clearly felt with Shaun caused an uncertainty to twist within her.

'I guess that means he doesn't want me to go, either,' Shaun said, reading Daisy's mind and offering a tight smile before he looked to Yvonne. 'Who knows, perhaps we'll bump into each other again soon?'

'That would be lovely, and best of luck with everything.'

Before any of them could say any more, Shaun had turned on his heel and was practically sprinting out of the beer garden.

'Well, I hope it's not too serious,' Daisy said.

69

Given how there was still three-quarters of a bottle of wine to go, and how nice the evening was, it seemed silly to let it go to waste. And so, as Shaun disappeared out of view, Daisy picked up the bottle and tilted it towards Yvonne.

'So, I guess it's just you and me. Again,' she laughed, only to remember Johnny at her feet. 'Don't worry, I haven't forgotten about you,' she added as she topped up the glasses.

For a couple of minutes, the pair sipped their drinks in silence. It wasn't surprising. They had spent so much time together over the last week that they had grown this ability to just be quiet and at peace in one another's company. And yet there was a question Daisy was still desperate to ask. A question she thought, that if Yvonne was ever going to answer, then it would most likely be with a glass of wine to loosen her tongue, and yet it was another question that left her lips.

'Do you think there's something going on with Shaun?' she said.

'What do you mean?' Yvonne replied. 'He said it was a family issue, didn't he? That's why he had to leave.'

'No, not that,' Daisy said, realising she'd not expressed herself properly. 'I mean, about him and Johnny?'

'Johnny?'

Daisy looked down at the dog. It had only taken a day, but it was already clear he knew what his name was, and she didn't know if the thought made her happy or sad.

'I don't know. There was that whole thing with Johnny not wanting him to leave just now. And the only other person Johnny's taken to like that is me. He wasn't like it with you, or the vet. It was like they knew each other.'

'What are you saying, you think Shaun is Johnny's owner? *Was* Johnny's owner?'

Daisy felt her face scrunch up as she took a sip of her wine. Was that what she was saying? She didn't think so, but she was sure that Shaun's bumping into them wasn't accidental, and if he'd actually been interested in her, the way she'd first thought, then wouldn't he have at least asked for her number? It didn't make sense.

'Forget it. I'm just hearing hooves and thinking zebras.' She put her glass down on the table, and that other question reappeared in the back of her mind. The one she'd been wanting to ask for some time now. Daisy looked her shipmate in the eye and pressed her lips together before finding the words to start.

'You don't have to tell me if you don't want to,' she said, hoping Yvonne knew she meant it. 'But what happened to Harry was an accident, wasn't it? I heard you having nightmares.'

Yvonne lifted her hand and covered her mouth.

'I'm sorry, love, I didn't realise. Bloody things... I thought they'd stopped. For years. Couldn't remember the last time I had one and then...' Her words drifted off, and she lifted her glass to her lips, then nodded her head. Before she'd even taken another sip of wine, she carried on. 'It was a motorbike accident. Two days before Christmas.'

'I'm so sorry,' Daisy said. Losing someone you loved would be unbearable at any time of year, but somehow it being Christmas made it all the worse. It wasn't like you could forget the date, and the entire world would be happy and wanting to celebrate while you were lost in your grief.

'I'd asked him to take the car,' Yvonne continued. 'We were having Christmas on the boat, you see. With his niece and nephew. And my mum – she was still alive back then too, bless her soul – and we'd realised we'd not got crackers. Well, a Christmas table isn't a Christmas table without Christmas crackers, is it?' She looked at Daisy with her mouth turned upwards in a smile, but Daisy could see through it to the pain that was fixed in her eyes. And so she stayed quiet and waited for Yvonne to continue. This time, she needed a long draw of wine before she carried on. 'We still had another day to do the shopping, but he didn't want to do that because it would have been Christmas Eve and the shops would have been packed. That's what he'd told me. And he didn't want to take the car, either, because he said it was going to be hard enough to park with the bike. And of course, I just let him have his own way, like he always did. After all, he'd motorcycled down the Swiss Alps. Down the Stelvio in Italy. He knew what he was doing. He was safe. That's what I thought. Only there was black ice, and the driver of the truck didn't see it. Harry didn't stand a chance.'

'Yvonne, I'm so sorry.' Daisy wished there were more words she could offer. Almost as much as she wished she'd never asked what had happened. She'd wanted to know out of nothing more than a sense of curiosity. Only now she realised what that had meant for Yvonne. 'I shouldn't have asked.'

'It's fine. I need to talk about it. People say it makes it easier, don't they, if you can talk about it? I don't know if that's true or not. Maybe it is, though I don't think so.' She drew in a long, deep breath, and all Daisy could do was sit in silence and nurse her drink, the guilt rippling within her. She thought that at some point, she would have to break the silence, but before she could even think how to start, Yvonne was speaking again.

'People still came for Christmas. I forgot to tell them, you see. Sounds ridiculous. Of course it does, but I couldn't. I couldn't speak to anyone. I couldn't think. I don't even know what I did. I think I just sat on the sofa the entire day in disbelief. Waiting for him to walk through the door with those blasted Christmas crackers. His niece and nephew found me in the same clothes I'd been wearing when the police came and told me what had happened. It's safe to say that Christmas wasn't quite the one anyone had expected.'

Daisy didn't want to think about it, and yet the image rose in her mind. People arriving at the *Ariadne* full of joy and ready to celebrate the biggest day of the festive season, only to find Yvonne there, staring blankly at a photo of her husband.

'I would've died from a broken heart,' Yvonne said, sounding as though she was speaking as much to herself as she was to Daisy. 'I believe that, you know. I would have died from a broken heart had they not come that day. But they saved me. Well, they saved my body, at least. I know a small part of me never lived again after that day.'

Daisy wanted to offer deeper condolences. To say how she was glad Yvonne was still here. How she had learned more about her father from her than from anyone else on the planet, because it was true, and because she thought it might bring Yvonne just the slightest flicker of joy, but this time, it was her phone that rang. Theo.

'You should get that,' Yvonne said, wiping away the tears that had surreptitiously dripped down her cheeks. 'I'll just pop to the ladies', give you two a little bit of privacy.'

* * *

As Yvonne left, a heavy weight filled the pit of Daisy's stomach. Love was great until it wasn't. Daisy had learned that long ago. But the idea of being left with scars like Yvonne's after all the years made her wonder how some people ever picked themselves up again.

Suddenly remembering that her phone was still buzzing in front of her, she swiped the video call open, only to immediately regret her decision.

'Hey, you!' Theo's face beamed at the sight of Daisy in front of him. 'You got your phone fixed.'

Daisy could feel her mouth bobbing open like a fish as she tried to figure out what he meant. Of course – she'd told him it wasn't working. That was why they hadn't been doing face calls. She cursed herself for not thinking properly, but Yvonne's story had made her forget what she was doing.

'Yes.' She smiled as broadly as she could. 'Mum took it to be fixed. I still think it's a little dodgy though,' she added, hoping she could cover herself for future video calls.

'Well, it feels like forever since I've spoken to you like this. Where are you?'

'Where am I?'

Again, she gawped. This was why she needed to be the one to ring Theo, so that she could plan answers for when he sprang questions on her. 'Oh, it's someplace near Maldon,' she said, hoping he couldn't hear the lie straining in her voice.

'Maldon?'

'Yes, some beer garden. Nicholas recommended it to me,' she added randomly, hoping that more details made a lie more convincing.

'You're taking recommendations from Nicholas. Wow, that's something I didn't expect to hear. Does that mean he's there with you?'

'No, no. It's just me.'

'You went to Maldon to go to a pub on your own? How come?'

Daisy could feel herself getting flustered. It felt like an interrogation, and one she was certain to fail.

'I came with Mum,' she said, trying to swallow as her throat got drier and drier.

'Oh, right, so Pippa's there with you?'

'Yes, well, no. She was. She's just gone to the toilet.' Her cheeks were growing redder and redder as she spoke. If the coffee shop ever failed, there was no way she could ever consider going to work as a spy. She was terrible.

'Oh, okay. Well, that's good though, you got out. I guess it was a busy one at the coffee shop this morning. That's why you didn't reply to any of my messages?'

'Oh...' Daisy was drowning. She could feel it building in her, the urge to say something. To let the whole truth spill from her lips. 'Sorry, Theo, I think I'm going to have to go. Mum's back from the bar and she's struggling to carry all the drinks.'

'I thought she'd gone to the toilet? And how many drinks can there be to carry if it's just you two?'

'She went to the bar and the toilet,' Daisy said. 'We'll speak later, okay? Love you.'

'Love you too.'

A second later, Daisy hung up the phone. She was going to have to work on her lying. A lot.

As she let out a long groan, Yvonne reappeared at the table.

'You know what, that walk here really took it out of me,' she said with a soft smile. 'What do you say we take this bottle of wine back to the boat and finish it off there? I'm sure this guy could do with some food too, couldn't you?'

As she reached down and stroked Johnny's head, the dog let out a slight whine. It was a sound Daisy hadn't heard from him before, even when he'd been soaking wet and shivering, and she wondered if he was injured, but as she stood up and took his lead, his tail beat against her leg.

'I guess that's a yes, then,' Daisy said. 'Home, wine and dog food it is.'

70

Daisy was worried that the walk back to the boat was going to be awkward. That the silence that had hung over the table when Yvonne had been talking about Harry would return, but Yvonne seemed happy enough. Or at least, she was putting on a good show.

'I'm looking forward to slowing the pace tomorrow,' she said as they reached the towpath. 'Don't get me wrong, I know we have a schedule to keep to and everything, but those last couple of days on the river were a little hair-raising.'

Daisy stopped so fast, she jerked Johnny's lead.

'You found it hair-raising? I thought you said it was all normal? Fine?'

'Well, it was an adventure, wasn't it?' Yvonne said, casually glossing over the issue.

They walked far more slowly on the way back. Even now, Daisy loved having a nose through the windows of the other canal boats, looking at the different layouts, where they put their galleys, how they had arranged the living room. Yes, that sudden urge to start another renovation project was back again. Perhaps this time, she should take a little longer to look at all the options out there. Who knows, if the coffee shop kept going through autumn, she might even have a bit of a budget this time.

'So, how do you think Theo is going to feel about you turning up at his workplace with no warning?'

'His workplace? I hadn't thought of it like that.'

Daisy hadn't considered that her surprise could disrupt Theo trying to do his job. Back when he lived at Wildflower Lock, he had worked on the canals there too, but his job had taken him all along the canal network, up as far as Chelmsford, not to mention some occasional work at local marinas. It would be the same in Slimbridge, she hoped. Her turning up at the canal wasn't like turning up at someone's office, was it? Daisy shook away the feeling of doubt that was creeping in. Theo would be thrilled to see her. She was sure of it.

As they approached the area of the canal where the *September Rose* was moored up, Johnny began pulling on his lead, barking loudly.

'Stop it, Johnny,' Daisy said sharply, tugging him back to heel, but unlike at the pub, where a simple word from her had been enough for him to toe the line, this time he wasn't stopping. 'Johnny, what's wrong with you?'

He was tugging her so hard, she could feel her arm straining at the socket. If he pulled any harder, he'd end up dislocating her shoulder, but she could hardly let go of him. There was no way she could drop his lead and let him run wild on a canal path where other dogs and children were walking. That just wouldn't be safe.

'Johnny, what is wrong with you? Stop it, now!'

His barking continued, though he lessened his force by just a fraction. Daisy looked down at him, crouching down to her knees.

'What is wrong with you? We're nearly home. You'll get your food in a minute. Really, the sooner we find you another home, the better.' Daisy got to her feet.

'It's like this dog's got a dozen different personalities,' she said to Yvonne, although rather than responding, Yvonne was squinting into the distance. 'What is it?' Daisy asked, following Yvonne's line of sight, although she couldn't see anything.

'I think somebody just came out of the *September Rose*,' she said.

71

Daisy stared along the towpath. People were coming towards them, walking in the same direction. Some business commuters, some people looking like they were on an early-evening stroll with their dogs. It was certainly a busy place to be. Although she could see the *September Rose* just a little way off in the distance, she wasn't even sure if she'd be able to tell whether someone had stepped out of it.

Johnny's barking continued, but Daisy was only half listening. It was probably just her imagination, but something didn't feel right. A nervousness buzzed within her as she quickened her pace, much to Johnny's relief, although he still tried to break out into a full-on run. Though she was a long way from sprinting, Daisy was doing a light jog by the time she reached the *September Rose*.

Before she'd even stepped foot on the stern, she spotted the door ajar and the nerves that had filled her expanded into a feeling of outright nausea. Never in all her life had Daisy left the *September Rose* unlocked. Not even in Wildflower Lock, where the towpath gossips knew every single going-on. She would never have done something like that there and most certainly wouldn't have done so in a mooring she didn't know. Particularly not in London.

Daisy's pulse hammered against her eardrums as she stepped onto the stern, though Johnny was continuing to bark and refusing to get on the boat behind her. Lacking both the patience and time to deal with whatever random bout of behaviour the dog was going through, Daisy handed the leash to Yvonne.

'Take him,' she said, her throat growing tighter and tighter.

Yvonne nodded meekly. Daisy stepped onto the stern of the boat, only to let out a gasp as she covered her mouth. The glass panel in the door – the original one from when she had taken over the boat – had been smashed. Any doubts of a once-in-a-lifetime bout of forgetfulness disappeared. Someone had forced their way into her home.

Daisy slowly pushed the door open, hearing the creak of the hinges as tears trickled down her cheek.

'Perhaps we should wait,' Yvonne said. 'Perhaps you shouldn't go inside until we've called the police.'

She was probably right, Daisy thought. Waiting for the police would definitely be the sensible thing to do. But she couldn't. She needed to see inside.

With her hand still covering her mouth, she stepped into the *September Rose*.

At first, Daisy frowned at how normal everything looked. No tables were overturned, no cupboards flung open. Everything looked exactly as it should have. Almost. It took her a second to realise why her home didn't feel the way it normally did – all the paintings were gone.

'What...' she said, stepping inwards. Bare hooks stuck out of the walls where her pictures had previously hung, though as she stepped further inwards, she discovered those weren't the only things that had been taken. The folder where she kept her artwork was gone, every painting taken, including those for the visual diary of the trip that she had been working on.

Nausea rippled through her as she moved over to the table and pushed the notepad aside, finding that the portrait of Yvonne was gone. All her paintings had been taken.

Her tears were streaming now, not because of the missing paintings, not entirely. Someone had been in her home. Someone had taken her things. Personal things. With that, another thought jolted in her mind, and for the first time since entering the boat, she half-sprinted as she dashed towards the bookcase. She moved the books one by one, taking them out and tossing them to the side, knowing it was a lost cause.

'No, no, not that,' she said. 'Please. Please don't have taken those.'

But she knew it was hopeless. Her father's paintings had gone, just like her own.

72

Tears stung the back of Daisy's throat as she stared blankly into the space. Her father's paintings were gone. The one true connection she had to Johnny stolen from her and her heart was breaking because of it. They could have taken every one of hers. Every single item in the boat, if they had only left one picture for her to remember him.

'I don't understand why?' she spoke aloud, though there was no one in the boat to listen. Yvonne was still waiting outside with Johnny.

Yvonne. The thought struck Daisy like a hammer in her gut. She had brought all her most precious items aboard the *September Rose*. All the treasures that she had collected throughout the years and not wanted to leave in Wildflower Lock, because she had thought they would be safer with her here. And now Daisy had let her down.

Daisy darted to the cabin, gulping deep lungfuls of air as she tried to steady her breath.

It was difficult to work out whether anything was missing. There were still dozens of crystals on the surfaces of the cabinets and bedside tables, while the lid of the heavy trunk was closed, and Daisy had no intention of opening it. Yvonne would need to do that.

Going into the room offered little in the way of relief. Until Daisy knew for certain whether any of Yvonne's belongings had been taken, her feeling of absolute guilt would remain. Nausea struck again, so fiercely it caused her head to spin with dizziness. Dropping herself onto the corner of the bed, she buried her head in her hands, allowing her palms to stifle her sobs as tears dripped through her fingers. Why had she thought this trip would be a good idea? It was a miracle they had survived the journey on the Thames. And now this? It was like the universe was giving them a sign that they should turn around and go back. Daisy wanted to stay there, in that spot, and let the world swallow her up. But it was a selfish thought. She needed to face the music.

With her heart in her throat, she stood up, wiped away her tears the best she could, and headed back out onto the stern.

'It's a break-in,' she said. 'All my paintings have gone. Even the ones in the folders. And they took my dad's too. I'm sorry, Yvonne, I don't know if they took any of your things. Hopefully, we startled them. You'll need to look.'

'I will, love, but first I'll ring the police.'

'Yes, yes of course. I guess the more detailed a list we can give them, the better, right?'

Daisy stopped speaking, expecting Yvonne to respond, but the old woman's lips were pressed tightly together. Rather than looking at Daisy, she was staring past her, into the boat, her eyes trained downwards as if she was looking at the floor.

'Yvonne, what is it?' Daisy said. Yet before Yvonne could reply, Daisy had followed her gaze into the boat. She knew exactly what part of the floor Yvonne was looking at.

After bringing Johnny in from the storm that morning, Daisy had mopped the entire kitchen and living area of the boat twice to get up all the dirt. By the time it had all dried, the floor had been practically sparkling. But it wasn't sparkling now. Instead, it was marked with footprints. Extremely distinctive footprints with a highly unique grip pattern of a small, coiled-up snake.

73

One of the police officers said yes to a cup of coffee, while the other said no. Still, they had come all this way out, so Daisy placed a plate of biscuits between the pair, along with the drink, and two glasses of water just in case.

'And you're sure that this footprint couldn't have been from earlier in the afternoon? You did say that this man, Shaun, came to the boat to invite you for a drink.'

'But he didn't come inside. I'm positive. Johnny was jumping up at him.'

Daisy had wanted to believe she was wrong. That the footprints had, like the police officer suggested, been placed there earlier in the day. But she could remember the moment Shaun came round. Yvonne speaking through the doorway as the dog blocked it. Besides, that snake footprint was fresh.

'He said he was travelling by campervan, around the country, but I don't know if that's true,' Daisy said, wanting to give the officers as much information as possible.

'He was nice. He helped me when I slipped down in the marshes by Burnham-on-Crouch. I checked online, and apparently there was a spate of robberies in Burnham at the same time he was there. I don't know if you want to check that out, too?'

'We will explore all avenues,' the female officer said gently as Daisy let out a long groan.

'I wanted to see him again to thank him. I thought he was a genuinely nice guy. God, how could I have been so idiotic?'

Once again, the female officer offered a sympathetic smile, while the man tucked into the biscuits.

'You say it's just the paintings that he took?' she said. 'I assume they were valuable?'

'He believed they were valuable.' Daisy replied. 'We told him before how much some had sold for at auction, even though it was a one-off. He obviously thought he could get some money from them.'

Daisy scoffed. If making money selling her paintings had been that easy, she would have sold them all already. But there was one saving grace to the situation.

'I guess Johnny's barking warned him we were coming back,' Daisy said. 'Before he'd reached the cabin and Yvonne's things.'

Yvonne had tried to hide her tears of joy at discovering that none of her belongings were missing, but Daisy had wept over them for her. Daisy's paintings were personal to her but had no real history, other than from the last couple of years. There were probably mugs and pictures she had of far more sentimental value, but that wasn't the case with all the items Yvonne had brought and Daisy would never have forgiven herself had they been stolen.

'Well, I think we've got all we can, but I'll be honest, I don't hold out much hope. Someone like that clearly knows what he's doing. He's probably a pro at it. It might be a good idea to keep your eye out, though, to see if any of your work pops up at galleries or auctions. You never know.'

'Thank you, but I think he's going to be disappointed when he goes to sell them on.'

'Either way, we'll keep you updated if we hear anything.'

'Thank you.' Daisy stood up and shook the officer's hand. Then she reached for the male officer's only to find it was once again reaching for the biscuits.

'And that's a good dog you've got there,' the woman said as she stepped onto the towpath, offering Johnny a quick rub. He tipped his head to the side and didn't even offer the slightest hint of a bark. 'I'd make sure I keep him on board, if I were you.'

Daisy let out a little groan before looking down at him.

'Come on, then. I guess you're sleeping inside tonight.'

As the police officers disappeared down the towpath, Daisy and Yvonne fell into silence. It was only then Daisy realised she hadn't eaten anything since breakfast.

Her stomach growled, reinforcing this point. The half bottle of wine sat on the table. Daisy wanted to throw it out of the window into the canal, but she wouldn't waste wine. She would save it and cook with it later in the week.

'I'm going to do some toast; do you want some?' she said, moving across to the kitchen.

Yvonne nodded. 'I think that sounds like a good idea,' she said.

Silence encapsulated them, the weight of what had transpired hanging tangibly in the air.

Daisy slipped the bread into the toaster and had moved to the fridge when Yvonne spoke.

'Do you want to head back?' she said gently. 'You know, I understand. There's no shame in it. And from what I remember, there's a marina up here. You could put the *September Rose* on the back of a lorry and have her home by next week. I don't mind paying for it if you're worried about money.'

Daisy smiled sadly. It was the sweetest offer, and one she genuinely considered for a moment, only to dismiss it. Leaving now would feel like Shaun had taken even more from her.

'One of the pictures was of you,' Daisy said when she swallowed the lump in her throat. 'I wanted to keep it as a surprise. It was a pencil portrait of you on the Thames.'

Yvonne's eyes filled with tears.

'Thank you. Thank you so much, Daisy. Honestly, what you've given me these last few days has been life-changing.'

Daisy shook her head, about to say that without Yvonne, she would never have got this far, but before she could say something, her phone rang.

Theo.

74

Daisy wanted to smile. She needed to smile. If Theo saw that something was wrong, he might do something stupid like head down from Slimbridge that night, and that was the last thing she wanted. She needed to keep up the pretence of being at Wildflower Lock, the doting girlfriend, missing her boyfriend. But she couldn't. She couldn't make herself smile. And so she let the phone ring out. A minute later, silence filled the boat as the ringing finally stopped and flicked to voice mail.

'Why don't you tell him?' Yvonne said. 'You can at least tell him some of it? Tell him about the paintings?'

'I just need a little head space, that's all,' Daisy said. 'I'll talk to him later.'

She was right. Now that she'd said it, she realised how much she needed space. Before that evening, she'd loved being inside the *September Rose* more than anywhere else in the world, but that was because until that day it had held only positive memories. All of a sudden, it felt different. Like Shaun was still lurking in the shadows.

'What do you say we go for a walk?' Daisy said, looking up at Johnny, who tilted his head expectantly. 'Would you like that? Walkies?'

His tail wagged hard as he saw Daisy grab the leash from the side.

'You don't mind me heading out for a bit, do you?' she said to Yvonne, recalling the bread she had just placed in the toaster. 'I won't go far.'

'I'll be just fine,' Yvonne said.

Outside, Daisy's eyes once again filled with tears. It was the fact she couldn't see it that really got to her. The fact that Shaun had clearly been playing her from the very first moment they met. She remembered the bag that seemed so out of place with the rest of his outfit, and the dog treats when there was no sign of a dog. Perhaps he didn't do any kind of housesitting at all. Perhaps he'd stolen the bag earlier in the day. That seemed like a far more viable idea now that Daisy knew what type of person he was.

Daisy's chest ached, not with the loss of objects, but with the loss of pride. She had always thought she was such a good judge of character. That she could spot a rotten egg from a good one at fifty paces, but clearly that wasn't the case.

'You didn't know either, did you?' she said, looking down at Johnny. Every interaction the dog had had with Shaun had been so friendly. Daisy wasn't the only one Shaun had fooled. Perhaps the fact they saw the best in people was a sign that she and Johnny were meant to be together. Daisy shook the thought away. She wasn't keeping Johnny. She was finding him a home. There was no way she was going to get any more attached to him. It wouldn't work. Not when she had to run the coffee shop from the boat. But the thought of leaving him, handing him over to someone else, when every day, she and he seemed to learn a little more about each other, was feeling harder and harder.

It was only when she was a fair distance from the boat that Daisy realised how selfish she'd just been. She might have needed space, but she had left Yvonne alone in a place that was clearly not the safest area of the city, and without Johnny. She turned back, ready to go, when her phone rang again. Theo. Once again, she let it go to voicemail, but this time, when the phone stopped ringing, a text pinged through.

Hey, I know you're busy. Would love to chat, though.

There was something about the message that made her heart ache.

She wanted to talk to him, too. She wanted nothing more than to hear his voice and tell him about Shaun and the locks and everything she had done. But then that would ruin the surprise.

She went to text back, only to change her mind. There were plenty of bushes around her. She could do a quick video call now and ring him properly later when she was back on the *September Rose*.

A second later, she was holding the phone up in front of her.

'Hey,' she said, her smile rising at the sight of him. It looked like it had been a tough couple of days for Theo, too. She hadn't noticed when they spoke earlier just how dense his stubble had grown, almost to the point of a semi-beard. And dark circles ringed his eyes.

'Hi, how are things going?' he said. 'I thought you were going to ring me back?'

'Sorry,' she said, only then recalling how they had finished their previous conversation. Though it wasn't like it was her fault. She had a valid distraction, what with the break-in then giving their statements to the police. 'It's been a crazy evening.'

'You mean after the pub in Maldon?'

Her brain was on delay, trying to play catch up with the lies she had told him.

'Yes, yes, that's right. Look, Theo, I'm just taking Johnny for a walk. Can I give you a ring when I'm back at the boat?'

'Because you've got something more important to do.'

There was a terseness to his voice. A tone that Daisy couldn't remember ever hearing from him before.

'It's not that, it's just—'

'Look, I'm sorry, Daisy, but I need to say this. Are you just not into me? Is that what the problem is? Because if that's the case, then I'd rather we ended it now. Before I get any more hurt than I'm already going to.'

75

Daisy couldn't think. She couldn't hear. All she could feel was her heart drumming hard against her chest and the sound of her breath wheezing in and out of her lungs.

'You want to end this?'

She watched as Theo took a deep breath in and looked down at his feet before he lifted his gaze again to meet hers.

'That's not what I said. What I said is, if you've lost interest, then I don't want to be strung along. Because that's what it feels like right now. It feels like I'm being strung along.'

'What?'

Her mouth hung open as she tried to swallow back the tears she could feel building behind her eyes.

'No, Theo. I'm not... I promise. I told you. I love you.'

'Yeah, about that...'

She felt queasy. Like the nausea she had felt upon discovering the break-in, only a hundred thousand times worse. Was he going to tell her he'd made a mistake? That it had slipped out without thinking, and now, having reflected on it, he didn't love her at all? Perhaps he didn't even like her. Perhaps he'd met someone new in Slimbridge. Someone who actually knew what they were doing with boats and could cook him fancy meals and was actually there in the evening. It wouldn't be the first time he'd fallen for someone when he was with someone else. The thought was enough to set her stomach churning.

'It feels like ever since I told you how I feel, you've been pushing me away,' he said.

'It does?'

He hadn't said he didn't love her. That was something. But it was hardly a good response.

'You don't seem to have time to talk to me. Every conversation is less than five minutes long. It's like you can't wait to get off the phone fast enough. That's hardly the action of someone in love.'

'I... I...' Daisy struggled to work out what she wanted to say. It was true. She had tried to get off the phone quickly when she spoke to him. But that was only so she didn't ruin the surprise. A surprise that was taking so much out of her, she wasn't entirely sure why she was going through with it. Only she had come so far, she had to.

'The *September Rose* got broken into,' she blurted out, unable to stop the tears from tumbling down her cheeks.

'What?' Theo looked at her, aghast. 'When? What did they take?'

Daisy took a deep breath in. She wanted to tell him the truth. But if she told him the break-in had only happened that day, it wouldn't explain why she'd been acting so oddly beforehand. And so she altered the truth as minimally as she could.

'A little while ago.'

'Why didn't you tell me? I would have come back.'

'I know. I know. That's why I didn't want you to know. I didn't want you to worry. It's fine. I'm fine. And I know you have so much to do. So I'm sorry, I just didn't want to be a distraction. I thought it was best if you didn't know.'

'Daisy.' Theo dropped his head as he let out a long sigh. 'I'm so sorry. And I acted like such an arse. What did they take? Did they get other people on the lock too? Where were you when it happened?'

It was a lot of questions to deal with at one time, particularly as Daisy knew she had to lie for a fair few of them, but she did the best she could.

'I was walking Johnny,' she said, grateful she could have some truthful lines in there. 'It was during the day. No one else. Just me. And they only took the paintings.'

'Your paintings? Why?'

Daisy drew a long breath in. 'I think they thought they were worth more than they actually were. They might have known about the auction. You know how much some people paid for the paintings.'

She couldn't bring herself to say Christian's name. The last thing she needed was to bring him into this complication.

'Daisy, I'm sorry.'

'They took my dad's paintings too,' she said. 'Yvonne found a couple in her things and gave it to me. I hadn't even taken any photographs of it.'

Theo's face was a mass of creases as he looked on helplessly.

'I'm coming down tonight,' he said, standing up. 'I'll take the day off tomorrow. They owe me that, the amount I've been working.'

Daisy shook her head, her pulse pounding in her chest.

'No, you can't.'

'I can. And I will. I'll help in the shop.'

'Please, Theo. That's not what I want. Not yet. I need to work my way through it. Okay? I love you, I promise. I love you so much, and I'm so sorry if you think I've been distant. It's just that I'm not used to having someone there who wants to know everything that's going on in my life. It's been a long time since I was in a relationship and the last thing I want to be is a burden.'

'Daisy, please, you don't need to explain, and you can never be a burden. I was in the wrong. Being paranoid.'

'No, no. You weren't. But trust me, I love you, okay? I promise I love you and I will see you soon. Is that okay?'

'Of course it is. I'm so sorry I added to your stress.'

'It's fine. Really. Speak tomorrow?'

'Absolutely. I love you.'

'I love you too.'

As Daisy hung up the phone, she crumpled into a mess. The truth was, without Theo there, she felt alone. This whole trip felt like a pointless disaster. As she was wallowing at her sorry state, Johnny pushed his head into her chest, snuggling up to her as if he wanted to give her the closest thing he could to a hug. Minutes ticked past, and he stayed there. No whining, no moving, just letting Daisy rest against him. When she finally sat up and wiped away her tears, she rubbed the dog's head and looked down at him.

She sniffed. 'Maybe I can find you a home at Wildflower Lock.'

76

Daisy didn't know how she was going to sleep on the *September Rose*. The closer she got to the boat, the more she worried that the unease which had filled her when she'd left to walk Johnny would return the moment she climbed back aboard. But when she stepped down into the boat, she found it looked decidedly different to when she had left it. Warmer, even. And it took her a moment to realise why. A sad smile lifted her lips.

She stepped inwards, the smile causing tears of gratitude to prick her eyes as she tried to locate all the small differences, which went well beyond the boarded-up window. They were in the kitchen, by the doorway, everywhere. But it was when Daisy was looking over at the living room that she noticed Yvonne, fast asleep, on the sofa.

Daisy padded towards her. While Yvonne wasn't having an outright nightmare, her lips were twisted and her eyebrows knitted as though the dream were far from relaxing.

'Yvonne?' Daisy said, gently rocking her by the shoulder. She knew she could get a blanket, cover Yvonne up and just let her sleep, but she didn't want her rolling off the sofa and hurting herself. Besides, she needed to thank her. 'Yvonne?'

After a moment of blinking, Yvonne finally opened her eyes and, after seeing Daisy standing over her, slowly sat up.

'Sorry, did I drift off?'

'You have nothing to apologise for.' Daisy took a place next to her on the sofa. 'Thank you. Thank you so much.'

A smile widened on Yvonne's face. 'I didn't want to go to bed until you'd seen everything. In case you didn't like it. I know it's not the same, but it's something, isn't it?'

'It's perfect,' Daisy replied.

In every place where Daisy's paintings had previously hung, Yvonne had placed one from her own collection. Daisy hadn't realised how many paintings there were in that battered old trunk of hers, but now it made sense why it had taken so long to find the picture by Johnny; there must have been hundreds. There were at least a dozen currently hanging on her walls. There were boat scenes, landscapes, portraits, and even, where Daisy had previously had her children's characters, there was a risqué life drawing of a woman wearing only two red roses. It was definitely a change.

'That's not you, is it?' Daisy said, looking up at the woman and suddenly feeling the need to ask the question. She loved Yvonne dearly, now more than ever, but that didn't mean she wanted a picture of her naked in the centre of her home.

'No, no. Don't be silly. It's my aunt,' Yvonne replied with a smirk.

That was marginally better, Daisy decided.

Daisy took the paintings in one by one. 'Where did the other ones come from?' Daisy said, looking at a landscape of a desert scene beneath a star-filled sky. She had no idea where it could have been.

'You want to know the story of all of them?' Yvonne asked.

Daisy was about to say no when she saw how Yvonne's eyes glinted at the question.

So she moved over to the kitchen and grabbed the remainder of the wine that Shaun had paid for.

'Yes,' she said, before grabbing two wine glasses from the cupboard. 'I would love to hear the stories behind each and every one.'

77

They finished the bottle of wine and then opened another, which they polished off too. Given how they hadn't eaten anything, the result was two very giggly women. Yvonne had a story to go with every painting. Some were so ridiculous that Daisy could barely believe they were true. Like the time Yvonne had gone to a hotel and her luggage had been swapped with that of a sheikh. When the baggage was sorted, he had tracked her down, and given her the landscape to ensure she told no one what was in his case, threatening her with a punishment worse than death if she did. Yvonne took the painting, though according to her, she'd never even opened the case, having realised from the tag it wasn't hers. She didn't tell that to the sheikh, of course.

There was another painting from a trip to Thailand, that of the train across the river Kwai and one of the Seine in Paris.

Every so often, Yvonne would yawn and take in a deep breath that caused her chest to heave, and Daisy would suggest they stop, but Yvonne wanted to keep going. Even when she finished telling Daisy all about the pictures hanging on the wall, she took several more out of the cabin, including a black and white photograph of a girl on a fishing boat, which Daisy tactfully suggested they swap out for the naked picture of Yvonne's aunt.

It was gone midnight when they finally called it a night.

'Thank you,' Daisy said as Yvonne headed to her cabin. 'And not just for the paintings. You really turned the day around. Thank you.'

'You're most welcome. Now, I should head to bed. I think I'm going to sleep well tonight. I haven't drunk like that in a long time.'

When Daisy headed to her cabin, she picked up her phone. There was only one message from Theo. Another apology that he didn't need to send.

With her heart strangely full, she pressed dial.

'Hey,' Theo said sleepily as he answered the call. 'Everything okay?'

'Yes, I just wanted you to know I really love you. Really, really love you.'

'Are you drunk?'

'A little bit. But I still love you when I'm sober. And I've got a surprise for you.'

'You do?'

'Yes, but you have to wait.'

'Okay, well, I'll look forward to it.'

She could hear the sleepiness in his voice. The way he wanted the call to end, even though she would have happily chatted with him for hours.

'We'll speak tomorrow,' she said. 'Love you.'

'Love you too.'

When she hung up the phone, Daisy had a feeling of lightness in her chest, which lasted until the moment she thought about her father's paintings again. Everything else she could deal with. The invasion of her home. The theft of her own art. Even Shaun's manipulation of her. All that she could get past. But Johnny's work was something she would never be able to replace. Perhaps, she thought, she could ask Yvonne if there were any other people who might have had some of his work. Some people from the funeral, perhaps. It was worth a try. Even though she doubted anyone hoarded things like Yvonne.

Her plan was to ask Yvonne for a list of names of people she could contact during breakfast the next morning, and then she would fire off as many messages as possible during the day while they were travelling.

Even when morning rolled around and Daisy found herself swallowing several painkillers to combat the effects of the wine, the plan remained etched within her mind. There was just one problem – there was no sign of Yvonne.

78

Not seeing Yvonne first thing in the morning wasn't unusual. Daisy had grown used to her sleeping in and taking naps at all times of the day, and after the shock of the previous night, it was no wonder she wanted a little more rest than usual. Wanting to spend the time productively, Daisy opened up the coffee shop and decided to serve drinks for an hour or so until Yvonne was up and they could decide how far they were going to travel.

There was another reason, beyond earning money, that made Daisy want to open the coffee shop, too.

'Make sure you haven't got any valuables on display,' she said to anyone who told her they lived on the canal. 'I'm pretty sure it was premeditated, but you can never be too sure. You need to be careful.'

Several customers made comments about things like Daisy's break-in being all too common, while others shook their heads and said how they'd never heard of something happening like that along this stretch before. Either way, it was a fairly constant stream of customers and Daisy was surprised when she looked down at her watch and found it was gone ten.

Johnny had spent the night in the boat with no messes. Daisy had let him out briefly as soon as she'd woken up, after which he went straight back to his spot under the table, where he stayed without complaint, until just before ten-thirty, when he started whining loudly.

'I know. You need to go out for a proper walk,' Daisy said, throwing him a quick glance. 'I'm sure Yvonne will be up in a minute. She can take you out. Or you'll just have to wait.'

Given how long Johnny had gone without toilet breaks when they were on the Thames, Daisy expected him to manage for just a bit longer, but within two minutes, he was on his feet, scratching at the door, although not the door that led outside, but the cabin door. Did he know there was a route outside through there onto the bow? Maybe, but it wasn't as if he'd ever been in there before.

Soon his whines were so loud, they were attracting the attention of customers outside the hatch. All she needed was for one of them to call a health and safety officer and it would be the end of her.

'Fine, let's go,' she said, the minute there was a break in customers.

She put up a *back in two minutes* sign on the hatch, then grabbed Johnny's leash, though rather than bounding to join her, the way he'd previously done when it was time to go out, Johnny sat down on the ground, his whining increasing.

'What do you want, then?' Daisy said, making no attempt to hide her frustration. 'I thought you wanted to go out. I don't know what sort of game you're playing, but I'm not playing it.'

She clipped the lead to his collar and turned away. Johnny's eyes widened and his head turned back towards the cabin door, but he relented, stood up, and headed outside.

In less than two minutes, he was back in the boat. The whining recommenced.

'Do you want to get moving?' Daisy asked as if she expected him to give her a genuine answer. 'That's what it is, isn't it? Well, you're right. We probably need to leave soon.'

She glanced at her watch. The morning was running away from her. That was always the case when it was busy, though. Those days flew by. It was the slow ones that dragged.

With a groan, Daisy looked down at Johnny, who was still emitting his whine while pawing at the cabin door.

'I know. She needs to get up. You're right. You're right.'

Last night, Yvonne had said she wanted to get in at least seven hours of driving to get through the mass of locks that awaited them. If they didn't leave soon, they'd been mooring up near sunset. And yet there was still no sign of her.

Deciding that making headway was now her priority, Daisy closed the hatch and knocked on the door of the cabin.

'Yvonne?' she said. Nothing.

Daisy listened closely. She hadn't heard any nightmares seeping through that morning, but with the coffee machine constantly whirring away, it was hard to hear anything at all. She knocked a little harder and, upon hearing nothing, cracked the door open.

Daisy looked into the space, struggling to make out Yvonne in the shadows. The curtains were still drawn, the darkness of the cabin a contrast to the bright sun of the sky outside. With her eyes straining, she took another step inward.

'Yvonne!' she screamed.

79

Daisy called an ambulance.

One look at Yvonne was enough to tell her that was what was needed, although beyond that, she had no idea.

'Is she breathing?' the person on the end of the line asked.

'I... I think so?' Daisy stood over her friend, searching for some sign of life. There was something you did to check someone was breathing, wasn't there? Something with a mirror. At least, that was what she remembered from first aid at school. Not that it helped her now. Instead, Daisy put her ear to Yvonne's mouth, where the softest, shallowest wheeze floated from her lips.

'I think so. Yes, yes,' Daisy said with certainty. 'She is. But not strongly. It's very quiet.'

'And she's unresponsive, you say?'

Daisy didn't need to check this one. She had tried shaking Yvonne by the shoulders several times, only for her body to flop around like a rag doll. And Johnny had been licking her hand since he'd been allowed into the room. So far, Yvonne hadn't so much as blinked in response.

'Definitely unresponsive. What should I do? How long are they going to take to get here?'

'The ambulance is on the way,' the responder assured her. 'Just a few more questions while I've got you here. Was she unwell, that you know of? Any history of heart attacks? Hereditary illness?'

'No, I don't know,' Daisy said, tears welling in her eyes as she struggled to keep control. 'No, wait, she's on some medication. I think I saw it in her drawer.'

'That's great. Can you find it and tell me what it is? The paramedics will need to know.'

'Yes, yes.' Daisy felt relieved to have something productive to do as she left Yvonne's side and opened the drawer beside her bed, revealing a medley of medication.

'Okay, this is what I've found...' Daisy read off the list of the medications, her chest growing tighter with each one. Medication always sounded serious when you read out its proper name, even for something as straightforward as paracetamol. But somehow Daisy knew that wasn't what these were. 'Do you think she'd forgotten to take one of them?' she asked, voicing her thoughts, mainly because the silence was so unbearable. 'We had a bad day yesterday. Someone broke into the boat. She could have forgotten. Could that have caused this to happen?'

'Possibly.' The responder was utterly non-committal in her response, but now the thought had formed, a surge of guilt flooded Daisy.

Why had she not asked Yvonne more about the medication she was on? Why had she not dug deeper when Yvonne had been struggling? But her bad days seemed so sporadic.

'How long now?' she asked. 'Will they be here soon?'

If this had happened on Wildflower Lock, Daisy would have known what to do. She would have had people around her. People who knew Yvonne. But here, she had no one. She was utterly on her own.

'Don't worry, they won't be long,' the woman said. 'You're doing a great job. Just keep her head up and make sure her airway is clear. They'll be there soon.'

Daisy blinked away her tears and nodded silently. There was nothing she could do but wait.

80

Daisy didn't know how long it took the ambulance to arrive. It felt like an hour, and maybe it was. All she knew was that with every passing second, she prayed they weren't too late. When she finally heard a knock on the door and a voice calling out her name, she stood up and looked down at Johnny.

'Stay with her, okay?' she said to the dog, who had been holding a vigil by her side. 'I'll just be a minute. The people have come to help Yvonne, all right?'

Johnny lifted his head for a moment before dropping it back down by Yvonne's arm, although when Daisy returned to the cabin with the paramedics following her, Johnny was on his feet. His eyes were wide and locked on the strangers, and for a split second, Daisy feared he might start snarling at them.

'It's okay, Johnny,' Daisy said, crouching down as she moved towards the dog. 'They're here to help, okay? They won't hurt her. These people are here to help.'

The dog's head tilted slightly like he was taking in what she had just said, and while Daisy knew he was still wary about the strangers in his home, she was also fairly certain he wasn't a risk to them.

'He's fine, he'll be fine,' she assured them, as they looked apprehensively at the border collie. 'He's the one that found her, that's all. I promise he'll be fine. He just doesn't want to leave her.'

To make the paramedics feel more comfortable, Daisy shifted over to the other side of the cabin to a small tub chair in the corner, taking Johnny with her. When she sat down, she promptly lifted him onto her lap. Until that moment, she'd have thought sitting with a dog that size on her would have been utterly ridiculous and possibly quite painful, but it turned out it was exactly what she needed.

Holding Johnny tightly against her, Daisy watched on helplessly as the paramedics lifted Yvonne onto a stretcher, then manoeuvred her out of the cabin. It wasn't easy, given how narrow the doors were, but, Daisy considered, it would have been even worse on the *Ariadne*. That boat was even narrower than hers.

When they were out of the cabin, she lowered Johnny onto the ground.

'It's okay, I'm just going to go with them, and make sure she's all right. You'll be okay here, won't you? You can keep the boat safe for me.'

Outside, a crowd had gathered on the towpath, watching on with morbid interest as the paramedics carried Yvonne.

'Can I come in the ambulance?' Daisy said as they opened the doors and placed Yvonne inside. 'Can I come with you? I don't have a car here. I'm not sure how I'll get to the hospital otherwise.'

The younger of the paramedics nodded.

'No worries. Is there someone you need to call, though? Someone who can meet you at the hospital, maybe. Someone for you? I know events like this are quite a shock.'

Daisy nodded. Her body felt numb. Cold and shivery despite the warmth of the summer day. She was utterly drained, in a place she didn't know, after a week of highs and lows that had taken every bit of her mental and physical strength to get through. And the only person who had been there with her was being carted off in an ambulance. She knew from their conversations that Yvonne's family was limited, but Daisy would try her hardest to get hold of them. Still, there was someone she needed at that moment, like the paramedic said – someone to look after her. And so she picked up her phone and called.

81

'Daisy!'

Her mother raced across the hospital foyer. The minute the two were together, Daisy collapsed into her arms, buried her head in her chest and sobbed. It didn't matter what they had gone through in the last year or how much healing Pippa and Daisy still had to do. When a disaster struck, there was only one person she wanted by her side.

Daisy had phoned her mother from the ambulance as soon as she knew which hospital they were heading to. Though she was barely coherent as she stuttered out words between her sobs, she must have said Yvonne's name at least a dozen times, and the name of the hospital. She hadn't needed to ask her mother to come and meet her, though. It hadn't been necessary. Pippa had known exactly what Daisy needed.

'I'm coming now.'

Those were the only words she'd said before the line went dead. Relief had flooded through Daisy. She had no idea how long it would take her mother to get to them, but she was coming. That was what mattered.

Two hours later, when the hospital doors opened and her mother ran across to her, Daisy noticed that she was still dressed in her whites from the kitchen, having clearly raced straight out of work to come to her.

'My darling girl.'

Her mum's voice was all it took for Daisy to crumble again. It was like she was a teenager. Or worse still, dealing with that first proper break-up that had made her feel as though her heart would never be whole again. They stayed there, standing in a room full of strangers, until Daisy finally stood upright, and brushed away the tears with the back of her hand.

'I didn't know how sick she was, Mum,' Daisy said, her words still staggered from her shallow breaths. 'The doctors said it's cancer. Late stage. And she knew about it. She was on meds. So many of them. I should have never asked her to come. This is all my fault. She was sick, and I asked her to do this.'

'Tssh,' her mother said, stepping back and wiping Daisy's cheeks as if she were a child who had scraped her knee at the park. 'Yvonne knew exactly what she was doing. She's a grown woman, and she was aware of any risks she was putting herself under by taking that trip. What have the doctors said now? Is she doing okay?'

'She's responsive,' Daisy said, her words still warbling slightly. 'But they need to keep her in. At least for the night. I'm such a fool. I should have known. Johnny knew. That was why he wouldn't stop whining. He didn't want to go out at all. He knew something was wrong.'

'Johnny?' Her mother frowned.

Daisy let out a long sigh. There was so much she had to tell her mum. So much she needed to say, but she didn't want to do it under the sterile white lights of a hospital foyer.

'Do you think you could give me a lift back to the *September Rose*?' she asked, the pressure of the day falling on her shoulders like a physical weight. 'I'll explain everything then.'

82

'So this is Johnny,' her mother said as she sat down on the sofa.

Immediately, the collie dropped his head onto her and lapped up the attention.

'I know I need to find him a home, but honestly, I'm not sure I can now. At least, not with someone I don't know. He's special.'

Daisy had filled her mother in during the car journey back to the boat, and now she was home, there was nothing left to do but stew over what a mess she'd made of things.

'You can't play that game with yourself,' her mother replied. 'There are a hundred what ifs, and not a single one matters. The only thing that matters is now. And Yvonne is in hospital. She's in the best possible place. You made sure that happened. I've rung Nicholas too. He's going to ask around the lock, see if there's anyone there who can put us in touch with Yvonne's relatives. He thinks she's got a nephew down in Heybridge that he's going to check out too.'

'Thank you, Mum.'

Daisy didn't have any more words to give. She was exhausted. Her whole body felt drained. It wasn't even seven o'clock, and she was ready for bed. Though what she was going to do in the morning, she had no idea. She could hardly get to Slimbridge without Yvonne on the boat with her, which left only one option – telling Theo. The thought filled her with dread. He wouldn't blame her for what had happened with Yvonne, she knew that, but she couldn't help thinking how cross he would be at the constant stream of lies she had told him to keep the trip a secret. Not to mention all the risks she had taken. He was likely to be furious at her for being so irresponsible. And he would be absolutely right. She had been irresponsible. The entire trip was rash and reckless and now she was going to have to spend money she didn't have getting the boat back to Wildflower Lock. She just had to pray the weather stayed good, so she could earn enough money to cover all her bills when she got back.

'Well, I should head back,' her mother said, putting her mug down on the coffee table as she stood.

'You're going?' She didn't mean to sound like a whiny child, but she hadn't expected her mother to drive all the way to find her, only to turn around and drive back home again. And she knew the boat held some pretty strong memories for her, but surely she could push them aside for one night?

Her mother's face dropped as she read Daisy's expression.

'I'm sorry, love. I'll be back in the morning, but I've left a load of stuff at work that has to be sorted by the end of tonight's shift. I didn't give them much warning when I left.'

'Sorry, you're right. I wasn't thinking,' Daisy said. She knew she should feel gratitude for the fact she'd come at all, but she didn't want to be left on her own. Even with Johnny by her side.

'I'll be back first thing in the morning,' her mother assured her. 'You need an early night. Fix yourself something to eat and get a proper night's sleep. I might be up before you're even awake.'

Daisy smiled, grateful that her mother wasn't abandoning her altogether. And it wasn't like she would be the best company, anyway. All she wanted to do was curl up and close her eyes.

'Thank you, Mum,' she said, wrapping her arms around her in a tight hug. Her mother was right. Daisy needed sleep. And then she would face tomorrow head-on. Whatever it brought.

83

Daisy walked her mum back to the car, partially so that she wasn't on her own in the boat but also to give Johnny a chance to stretch his legs. The poor dog had had nothing more than a couple of quick toilet strolls all day and had spent the entire time Daisy was in the hospital locked inside the boat – and there hadn't been a single mess. It was a far cry from the way he'd been racing along the coast to keep up with her when they'd first met. When she found him a home, it would have to be with someone who could give him the time he needed to go on proper long walks. Who could spend their days with him outside, giving him the freedom he had known for so long. And as much as it hurt her heart to think about, she didn't think that was her.

'Come on,' she said to the dog, as she waved her mother away. 'I think you deserve an extra big dinner tonight.'

Back on the boat, she gave him an entire tin of dog food, which he gobbled hungrily. She'd also make sure that whoever took him on had a far better routine than she did. It wasn't just a case of not walking him that day. While there was a big bowl of water under the table where he liked to sit, she hadn't even thought to leave any biscuits down for him when she went with Yvonne in the ambulance. No wonder he was so hungry.

'What a day, hey?' she said as he finished his food and flopped down at her feet. 'You know, my life isn't always this chaotic,' she said, only to change her mind. 'Okay, my life didn't used to be chaotic. It's just recently that it's all gone a bit crazy. And I'm not saying I want to go back to the way it was or anything, but I think this week has had a bit more stress than I'm able to deal with.'

Johnny didn't reply, but he snuggled his head into Daisy's leg. As she sat there, with the sounds of city life buzzing outside her window, she picked up her phone. The fact she couldn't go on with the journey hurt even more, as it meant that all the lying to Theo had been pointless. It was time she came clean and hoped he wasn't too mad at her.

She picked up the phone, holding her breath. She planned on blurting out the truth the second he answered. Although rather than the normal ring tone her phone gave when she called, the higher-pitched sound told her the line was busy.

Perhaps that was a good thing, she thought, standing up and heading to the shower. She would try again later. Maybe when she'd figured out exactly what she was going to say.

Only it wasn't that straightforward. After showering, drying her hair, and finally plucking up the courage to try Theo for a second time, Daisy held the phone to her ear. It rang twice, only to go to answerphone again. She checked the time. Seven-thirty. Normally he would be in the *Narrow Escape* by now, after a full day on the canal. But he had said he wanted to make the most of the daylight hours and he might have been working late.

Deciding that she didn't have it in her to stay up any later, she left a message saying she needed to speak to him and would ring him in the morning, before she lay down on her bed.

She was asleep before her head even hit the pillow.

84

Given how abruptly Daisy had fallen asleep, she hadn't had the foresight to set an alarm to get some early-morning coffee shop trade in. And so, rather than waking up to the shrill tone of a phone, or even Johnny barking to go out, she was woken by a hammering on the door.

'Hold on!' Daisy hollered, still rubbing her eyes as she moved through the boat. Johnny was sitting by the door, his tail wagging profusely.

'I take it that means it's someone nice,' Daisy said as she stroked his head. 'Don't worry, I'll take you for a walk. Just let me see to this, and then we'll go out.'

As well as forgetting to set an alarm, Daisy had also forgotten what her mother had said about returning early in the morning. And yet there she was, heavily laden with cups and bags. Daisy's eyes scanned her mother, taking in everything from the takeaway cups and paper bag in her hand to a large duffle bag over her shoulder.

'Mum? You know I have a coffee shop, don't you?' Daisy said as she looked at the drinks.

'I do. Just like I know you need a day away from work. It's not good living at your job like this. It doesn't give you a chance to switch off properly, and I think that's what you need to do. Now, why don't you take your mocha, go get dressed and I'll take Johnny here for a quick walk.'

It was ridiculous, her mother telling her what she should do, like she was a teenager, living at home again. But it was also amazing how relieved she felt to have her mother ordering her about in such a manner. She needed someone to take control of things. To stop her from having to think about every last detail of what had happened over the last few days.

After getting dressed, Daisy took a large gulp of the drink. It wasn't as good as she could have made, but she hadn't had to make it, and that was something. Her mother was still out walking Johnny, and Daisy took a moment to look at the other things her mother had brought, namely the big bag of pastries. Since moving to Wildflower Lock, one of the few things Daisy missed was the bakery she used to live above that would leave leftover pastries on her door at the end of the day. After a brief look at the selection inside, she decided on a pain aux raisins.

When her mother returned, Daisy was still chewing the first mouthful.

'Well, you look better,' she said.

'Thank you for taking him out, Mum. Was he okay?'

'Okay? He was fabulous. He's a very good boy. We passed a couple of other dogs who weren't on their leads and he didn't bat an eyelid. I can't believe you haven't found his owner.'

'I know,' Daisy said. 'I don't suppose you want to take him, do you?'

As she said the words, a hint of hope flickered within her, but deep down she knew what her mother's answer would be. There was no way she could manage a dog with the hours she worked. It wouldn't be fair. All the late evenings and time spent in an empty house weren't what he needed. And it wasn't like her mum could take him to work with her.

'I wish I could,' her mother said. 'He's lovely.'

'He really is.'

A silence swirled around them and Daisy wasn't entirely sure what had caused it. She didn't think she'd said anything that could have upset her mother. Did Pippa have a dog on the *September Rose* when she lived here before? She hadn't seen one in any of the photographs, but that didn't mean much.

Feeling the need to break the silence, Daisy pointed to the large duffle bag that her mother had placed on the ground when she'd come in.

'What's the bag for?' she asked. 'Are you going to stay with Nicholas after this?'

It was the only explanation Daisy could think of, though it didn't really make any sense. If that was the case, her mother could have just left the bag in the car.

'Actually, there's something in there for you.'

'For me?'

Pippa nodded again, but she didn't say any more. Neither did she move towards the bag. There was a bizarre tension building around her. Almost as if she was nervous.

'I don't know why I didn't give these to you before,' she said eventually. 'Well, I guess it was because I didn't know why I even kept them.'

Daisy stayed silent. She could feel there was plenty more her mother needed to say, and the last thing she wanted was to make her feel any more uncomfortable than she already did.

'I didn't take any of them with me when I left, obviously.' Her mother's eyes were on the bag, rather than on Daisy. 'I didn't take anything. But when Johnny died – your father Johnny, that is – Fred, your grandfather, came and brought me these. I won't lie, I thought about burning them. I really did. But by that time, you were already so in love with your art, and it seemed wrong to keep this from you forever. I kept telling myself, maybe when you finished your A levels, I'd give them to you, then when you got into college. But then I knew it would raise a whole host of questions I didn't want to answer.'

Daisy was only half listening to her mother now. Instead, she was staring at the duffle bag, wondering what on earth could be inside that was making her act in such a way. Soon, it became too much.

'Mum, what is it? What's in the bag?'

Finally, her mother reached up, picked it off the ground, and handed it to Daisy.

'Why don't you have a look yourself?'

85

Daisy was too stunned to speak. Instead, her heart was racing as she pulled the paintings out of the bag, one and then another. All of them signed in the corner with the exact same signature Yvonne had shown her only days before. *Johnny.*

'He painted them all?' Daily said in near disbelief. She'd thought *she* was a prolific artist – once she'd got back into the swing of things, that was – but there were dozens of paintings here. In all different mediums, although watercolours appeared to be his most popular choice.

'Well, I never thought I'd see this one again,' her mother said, plucking out a vivid purple painting of a boat with a single figure standing on the stern. 'I don't think I even knew it was in there. You know, he painted this when I was pregnant with you. That's me. Or it's supposed to be, I think.'

Daisy looked at the figure more closely, noting the way the person's stomach bloomed outwards. Her father had painted her. Not directly, of course, but the thought alone was enough to make her chest soar. There were dozens of paintings in the bag. If he'd painted one when her mother was pregnant, there was a good chance he'd painted one when Daisy was a baby, too. She wanted nothing more than to tip them all out onto the floor and take them all in, but her mother was still speaking.

'They're not in the best condition, I'm afraid. They've been up in the loft, and I think a couple of them have got a bit of damp, but maybe you can have a look on the internet and see if there's some way to sort that out.'

Daisy didn't know whether to laugh or cry. All these years, she had been desperate to learn more about her father. About what type of man he was. And the answers – at least some of them – had been up in the attic all along.

'This is probably a lot for you to take in, after the last couple of days, especially,' her mother said. 'Why don't I give you some space? I'll go ring the hospital. See if there's any news on Yvonne.'

'Thank you,' Daisy said, though she barely even lifted her eyes to look at her mother.

As Pippa headed outside, Daisy sat on the sofa, lugging the bag with her. There was so much to look at, she didn't know where to start. One by one, she pulled the paintings out, wiping the tears from her eyes, struggling to make sure the water didn't get close to the paper.

After studying the first half dozen, she realised that perhaps taking photos of them might be a good idea. While she didn't believe lightning would strike twice in terms of Shaun, there would be no third chances after this. These were the paintings Fred had given her mother. These were all that remained, and she needed to preserve them, one way or another.

As she stood up to fetch her phone, there was a knock on the door.

'It's fine, Mum, you can come in,' Daisy said, a sense of sweet nostalgia sweeping through her. There was a time in her life when her mother would have let herself into Daisy's personal space, whether Daisy wanted her there or not. Only a few months ago, she had turned up outside her workplace. It was a good sign of how far their relationship had come that she was respecting Daisy's privacy again.

As the door creaked open, Daisy turned back and picked up her phone, only for Johnny to jump up from the ground and start barking madly. He was turning on the spot, chasing his tail as he moved.

'And this must be Johnny.'

It was only five words. Five short words, yet it was enough for Daisy's throat to close with tears and her heart to near leap out of her chest. Forgetting about the phone, the paintings and everything else, she spun around, finding herself face-to-face with Theo.

'Well, it sounds like you've got yourself into a bit of a mess while I've been away,' he said.

86

'You're here?' The first words out of Daisy's mouth were somewhat superfluous, yet she didn't know what else she could say. It didn't feel real. Theo was standing there, on the *September Rose*, in the middle of London. 'How? Why?'

'How?' Theo said, taking a step closer to her. 'Well, you have your mother to thank for that one.'

'My mother?'

'She rang me last night, after leaving here. Told me all about your trip. And Yvonne.'

'Theo.' Daisy's stomach plummeted. 'I didn't know she was sick. I really didn't. I never would have—'

'I know. You don't have to explain. No, actually, you do. You know that it's crazy, right? Thinking you could travel all the way here. I can't believe you got this far.'

'It was mostly down to Yvonne,' Daisy admitted. 'Although when she gets out of hospital, we are getting her a smartphone that she can access the tide times on.'

Theo stepped forward, slipping his hands into hers.

'I can't believe I didn't work out what you were doing,' he said. 'I mean, I knew something was up, but I just thought you were having second thoughts. About us, you know?'

'No. I couldn't. Not ever. I just missed you.'

'I get it,' he said, then for the first time since he'd set foot on the boat, he leant forward and kissed her. For a split second, it was like all the stresses of the last two days had disappeared. It was just her and Theo, back together again. And it was exactly how Daisy wanted it to be.

Only a moment after they started kissing, a loud bark interrupted the moment.

'So.' Theo broke away and looked down at the dog that was by his leg, wagging his tail. 'I take it you didn't find this guy on Wildflower Lock either?'

'I think it's safe to say that I didn't find him at all. He found us. But I don't know what I'm going to do now. I have to find him a home. I know I do. There's no way I can keep him, not with the coffee shop. But he's done so much for us, Theo. Honestly, I'm not sure I can bear parting with him.'

Without another word, Theo knelt down and rubbed Johnny under the chin.

'You've made quite an impression on my girl, haven't you?' he said, scratching a rough bit of fur and causing Johnny's tail to beat harder and harder. 'You know, it's quite funny, actually. I was thinking only the other day how much nicer my job would be if I had some company. You know, someone to head out to work with early in the morning. Spend the day out on the canals with and keep me company on the long drives. He'd have to be good on boats, though.'

'Are you serious?' Daisy said, not daring to believe Theo wasn't just winding her up.

'Can he do boats?'

'Can he do boats? He's amazing on boats. He did the Thames with us. I mean, you have no idea how fast that was. It was crazy. Insane. I actually thought we might die, but Johnny loved it.'

'You didn't travel when the tide was going in, did you?' Theo said, a sudden look of terror on his face.

'We're not talking about me right now,' Daisy said, realising her slip-up. 'We're talking about you taking Johnny. Do you mean it? He's perfect. Well, that's probably an exaggeration, but you won't regret it. I know it.'

Theo opened his mouth, but before he could reply, a rhythmic knock on the door was accompanied by her mother's sing-song voice.

'Knock, knock. Can we come in?'

As the door opened, her mother stepped forward and Daisy saw the shadow behind her. For a moment, she thought it was Yvonne, somehow out of hospital and back on the boat, but as the view cleared, she saw it was Nicholas. Her mother's boyfriend. Before now, Nicholas had barely spoken two words to Daisy, other than to yell at her for opening the Coffee Shop on the Canal. And yet here he was, holding two large bags in his hand.

'So, the good news is that Yvonne can go home tonight,' he said.

'Thank goodness.' A gasp of relief cascaded through Daisy's body, so strong her knees almost buckled. Yvonne was going to be all right. Nothing else mattered. Not now. 'Thank you so much.'

'No problem. Now, where do you want me to put these?' Nicholas said, looking directly at Daisy while lifting the bags.

'Are they more paintings?' Daisy said. She couldn't believe it. She didn't know how long it was going to take her to go through all the ones her mother had already given her. The last thing she was expecting was more.

Yet her mother shook her head.

'No, they're not paintings. They're my clothes.'

'Clothes?' Daisy said, confused.

'Well, you're not going to make it to Slimbridge on your own, are you?'

87

Daisy listened on with a mixture of disbelief and awe. They had it all planned. Apparently, Nicholas had driven to the *September Rose* that morning so he could drop off Pippa, then pick up Yvonne from the hospital to take back to Wildflower Lock while her mother stayed onboard the boat and carried on the journey with Daisy.

'What about work?' Daisy asked, still not able to believe this was really happening. 'You can't just not work.'

'No, you're right, but I'd already booked next week off work, anyway. Nick and I were going to take a little trip, but this one sounds even better. And work was all right about it, not that I gave them much choice. They owe me after all the years I've worked there. And Theo reckons we can make it in a fortnight.'

'But... but... You know about this too?' Daisy said, looking at Theo. The disbelief was growing more and more by the second. It was one thing for her mother to ring Theo to tell her what had happened to Yvonne, but making these sorts of plans without even discussing it with her was next-level meddling, though it came from the loveliest of places. Daisy wasn't sure whether she should be grateful or angry, though one of those emotions was definitely more prevalent.

'Unless you've changed your mind and don't want to come up to Slimbridge?' Theo said with a twist of a smile on his lips.

Of course she wanted to. All the fear and worry of Yvonne had meant Daisy had pushed aside how heartbroken she'd been about having to cut the journey short. Even if she had hated lying to Theo about it, the trip itself had been nothing short of incredible, and she was only halfway through.

But it wasn't as straightforward as whether she wanted to do it.

'Are you sure?' Daisy said, looking at her mother. 'Will you be okay here? On the boat?'

'Well, you've already done the hard bit. A few locks and canals are nothing compared to the open waters and the tidal Thames. And I've made sure I've packed my wellies. I know how muddy these towpaths can get, even when it isn't raining.'

'That isn't what I meant,' Daisy said.

Even though she'd never seen her mother out on the canals, Daisy didn't doubt her ability to hitch a knot or open a gate. Once you learned something like that, it was ingrained in you. Like riding a bike. It was the emotional side of things that worried her.

'I mean, are you going to be okay here, on the *September Rose*? On this particular boat.'

'You know what, I think this boat and I need some more memories,' she said, stepping forward and taking Daisy's hands. 'So if you're asking me if I am going to be okay with spending two weeks with my daughter, helping her run her business, seeing parts of the countryside and telling her about my life on the canal, then the answer is yes, absolutely. Now, why don't we go get Yvonne's things packed up and you and Theo can go grab some breakfast together before we have to set off? How does that sound?'

88

Daisy and Theo picked up breakfast sandwiches from a local deli, which they sat and ate on the back of the boat, while her mother and Nicholas finished packing up the last of Yvonne's belongings.

'You know, I feel like I should be mad at you for keeping this from me,' Theo said, his hand resting on Daisy's leg. 'But somehow, it makes me love you more.'

'Really?' Daisy said, swallowing a mouthful of food. 'Me lying makes you happy?'

'I don't think that's what I said exactly,' Theo said, raising his eyebrows. 'The lying doesn't make me happy, but the fact that you would do this does. And that you would try that hard to surprise me. I think it's amazing. I think you're amazing.'

He gazed into her eyes, and Daisy knew he was about to kiss her, but she shifted back ever so slightly.

'So amazing that you're going to keep Johnny?' she said, raising her eyebrows expectantly. Her mum and Nicholas's arrival meant Theo hadn't actually confirmed whether he was going to take the dog and while Daisy didn't want to be greedy – she had already had more good news in the last three hours than she could ever have imagined –

knowing she had got the best possible home for Johnny, where she could still spend time with him, would be the absolute icing on the cake. As she waited, she stared up at Theo expectantly. A small grin twisted on his face.

'I guess that sounds like a fair deal.'

'You mean it?'

'I mean it. What do you think, buddy?' Theo said, looking down at Johnny, who was bouncing on his feet as his tail wagged non-stop. 'You think you'd like to come live with me?'

As perfectly timed as always, Johnny let out a single bark, causing Daisy and Theo to burst into laughter. They both reached forward and gave the dog some much-deserved fuss.

For a moment, everything felt right with the world. What could have been the worst week of Daisy's life was turning out to be the very best. She had the links to her father back with the painting, a chance to bond with her mother like she hadn't done in years. Her friend was coming home from the hospital. And her boyfriend... Well, there weren't words enough to describe how grateful she was to have someone like Theo in her corner.

Having stopped stroking Johnny, Daisy was just about to say as much when Theo glanced down at his watch. A familiar knot twisted in Daisy's stomach. The next words out of Theo's mouth would be him saying he needed to leave any minute now and get back to work. That was the way their relationship had to be at the moment.

'You need to get going?' she said, anticipating the moment before Theo spoke. Only to her surprise, he shook his head.

'Not yet,' he replied. 'I was thinking that we could get the map out and have a look together? Plot out your route and work out where I can come and meet you on my days off. Maybe some evenings too, when you get closer. I could give Pippa a bit of help with the locks.'

Daisy's heart felt as though it was going to burst from her chest. 'You'll do that? You'll come and meet me?'

'After what you've done for me, I think it's the least I can do. I'm in this for the long run, Daisy May. You and me against the world forever.'

As they leaned in to kiss, another bark resounded into the air, and Theo let out a short chuckle.

'You, me and Johnny against the world,' he corrected.

ACKNOWLEDGEMENTS

Countless people are involved in the process of turning the stories in my head into the pages of a book and I am so grateful to them all.

First of all, I have to extend my heartfelt thanks to Kate, who willingly gave her free time to talk to me about her life on a narrowboat and the trials of navigating the tidal Thames. I would not have managed to bring this story to life without your expert knowledge and am sincerely grateful for your guidance.

To Emily, my editor, who helped me to shape this story into what you have read today, your expertise is truly appreciated in all my work. Thank you.

To the various canal and boatyard workers, whom I would ring whenever I needed to know whether something I had plotted was feasible, I am sorry I did not get all your names, but I appreciate how you gave your knowledge so freely.

To Jake, who navigated our way around the South Oxford Canal so I could get as much hands-on research for this book as possible. Thank you. I know I'll persuade you to move onto a narrowboat soon!

Lastly, to my readers. I want you to know that I never forget how truly privileged I am to write stories as a living, and I would not be able to do that without you and your support. I am grateful to each and every one of you. You are the people who made my dreams come true.

ABOUT THE AUTHOR

Hannah Lynn is the author of over twenty books spanning several genres. Hannah grew up in the Cotswolds, UK. After graduating from university, she spent 15 years as a teacher of physics, teaching in the UK, Thailand, Malaysia, Austria and Jordan.

Sign up to Hannah Lynn's mailing list here for news, competitions and updates on future books.

Visit Hannah's website: www.hannahlynnauthor.com

Follow Hannah on social media:

- facebook.com/hannahlynnauthor
- instagram.com/hannahlynnwrites
- tiktok.com/@hannah.lynn.romcoms
- bookbub.com/authors/hannah-lynn

ALSO BY HANNAH LYNN

The Holly Berry Sweet Shop Series
The Sweet Shop of Second Chances
Love Blooms at the Second Chances Sweet Shop
High Hopes at the Second Chances Sweet Shop
Family Ties at the Second Chances Sweet Shop
Sunny Days at the Second Chances Sweet Shop
A Summer Wedding at the Second Chances Sweet Shop

The Wildflower Lock Series
New Beginnings at Wildflower Lock
Coffee and Cake at Wildflower Lock
Blue Skies Over Wildflower Lock

LOVE NOTES
LOVE IN EVERY CHAPTER

WHERE ALL YOUR ROMANCE
DREAMS COME TRUE!

THE HOME OF BESTSELLING
ROMANCE AND WOMEN'S
FICTION

WARNING:
MAY CONTAIN SPICE

SIGN UP TO OUR
NEWSLETTER

https://bit.ly/Lovenotesnews

Boldwood

Boldwood Books is an award-winning fiction publishing company seeking out the best stories from around the world.

Find out more at www.boldwoodbooks.com

Join our reader community for brilliant books, competitions and offers!

Follow us
@BoldwoodBooks
@TheBoldBookClub

Sign up to our weekly deals newsletter

https://bit.ly/BoldwoodBNewsletter

Milton Keynes UK
Ingram Content Group UK Ltd.
UKHW041117200624
444314UK00002B/11